FALLEN

THE CURE CHRONICLES, BOOK FOUR

K. A. RILEY

To those I've met and yet have never met, the lovely readers of Booktok who regularly make my day...

Thank you so much.

SUMMARY

When Ashen heads east to New York City to find Finn's brother, she finds herself confronted by an entirely new set of problems.

The city is a war zone overshadowed by the Behemoth, the largest Arcology in existence. Few are allowed entry, and those who go in never leave. At first, Ashen assumes the power structure is one she knows well: Directorate vs. Dregs, Wealthy vs. Poor.

She's seen this fight before, and she knows how to win it.

She soon discovers that the power in New York is held entirely by one young man. Known only as the Bishop, he's mysterious, unnervingly handsome, and smooth-voiced. His allure is undeniable, despite his tendency toward cruelty.

But as Ashen gets to know him, she begins to question how he managed to gain so much power at such a young age. Who is the Bishop, really? And where did he come from?

The even more mysterious question is....

What exactly goes on inside the Behemoth?

DARKNESS

MY EYES ARE OPEN. At least, I think they are.

An all-encompassing blackness surrounds me like a thick woolen blanket, suffocating and disorienting. I can't make out a single speck of light or flicker of movement.

The air smells faintly of smoke, as if there's a fire raging somewhere in the far distance.

What's burning?

Where the hell am I?

I can't answer either question. All I know for sure is that I'm lying on a remarkably comfortable bed.

I try to lift my hand, hoping to reach out and feel a wall, to feel *anything*, but I realize with a hit of anguish that both my arms are tied down. Some kind of bond is tightly fastened around each of my wrists, winding around my forearms and preventing me from moving them.

When I attempt to move my legs, I immediately encounter the same difficulty.

Someone wants me isolated, helpless. I'm a prisoner, for what feels like the thousandth time.

But this time, I don't have the first clue who my captor is. Am I in a Directorate stronghold?

My head is swimming, and I feel...intoxicated. Yes, that's it. Like someone has drugged me, or maybe they've plied me with alcohol. Aside from the helplessness of it, it's not an entirely unpleasant feeling. The trouble is, I can't seem to focus on anything. I trip over every new thought as the previous one meanders away in a fog.

I don't have time for this.

Think, Ashen. Think.

Try to remember how you got here.

Breathing deeply, I force my mind to settle, pushing away the effects of whatever mind-altering substance has been introduced into my system.

Piece by piece and morsel by morsel, bits of errant memory begin to float their way into my mind.

I can see Finn's face now. He looks...happy. *Yes, I remember now.* He and I were heading to New York to find his brother, Merit. We were in a drone, a flying machine called an Air-Wing. My friend Rys had provided the drone for us, telling us it had once belonged to the man known in the Arc as the *King* —a quiet, cruel figure who had single-handedly developed much of the technology used in every Arcology in the country.

As the scene unfolds in my mind, I interrogate myself, hoping to uncover more than the mere basics.

Who was flying it? Was it Finn?

No. It was Rys.

But he wasn't with us. He was piloting it remotely from the King's Guard's headquarters in the Arc. Before we left, he assured us that it was all perfectly safe—the aircraft had been checked over, he said, and it was in excellent shape. Given that

Rys is an expert at controlling a hundred drones at once, we figured nothing could go wrong.

Rys did indeed keep us safe as we soared over state after state, the country unfurling below us like a beautiful, ever-altering quilt. With a brief smile, I recall that for much of the journey I held Finn's hand, my head resting on his shoulder as we watched in wonder, reveling in the beauty of the landscape far below.

After several hours had passed, Rys announced that we were nearing Manhattan, though he hardly needed to tell us. We were close enough to see New York's famous skyline in the distance, complete with its monstrous recent addition.

The Behemoth.

The largest Arcology in the country and a blight on the horizon, it looked like an enormous, horrifying intruder casting a grim shadow over a once iconic skyline.

I was still staring at it in a sort of petrified awe when Rys's voice boomed over the speakers once again, imitating an airline pilot. He informed us with glee that we would soon begin our descent and that he hoped we'd had an enjoyable flight.

"Don't forget to grab an extra bag of peanuts as you disembark at the gate," he all but sang as we banked hard to the left, the drone preparing for its landing. Rys had already told us he would find a quiet street—one not overrun with Directorate vehicles—and put us down gently.

I remember grabbing Finn's arm and pointing to the Statue of Liberty far below us, delighted to find that it still existed.

The image of his smiling face floods my mind now like a pleasant dream crafted out of liquid smoke, and I try with all my willpower to hold onto it.

But then, as if my mind is protecting me from a trauma too painful to bear, the memories end.

No, no, no.

Finn is alive. I'm certain of that much; I can feel it deep in my chest, though I'm not sure why I'm so confident. I suppose it's that I've been through this before. I thought I lost him once. I came close, even, to accepting it. But the whole time, I felt somewhere inside my soul that he was still with me.

I feel it now, too.

He's alive. He's out there.

I just need to find him.

I slam my eyes shut and force myself into renewed focus. Traumatic or not, I need to remember what happened. I need to figure out why I'm now alone in this dark place.

There has to be more to my memories—a scrap of information that can prove to me nothing terrible has happened to him. Something that tells me where he went...

Think.

Think.

Think.

As I lie motionless, my eyes begin to adjust to the room's darkness, and my mind veers temporarily away from thoughts of our journey.

I need to figure out where I am, if I'm to have any hope of escaping this place.

By now, bits of light have begun to seep in around thick, dark curtains covering two large windows to my left. I can see enough to tell that the ceiling is high—fourteen feet, at least—and I get the impression that I'm in a bedroom. Even in the shadows, I can make out an ornate mirror leaning against the far wall, as well as an antique dresser.

I appear to be in a rich person's home.

But as my eyes continue to adjust to the meager light, I begin to realize that I'm wrong about that.

I'm in a rich person's *former* home.

The plaster and paint on the ceiling and walls are cracked violently in places, as if the house is trying to split itself apart. The floor, I notice as I twist my head and glance down to my right, is a deeply worn and chipped hardwood in desperate need of refinishing. It was probably beautiful once, but like so many things that were once lovely, it's been abandoned, left to wither and decay.

I wonder with a shudder of nausea if I, too, will be left in this place to wither until I fade to nothing.

When my eyes land on a picture hanging on the wall a few feet from me, I pull my chin up to study it. It's small—no more than six by six inches—but even in the shadowy room, its subject is unmistakable. A crudely-drawn rose, hanging upside down and dripping dark liquid onto the ground below.

The Directorate's rose, overturned and bloodied?

It has to be.

A flicker of hope ignites inside me as I wonder if I could possibly be among allies.

But why would allies tie me to a bed?

A second timid spark of hope twitches to life when I pull my eyes down to my body and note two things.

One, I'm still wearing my silver uniform. The garment grants me strength I would otherwise never possess—enough to throw a full-grown man across the room, should I feel so inclined. It's a reassuring thing to know I'll be able to defend myself if anyone tries to assault me.

Two, the straps holding my arms down look like nothing more than repurposed seatbelts quickly sewn together as makeshift bonds. They're not cruel or biting, but they are firmly attached to my arms, almost as if to protect me from myself. I realize as I examine the stitching that I could probably tear myself free if I wanted to.

But then what? Would I try and break my way out of this room and assault my waiting captors? I don't even know who they are, damn it.

I need a plan. But the thing I need most is to *remember*. I need to figure out how I got here. Where Finn is. What happened to us in the moments before...before...

Before what?

2

JOURNEY

CLOSING MY EYES AGAIN, I attempt to focus despite the fact that my head is suddenly pounding. I claw at my mind, trying to recall the last moments before Finn and I were separated.

After a few seconds, a dam somewhere inside me seems to burst, and the memories flood my mind in a torrent, coming fast and chaotically. They feel like vivid, colorful shards of the most graphic jigsaw puzzle, pleading to be sorted into some kind of order.

I snatch at the pieces and assemble them, watching the moments unfold as if I'm living them right now.

I see Finn's face, his contentment morphing into concern as we sit close together, the mutated skyline of New York City emerging from between thick clouds in the distance. With a sudden, shocking clarity, I recall our first detailed look at the Behemoth, taking in its imposing size and mass. A monster that could devour the entirety of the Arc and every person inside it in one tidy bite.

As the scene unfolds—the very moment when we realize what we're up against—terror begins to rise in my chest.

Something about the sight convinces me that we've made a mistake coming all this way. A gut feeling that if Merit is inside the Behemoth, we'll never see him again.

In the neighborhoods far below us, I can just barely make out the orange glow of what look like bonfires raging at random intervals along the city streets. Buildings have crumbled to the ground here and there, their grim remnants like decaying corpses, victims of an ongoing, brutal war.

"That's Brooklyn, I think," Finn tells me. "I'm not entirely sure why it's on fire. Rys—do you know anything about this?"

"Not a thing," Rys replies over the speaker. "This is the first I'm seeing of it. I don't have access to New York's drones or surveillance systems. Who is at war, exactly?"

"I can only guess it's the usual," I say. "Dregs versus Wealthies. It's a tale as old as time."

As we fly in the direction of a structure I recognize as the famous Brooklyn Bridge, the fires come to an abrupt end, the smoke clearing to reveal a series of khaki vehicles that seem positioned to halt any traffic that might want to cross the bridge.

I'm about to point this out when the Air-Wing's digital controls begin wavering, flickering, then shut down entirely.

"Something's wrong," Rys's voice bellows through the speakers. "I've lost control of the drone—someone has hacked into the system. They've cut me off!"

"Can't you do something?" I cry, feeling the Air-Wing dropping like a stone, a surge of nausea assaulting me. "Rys!"

He goes silent for a moment, and I'm convinced we've lost him. But as we plummet toward the ground at alarming speed, his voice comes once again.

"They've taken over," he says, the words eerily calm. "If you make it, look for Atticus. He'll find you. I—"

His voice cuts off as if someone has severed our connection.

"*Who* has taken over?" Finn says. "Rys? Rys!"

I let out a shriek as the drone's free-fall comes to an abrupt end.

At first, I'm convinced we've collided with the ground. But we couldn't have. For one thing, we're not dead.

For another, when I look outside, I see that we're still high in the air, hovering many feet above the street below. But almost immediately, the drone starts to fall slowly, heavily, as though Finn and I are being dragged to earth by a giant magnet. We grab desperately for the manual controls, trying in vain to steady the flying machine.

Realizing the futility of our efforts, I reach for Finn, squeezing his hand so tightly that I'm worried I'll break his bones.

I want him to promise we'll be okay. But I can see in his face that he knows as well as I do it would be a lie.

Somehow, the next moments pass both in slow motion and blindingly fast. *I love you,* I think desperately, my voice too strangled in my chest to utter the words out loud. I can feel in Finn's grip that he's as paralyzed by confusion and fear as I am.

Our last message to one another, it seems, will be conveyed through the touch of our hands.

We will not allow ourselves to scream or to despair as we surge downward. Our lives will end with dignity.

But death doesn't come for us.

Instead, the drone steadies with a jolt fifty or so feet in the air. Then, as if steered by an invisible hand, it edges toward a tall glass office building, a multitude of mirrored windows reflecting our vessel, almost as if the glass itself is mocking us.

I'm horrified when I see my own face looking back at me, my vulnerability written all over my features even as Finn manages to appear strong and calm at my side.

"Who is doing this?" I ask, my voice strained. "Who's controlling this thing?"

"I can guess," Finn replies, "though I can't imagine how it could be possible."

"Your mother." My voice is bitter. "You think she somehow knew we were coming."

"The thought crossed my mind, yes," he nods before hesitating. "But she wouldn't have the power to hack into this drone. Even if she and my father really brought Merit to New York, they haven't been here long enough to take charge of anything or anyone. It *has* to be someone else, Ash."

The drone continues its descent until we near the street below, slowing down to a crawl until I feel the Air-Wing land with a sort of muffled thud on the ground.

Relieved, I peer around, seeing no one at first. In fact, there's nothing here but an eerily empty street.

An optimistic thought occurs to me then: Maybe the drone has some kind of automatic landing system that overrode Rys's commands?

Yes. Maybe this was *supposed* to happen.

But almost immediately, a deep, nagging apprehension warns me not to get my hopes up.

As if to confirm my fear, the convex glass hatch above us flies open. Voices come at us, growing louder with each passing second—men shouting commands, their words aggressive and angry.

Ready to fight, I undo my seatbelt and try to rise out of my seat. But almost instantly, a shock of pain assaults the side of my neck like the vicious sting of an insect.

The world goes blurry and my legs give out underneath me as I collapse back into my seat.

Finn, too, seems to be having trouble moving. He tries to climb out of the aircraft but fails, and I watch helplessly as two men leap into the drone and grab him. One of them extracts a black device from a holster at his waist and holds it in front of Finn's face. A second later, a tidy red beam streaks over his features.

I hear four words then:

It's him. It's Davenport.

The men grab Finn and drag him out of the drone.

Struggling to keep my wits about me, I tell myself to follow. But when I try to push myself up again, the piercing, percussive sound of gunfire meets my ears. I drop down to crouch uselessly on the Air-Wing's floor, the world spinning.

More shouts echo through the air, only this time they seem to come from every direction.

I push myself up just enough to see the men in dark uniforms dragging Finn away. But he's not going without a fight. Pulling free for a few seconds, he turns back to shout something at me—something I can't quite hear.

The guards grab him again. Under normal circumstances, Finn could fight them off. He's strong enough in his uniform to take on ten men. But these circumstances are anything but normal. If he's feeling as disoriented and weak as I am, he can barely stand on his own, let alone fight.

Suddenly, a small crowd is rushing at the drone from behind me. When I use my remaining strength to turn and look, I can see that unlike the men who abducted Finn, they aren't in uniforms. Their clothing is bedraggled and mismatched, torn and dirty.

Rebels? I wonder. *Consortium members?*

"Grab her!" a woman's voice shouts. My eyes land on her face as she climbs into the Air-Wing, but I can't focus on her features enough to determine anything about her.

"Who…who are you?" I ask, my speech slurred. My tongue feels swollen in my mouth.

This isn't right.

"The more important question," she retorts, "is who are you, and what are you doing in a drone that belongs to *him*?"

"Him," I repeat, but I can barely manage the word. "You—you mean the King?"

"I—no!" she replies. "Look, we don't have time to chat right now. If we don't get you out of here, it won't end well for you or any of us."

I try to speak again. I want to go after Finn, to get him back before those men take him somewhere I can't follow.

But even as my mouth tries in vain to form the words, I lose consciousness.

3

NOW

THE MEMORIES HAVE ONCE AGAIN COME to an end.

Pulling myself into the present in the strange bedroom, I open my eyes again. Sweat beads my brow. My hands are clenched into fists as I let the images in my mind drift away to nothingness.

I'm still here.

If I could only figure out where here is.

"Hello!" I call out. "Can anyone hear me? I'm awake! I need answers!"

No one replies.

But after a minute or so, the curtains part as if by a will of their own, splitting open to reveal a surprisingly pleasant view of the outdoors. A row of red brick homes, their windows large and evenly-spaced, stare back at me from across a broad street.

There's something comforting and familiar about them. I remember my father telling me about New York City's famous brownstones, row houses joined by walls linking neighbor to neighbor. He explained that they were named for the type of sandstone used in their construction.

As my eyes move up the buildings' façades, I can see that some of their upper windows are blown out, and scorch-marks streak the chipped and cracked brick, as if a recent explosion has marred their perfection.

"The Directorate has been busy," I mutter under my breath.

Pressing my head back into the pillow, I let out a deep sigh. Finn and I could have stayed in the mountains. We could have started a new life, either inside the Arc or in a chalet somewhere in the foothills. We have plentiful options, now that the Consortium is in control of the Arc and most of its former Directorate members have either fled or been incarcerated for their crimes.

But when I pause to fully consider it, we *didn't* have a choice. Not really. The Duke and Duchess, Finn's parents, disappeared along with Finn's ten-year-old brother, Merit, and we have reason to believe this is where they ended up. Finn wants Merit back, and I can't say I blame him.

Finn, like me, would do anything to protect his brother.

I can't help but think of the last time I saw my own brother, Kel. He was being ushered inside the Arc by our allies in the Consortium, ready to begin his strange new life. Illian and Kurt, the two leaders, promised to keep my brother safe until my return, and I trust them as much as I've ever trusted anyone.

I never wanted my little brother inside the Arc. But he's safe, and that's all that matters. Kel is currently in my friend Kyra's care, living in a luxurious residence formerly inhabited by some wealthy Aristocrat on Level Two-Ninety. With them are two other families and several other children from the Pit, including Masha, a friend Kel met during his time in that subterranean stronghold.

Kel is safe, I tell myself. *There's no reason to worry about him. My focus needs to be on here and now. I need to figure out where Finn is...then we need to find Merit and get the hell out of here.*

Simple, right?

The problem is, Merit isn't the only reason I wanted to make this journey. I have a far more nefarious motive for coming east.

The Duchess.

The woman who has tortured and tormented me. The woman who killed my friend Peric with her bare hands.

She's twisted and cruel, and I want to see her suffer for it.

Even if she *is* Finn's mother.

I intend to find a way to bring her to justice one of these days. Whether it's by dragging her back out west for a trial or killing her myself, I don't know.

All I know is that she needs to pay for what she's done.

As rage heats my skin, I force my mind away from toxic thoughts of that woman, choosing instead to picture Finn's face. The excitement, the anticipation in his eyes back in the Arc when we spoke of our upcoming trip to New York.

He looked so at peace, so calm, so collected.

It wasn't so long ago that I thought I'd lost him...and when I finally got him back, the nanotech implanted in his body threatened to destroy his mind, assaulting it with a perpetual parade of cruel visions of a devastating future.

But he's reverted more or less to his former self now, and for a couple of blissful days and nights before we began our journey east, we were able to enjoy our time together without the haunting shadows of his visions torturing him.

Despite the potential danger that awaited us, I too was

looking forward to our time in Manhattan. We've always been a good team, after all. And recently, we've become almost unstoppable. I suppose the naive part of me thought this trip of ours would prove easy. We would land, extract Merit from wherever the Duke and Duchess had taken him, and, after I'd found a way to deal with the Duchess, we would escape.

Easy-peasy.

But in my blissful, idealistic fog, I conveniently forgot that nothing in this cruel world is ever easy. Nothing goes according to plan.

Think.

Staring up at the ceiling, I call out, "Is anyone there?"

It comes then. A low, amused laugh that sounds like that of a young man.

"Oh, great," I say under my breath with a wince. "Another psycho."

"Don't worry," a voice says. "I'm not going to kill you. At least, not just yet."

4

ADRASTOS

I GLANCE AROUND THE ROOM, hunting for any sign of the person who just spoke.

But there's no one.

I tell myself I only imagined the voice. I'm delusional, delirious with panic or fatigue, or both.

As if to confirm my madness, when I press my head back into the pillow, the bonds holding my arms and legs in place loosen then pull away, freeing me.

At first I tell myself I must be imagining it, but when I manage to raise my hands over my face, I feel reassured, if only a little.

Still, I hesitate to move, waiting expectantly for someone to storm into the room. But when no one does, I push myself up and twist around so my legs slip over the edge of the bed.

I ease into a standing position, my head swimming. For the first time, I realize that the sting I felt in my neck when the drone landed must have been from some sort of projectile. A tranquilizer, most likely. Someone drugged me with something—a substance that made my brain fog up like a window

K. A. RILEY

on a cold winter's day. It's why I'm so confused, why my mind keeps veering from one memory to the next, robbing me of the ability to formulate a coherent string of thoughts.

But the fog is lifting, and I'm able to look around the room properly now, to hunt for signs that anyone is watching me via camera or micro-drone. All I see, though, are the bed, the dresser, the large mirror leaning against the far wall. There's little else.

I slip forward, taking small, careful steps, my hands out in front of me in case I should lose my balance. I consider calling on the power known as the Surge—a power granted to me by Finn—to blast a hole through the door.

But I have no idea who or what is on the other side. For all I know, it's a Dreg, someone innocent and undeserving of assault.

My captors may not know it yet, but we're probably on the same side. Still, how can I blame them for being cautious? After all, I showed up here in the King's drone, and it's not like I'm wearing a sign on my chest that says, "I'm with the good guys." All they've seen of me is my silver uniform, which looks more like it might belong to a Directorate member than anyone else.

"Glad to see you up and about," the elusive voice says through some unseen speaker, startling me so that I leap backwards, ready to fight. It's the same voice I heard a few minutes ago—rich and almost unnaturally deep. "I hope your head isn't hurting too much. If it is, rest assured that it will feel better soon."

"Who is speaking?" I ask, narrowing my eyes accusingly toward the mirror, which I imagine to be the only possible vantage point my captors have. Is there a hidden camera behind it, or perhaps tucked into a nook in the wall?

"First things first," the voice replies. "I have no doubt you could use a washroom. Behind the mirror, you'll find a narrow door. Feel free to help yourself."

Realizing my captor is right—I'm desperate, actually—I do as he says, stepping cautiously over to the mirror and grabbing its sides. I lift it easily, shifting it a few feet to the left and quickly shooting a glance at its back in the process, only to see there's no evidence of a camera or any other electronics.

The narrow door my captor mentioned opens easily, and I step inside to find a small, simple powder room that contains nothing but a toilet and a small sink.

When I head back into the bedroom a few minutes later, the voice comes at me again.

"My name is Adrastos," it says in an unreadable tone. "And for the record, that's the *only* door you can open without my permission."

That sounds like a challenge to me, I think with a scowl. I'm almost tempted to prove my captor wrong, but I suppose it couldn't hurt to play nice for the time being.

"Now," the voice adds, "maybe you could tell me who the hell you are."

"Who do you *think* I am?" I ask, pacing the room, my eyes hunting for the source of the sound.

"You're not dressed like an Aristocrat," the disembodied voice replies. "But you're definitely not dressed like a Dreg, either. If I had to guess, I'd say you were some sort of super-soldier in training. That still doesn't answer the question about the drone you were in, though. Even super-soldiers aren't usually afforded such luxury. Then again, you probably stole it, so..."

"I take it you're not an Aristocrat, Adrastos," I say, staring into the mirror past my own reflection.

K. A. RILEY

"You saw the rose," Adrastos replies. "And obviously, you're no fool. You're quite right—I am far from an Aristocrat."

"Then why don't you let me out of here," I ask, "and we can talk like civilized human beings about what brought me to this city?"

The speaker lets out a laugh. "I'll tell you what—I'll come in there and we can chat. Be warned, though. I'll have a few friends with me."

"I don't mind," I reply. "The more the merrier, right?"

A few seconds later the door creaks open, revealing three figures silhouetted in the bright hallway outside the room.

In the center is a tall young woman, flanked by two men. They all appear to be around the same age—maybe nineteen or twenty. The men are carrying handguns. The woman is unarmed, but somehow manages to be the most daunting of the trio.

I take a step forward, and when the men reach for their guns, I grope instinctively to my side only to realize my dagger is gone, though its sheath remains firmly fastened at my waist.

"Your weapon is safe," the young woman says, holding a hand up to tell the men to stand down. Turning to them, she adds, "Don't worry, she's not intending to hurt us."

I wonder how she can be so sure, but I relax my shoulders and cross my arms as though to confirm she's correct.

I examine the two men, wondering if it was one of them who was just speaking to me. But it's the woman who says, "I'm Adrastos. Around here, they call me Adi."

Her voice is feminine, almost lilting. Completely unlike the heavy, deep drawl that was being projected into the room just a minute ago.

"Wait..." I reply, confused. "I thought you were...."

"You thought I was a man." She smiles. "What can I tell you? I like messing with people's minds."

I've been through enough mental manipulation to last ten lifetimes, and the words make my blood boil.

I don't think. I don't breathe.

I thrust both hands out and, with a shocking set of matching blue orbs conjured from nothing but my mind, I send her two companions flying back against the wall of the corridor, their weapons crashing to the ground as their backs collide with hard plaster.

Before Adrastos can react, I step forward, grab her by the neck, and press her into the wall between her companions, lifting her a few inches off the ground for good measure. Given that she's taller than I am, it proves somewhat difficult. But I'm reluctant to let her see the strain in my face as I tighten my grip.

Groaning, one of the guards manages to drag himself a few inches to reach for his gun, but I stop him with a snarl.

"Touch that weapon, and I'll kill her." Turning back to the woman, I add, "I'm not interested in games, Adrastos. If you're not going to cooperate with me, I will kill you, your guards, and everyone else who might be lurking in this house. Then, without so much as an ounce of guilt, I'll walk straight out the front door. Am I making myself clear?"

She musters a weak nod and I release her.

"Interesting," she croaks with a look of reluctant admiration as she presses back against the wall.

"Tell your men to leave their weapons and go," I command. "I have no intention of hurting you, but I'm not okay with having guns pointed at my face, either."

With her hand to her throat, she manages, "You can go. It's fine."

"But…" the taller of the two men protests. The way he's looking at her makes me feel a *little* guilty for what I've just done. I've seen that look before in Finn's face when he's determined to protect me.

You care about her, I think. *A lot.*

"Give us a few minutes, Cillian," she says sharply, pronouncing the name as if it begins with a K. "I'm *fine*."

When the men have set their guns on the floor and left, I pick up the weapons and allow myself to back into the room to assess the young woman. Her shoulder-length black hair is almost completely shaved on the sides. Thick brows arch above large hazel eyes, and on her lips is bright red lipstick that seems more about power than beauty.

There's something lovely about her, though I get the immediate impression she wouldn't want the word applied to her. She's all business, the expression on her face that of someone who is both mildly confused and desperately in need of answers.

"What do you want to know?" she asks.

"The young man I was with in the drone," I say. "Do you know what happened to him?"

I don't want to refer to Finn by name or as my boyfriend, to give Adrastos any leverage over me by revealing that I care deeply about him. Affection is a potent weapon in places like this—a sharp knife used to extract precious information or to hurt prisoners. And while I don't fear my captors, I don't want to offer them any ammunition.

"He was taken," she says. "Before we could make it to the drone. Your friend is an Aristocrat, is he not?"

"Why would you say that?"

"We were watching when they scanned him. If they'd identified him as a Dreg, they would have shot him on the spot—which is what I suspect they would have done to you if we hadn't shown up. There are a few ways to recognize a Krat—an Aristocrat, I mean. One is facial recognition, assuming what they're seeing is a *real* face and not an altered version of it." Adi hesitates for a few seconds, her eyes shifting away from mine when she adds, "The other is to...to look for their mark."

"Mark?" I ask. I've never heard of Aristocrats having a distinguishing mark of any sort, and Finn has never mentioned it.

"A tattoo—small, but unmistakable. Most Aristocrats receive one at some point in their lives. Some who are young don't recall getting them—the Wealthies began to administer them years ago as a means to distinguish themselves in case anyone ever questioned their lineage. It's possible that your friend doesn't have one, but it obviously didn't matter. They knew exactly who he was, which means they were looking for him. Lucky for you, because stealing one of the Bishop's Air-Wings is a pretty massive offense."

"Bishop?" I reply. The two syllables run through my blood like ice, though I have no idea why. "Who is he?"

"He owns New York," Adi says. "He's also the man who has your friend locked up behind fourteen layers of security as we speak."

5

REVELATIONS

"So, this Bishop person has Finn," I say. "But why would you say he owns the Air-Wing we were in? It was the King's. The man who ran the Arc. He's rich as hell and—"

Adi cuts me off. "At one point, I'm sure it was. But the man you call the King showed up here days ago, as a refugee. Even a man as powerful as he is doesn't just wander into New York City without paying a price. The Bishop basically owns the King now—and that includes everything in his possession."

"But the guy is incredibly powerful," I protest. "He's a tech giant. Why the hell would he ever agree to give everything away?"

"To ensure his family's safety." Adi gawks at me for a moment, then lets out a slow breath of disbelief. "You really have no idea what you've just flown into, do you? You came to New York expecting...what? To waltz across Brooklyn Bridge, wave hello to the madmen in charge, then go shopping on Fifth Avenue? *No one* comes here for pleasure. They either show up to escape or to hide, or both. Either way, they pay a huge price."

I stare at her, my chest tight.

She's right. Finn and I didn't know what we were getting into. We naively followed his family east, convinced we could simply infiltrate the Behemoth as we've infiltrated the Arc so many times—with Rys's help, of course.

But Rys, too, was naive. He hasn't seen this city up close. He has no idea what's going on here. In fact, I'm not sure *anyone* back home realizes what's going on here. New York is a war zone where Dregs are apparently armed, dangerous, and hiding in plain sight.

And from the sounds of it, the Directorate is run by someone far more powerful, even, than the Duchess.

"Are we in Brooklyn now?" I finally ask, desperate to figure out what I need to do to get to Finn.

Adi nods. "But most of us don't call it Brooklyn anymore. We call it *Broken*. You've seen enough by now to know why. There's not a single street in this borough that hasn't been bombed at some point."

My mind shifts to the devastated buildings we saw from the Air-Wing, to the piles of rubble and crumbling façades of once beautiful structures.

Yes, I understand perfectly why they would call this place *Broken.*

"Look, just do one thing for me, would you?" I ask, trying not to sound like I'm pleading with her. "Tell me who this Bishop actually is."

"That's not so simple as it sounds." Adi lets out another sigh. "No one really knows."

When I look like I'm about to respond, she holds up a hand to stop me.

"I don't mean no one's ever seen him. We see him all the time. He splits his days and nights between street level and the

'Moth—the Behemoth, I mean. He comes into Broken pretty frequently, probably because it's got the biggest Dreg population of any place on the east coast. It's an intimidation tactic on his part—he just wants to remind us he's always watching. So yeah. We all know his face like the backs of our hands." Almost as an afterthought, she adds, "Though if you ask me, it's not his *real* face."

"What does that mean?"

"Let's just say he's a mystery. He looks nineteen or twenty, but most of us Dregs are convinced he's a lot older. He's handsome—like, incredibly, freakishly handsome, in a way no one has any right to be. It's like he was created in a lab. The guy is perfect, if you don't count the fact that he's pure evil. What's gross is that people fall in love with him constantly, despite knowing what kind of man he is. If you ever meet him, you'll understand. I wish I could say I've never fallen victim to his charms, but I'd be lying through my teeth. He has this… effect…on people. It's like he gets into your head and convinces you he's the greatest gift the world has ever known…even when you know it's a lie."

"I take it he's Directorate?" I ask. "If he's pure evil and spends time in the Behemoth, he sounds like one of them."

Adi shakes her head. "He's not. It's like he's in a faction of his own making. He's more powerful than they are; the guy runs this city. But there's still a strong Directorate presence. They act like his henchmen. His own private army. Hell, the Bishop owns the entire east coast. No one comes or goes without his blessing. No one crosses the bridges into Manhattan without his consent. I tell you—he can see everything that goes on in every corner of New York. I'm convinced he loves the battles, the fighting, the fires. He gets off on the mayhem in his own twisted way."

"We saw the fires when we were flying in."

Adi nods. "There's fighting daily between us and the Directorate Guard. A constant struggle for territory. We're trying to keep our homes, our lives, and *they're* trying to make sure we have nothing. But I'm sure I don't need to tell you how it is."

"No, you don't," I tell her, though I can't say we ever actually fought the Directorate patrols in the Mire. We were always told they were our friends, our protectors, and we were foolish enough to believe it until it was far too late to do anything about it.

Adi looks me up and down and, seemingly not interested in the subject of battles anymore, says, "Your uniform contains stealth-silver and some other composite we weren't able to identify. I assume it's why you're so strong—though it doesn't explain the energy burst trick you pulled on my friends."

"The Surge…is a little hard to explain," I tell her. "Let's just say it was a gift from a friend."

"Show me how the uniform works," she says with a smirk, and for the first time, I understand why her people didn't remove it when they took me prisoner. Adi knows by now I could kill her in three seconds flat if I so desired. But she's not threatened by me. Which either means she *knew* I was an ally, or she strongly suspected it.

I push my shoulders back and, curling my hands into fists, press my fingers into my palms. The suit disappears, though my head, uncovered as it is, remains visible.

"Incredible," she breathes. "Really. I didn't know such a thing existed other than on paper and in scientists' imaginations. No one around here except the Bishop has enough money to work on developing that kind of tech."

"The Wealthies—Krats, I mean—they don't have money?"

"Not as much as you might think. The Bishop collects taxes every quarter. Massive amounts, which the Krats pay willingly, though no one really understands how he's managed to persuade them to do it. It's all very hush-hush."

"Protection money, maybe?" I speculate.

"Maybe. But I think it's more than that. I think they're paying for another service. I just don't know what it is."

I raise an eyebrow, more curious than ever about this Bishop character. As evil as he sounds, he also sounds like he enjoys taking advantage of the Aristocracy.

The enemy of my enemy is my friend.

Maybe.

"Tell me," Adi says, "if you're not a Krat, then how were you able to afford a uniform like that?"

The question throws me. I thought I'd made it clear that I'm not a Wealthy. I'm a Dreg, just like her.

I press my fingers into my palms again, disabling the stealth setting, and let out a laugh. Adi, however, does not look amused.

Crossing my arms over my chest, I reply, "If you took all the money in the world and burned it, the pile of useless ashes is how much I have. I'm a Dreg from the Mire. My family was poor. My parents are dead—both killed by the Directorate, who would love to kill me, too."

I'm well aware that my words are a gamble. Adi is unreadable, a frown on her lips as she studies me. I feel like she's trying to decipher me, to figure out how honest I'm being.

But after a few seconds, I get the impression she's already decided.

"If you're really just a Dreg, then why does he..." she begins, before stopping herself and shaking her head.

"He who?" I ask. "What are you talking about?"

She hesitates before saying, "You know what? Just come with me."

I stare at her, a sickening feeling of déja-vu working its way through my mind. I've been here too many times before. Not in this exact place, but in this exact, horrid situation, faced with someone I desperately want to trust—someone who appears to be on my side of the war.

But I've been betrayed far too often, and I've learned to trust no one in this world other than Kel and Finn.

And, when I'm feeling charitable, Rys.

Still, my choices appear to be:

One: Accompany my captor.

Or Two: Stay in the bedroom, where I'll probably be locked up indefinitely, curtains drawn, bonds strapping my limbs back to the bed.

Taking my chances, I decide to accompany the woman called Adrastos.

WELCOME TO NEW YORK

ADI WHISTLES as she moves into the hall.

The young man called Cillian appears a moment later, positioning himself protectively next to her. With a sigh of surrender, I follow Adi along the hall and up a long marble staircase to a large study on the second floor. Cillian follows me, his footsteps aggressive on the stairs as if attempting to remind me he would be all too happy to kill me the second his leader commands it.

When we reach the study, Adi takes a seat in a broad leather armchair and I plop down on a torn-up couch that's seen better days, its leather pulling apart at the seams to reveal a mass of yellowed stuffing intent on escaping.

An assortment of armed guards who seem more curious than antagonistic are now pacing the hallway just outside the room, their eyes alert. Every now and then I hear the crackle of static and what sound like distant communications via walkie-talkie.

"Look," Adi says, "I believe you're a Dreg, but I need you to tell me everything. Who are you really, and how did you gain access to that drone?"

"Wait—why do you suddenly believe me?" I ask, refusing to give her the satisfaction of answers just yet. "You literally strapped me to a bed in the dark when you thought I might be a threat. You were accusing me of being a Wealthy just a minute ago. Why the sudden change of heart?"

She narrows her eyes for a moment before seeming to resign herself to humoring me. "I have a way of knowing if people are lying to me," she says matter-of-factly.

I glance down at my wrists, my brow furrowing. "Did you put a monitor on me or something? How could you possibly know that?"

"I just know," she replies with a wry smile. "Look—you have your gifts, I have mine. Let's leave it at that, okay?"

The truth is, I don't particularly care how she knows. The important thing is that she knows she can trust me—which means, at least, that part of my work here is done.

"Are you rebels?" I ask.

"Rebels," she laughs. "Yes, I suppose that's what we are." She nods to her right, her eyes focusing on a window that looks out onto the same street I was staring at earlier. "You haven't answered my questions."

"I don't have time for that. I need to find—"

"The guy you were with," she replies. "I know you want to see him, but that's going to be impossible just now."

When she sees the dismayed look on my face, she adds, "Don't worry. They won't hurt him, at least not yet. He'll be in their care until they figure out exactly how valuable he might be."

"How long will that take?" I ask impatiently.

"A few days, maybe more. It depends on a lot of things."

She seems to sense the rage building inside me, because she continues. "Look, I'll do what I can for you. But it would help your cause if you told me exactly who you are."

I take a deep breath. "I told you, I'm a Dreg from—"

"The Mire. Yeah, I know. Tell me your damned name."

Adi is growing impatient now. *Well, at least she knows how I feel.*

Fine. I suppose I have no choice but to tell her *something* about myself. Anything to get her to stop asking her questions and start answering mine.

But do I lie or come clean?

A couple of options barrel through my mind. *Make up a name. Something that won't be too memorable. Susan Smith, maybe. Act like you're just some random, naive girl who got caught up in something larger than herself—who got dragged here by her reckless, wealthy boyfriend.*

Or...just tell the truth.

My instincts warn me against inventing an elaborate fable, if for no other reason than that Adi seems to have a built-in lie detector.

"My name is Ashen Spencer," I finally say, barely concealing the wince that contorts my features.

Adi tightens, pulling back for a second before forcing herself to relax again, and I know instantly this isn't her first time hearing my name. A palpable excitement dances through the air between us, as if something momentous has just occurred.

"You're the Crimson Dreg," Adi breathes, shaking her head and chuckling.

"How do you...?" Not only did she recognize my actual name, but she knows my nickname, bestowed upon me by the more rebellious residents of the Arc.

"Now I get it," she says.

"Get what?"

She shakes her head. "I'm just stunned, that's all. I guess I should have known your face. But it never occurred to me that you could possibly be here, standing in this wreck of a house. You're the last person I would have expected to see on this side of the country."

"I can't believe you've heard of me." My voice practically shakes with a cross between embarrassment and wonder. It was one thing to be famous inside the Arc, but for my name to have reached this far?

That's *insane.*

She nods, gesturing toward the door and the corridor beyond. Cillian eyes me with quiet surprise, though he still appears guarded and cautious.

"We've all heard of you," Adi says. "What happened in the Arc—the takeover by the Consortium—it's *legendary.* We've heard all about your so-called 'Quiet War.' We saw snippets of your videos, though they were a little scrambled and messed up—all bootlegs of bootlegs, which is why I didn't know your face immediately, I suppose. I have to tell you, it was incredible to watch from a distance. For a little while, you even managed to give us hope."

She looks wistfully toward the window.

"I'm glad," I say softly. "Really. All I wanted was to give the world hope."

She nods. "I wish it was enough. I wish we could use the same tactics out here that you used in the Arc, but believe me when I say nothing short of a nuclear holocaust would stop our particular brand of psychos from destroying New York—and we'd end up killing every Dreg on the East Coast in the process."

"I'm sure there's a way," I tell her. "You have weapons and from what I can tell, you have a small army. If we could get them into the Behemoth…"

But she shakes her head. "No one will be taking over the Moth. It's simply not possible."

"Why not? There has to be an entrance, right? And it sounds like there are thousands of Dregs fighting on this side of the river. You're armed, you're dangerous. You have what we never had back home—you have experienced fighters. That's huge."

"You don't understand." With another vigorous shake of her head, Adi says, "No army is getting into the Behemoth. The only—and I do mean *only*—entrance is a hundred stories above the ground. The only way into the Moth is by flying, and very few people have access to the drones required for entry. Every drone, like every person who's allowed inside, is highly vetted before being admitted. I mean, look—you saw what they did to the Air-Wing you were in. They hacked it remotely and brought you down. You were helpless. And they were *gentle* with you. It could have been so much worse. I've seen…" She stops talking and swallows, seeming to fight back tears. "Let's just say it isn't always pretty."

I stare at her, unsure how to respond.

If what she's saying is true, and if the Bishop's men have brought Finn into the Behemoth…I may never see him again. Not only that, but he'll be trapped with his wretched monster of a mother forever, in a prison worse than any I can imagine.

"Are you telling me I should turn around and head home?" I ask. "Because I'm afraid that's not an option for me."

"No. I definitely don't want you to do that. We need to get you into Manhattan." She says it with a determination that's almost frightening, and I find myself wondering why the hell she's so invested in my success. "Just…give me a little time to come up with a plan, okay?"

I grind my jaw. I don't want to wait. I want to leave this place now. To get to Finn as soon as possible.

But my view from the Air-Wing made one thing clear, and that is that New York is a disaster. I can't act impulsively if I want to navigate the shattered streets, the fires, the battles.

I need these people on my side if I'm to get to Finn in one piece.

"Okay," I finally say. "And…thank you. If you find a way to help me, I'll be more grateful than you know."

"Oh, I'll help you. It's not like I have a choice, even if I wanted one."

I don't know what she means by that, but I simply say, "Thank you. Again."

With a strange laugh, she replies, "Welcome to New York, Ashen Spencer. You may as well strap in, because you're about to go for a hell of a ride."

7

SECRETS

"Tell me something," I say, looking from Adi to Cillian and back again. "The Blight. The Cure. Does New York know…"

I'm not sure how to finish the question without diving into a long tirade about the truth of the "illness" that was created by biologists including my own father, then used as a weapon against millions of unwitting adults.

She lets out a half-stifled chuckle. "The Blight," she repeats. "The Blight killed a lot of New Yorkers. A *lot*. You won't see many people around here over the age of twenty-five, at least not Dregs. Our parents were targeted, just like the adults in the rest of the country. But it all backfired when the Directorate tried to convince the Wealthies to leave their homes and move into the Behemoth."

"Really? Why?"

Adi throws me a sideways glance and laughs. "You don't know a lot of New Yorkers, do you? We don't exactly like being told what to do—especially when it involves giving up a multi-million dollar house on Fifth Avenue. Most of the

Wealthies refused to budge when they were told to move to the Moth; they didn't want to upend their lives and move into an Arcology. They said they'd take their chances on the outside, and surprise, surprise, they survived just fine. Slowly, we Dregs began to piece it together—that those who were dying were being systematically targeted for elimination. And then, like some kind of wild miracle, the deaths just...stopped. That's when the Bishop rose to power. He was the one who finally came clean and told us the whole truth. I suppose it was an attempt to gain our trust."

"Then New York was a lot quicker to catch on than we were in the Mire," I reply.

"I suppose I should be grateful we've known the truth as long as we have," Adi says with a nod. "I don't envy you what you had to deal with—what you had to figure out while you lost so many. You were kept in the dark for years, weren't you?"

I nod. "Far too long. If we'd known..." I stop myself. The truth is, I don't know what we would have done. We had barely any food or water and no weapons. We had no communications, little electricity. Organizing a rebellion on the outside would have been all but impossible.

Adi pivots in the old, beaten-up armchair as a teenage girl strides into the room with two cups of what looks like extremely strong coffee. She hands one to me, the other to Adi.

"Tell me something," Adi says as she accepts the cup and nods a thank you to the girl before turning back to me. "Why did you leave the Arc? You were safe there, weren't you? Why on earth would you come to the most destabilized place in the country after you'd taken over that stronghold? It seems to me

—" With that, she shoots a look at Cillian, who's standing in the doorway.

Once again, I get the impression there's more to their relationship than Commander and foot soldier.

"Seems to us that you could have had a pretty sweet life there," Adi concludes.

I inhale a breath and take a sip of coffee.

"We're looking for someone," I finally tell her, hesitant to divulge too much. Somehow, I don't think Adi or her friends would be overly sympathetic if I told them we were looking for an Aristocrat child. "Someone we suspect was taken to the Behemoth. We—"

As I'm speaking, the room lights up in rapid, almost blinding flashes of red. My eyes wide, I stare at Adi, who quickly lays her cup on the floor, slips off the chair, and gestures to me to get down.

"Silent alarm!" she hisses. "We can't let them see us through the window!"

"Who?" I ask as I slip down and crouch behind the couch.

My question is answered when I turn my head toward the window and spot something hovering outside, two red eyes focused on the interior of the room, scanning the far corner.

"Don't move," Adi whispers. "Don't even breathe."

Though my legs are burning, I stay perfectly still, staring sideways at the drone, which is unlike any I've ever seen.

Rys's bird drones are magnificent and elegant. The Directorate's patrol drones are utilitarian and look exactly as devoid of character as one might expect.

But this one is horrifying.

It's large and menacing, with a set of threatening claws to either side of a pair of glowing eyes, and a jagged, razor-sharp tail curled up over its back. Its flying mechanism is hidden, and I can't quite fathom how it's even managing to remain airborne.

Nor do I want to know.

When it's scanned the room and determined that there's nothing threatening in here, the drone takes off with a loud, low buzz. I push myself to my feet and dare a step toward the window to see it disappearing into the distance.

"That was a Scorp," Adi says scornfully. "Nasty bastard."

"What does it do?"

"Nothing, usually. But if a Scorp decides you're a threat, it will happily come crashing through the window and shoot a poisonous dart into any part of you it chooses. It will kill you in a matter of seconds."

"Do you think it saw me?" I'm all too aware that if I could see it, the answer is probably yes.

"I can't say. If it did, it didn't deem you a threat, which is good enough for me."

"Where's Cillian?" I ask, turning to face the door. In response, he appears from the hallway, eyeing Adi.

"I'm surprised it came by," he says. "After..."

Adi shoots him a glare of warning, and he instantly clams up. She turns to me and speaks quickly. "He means they don't normally bother us. This house has been declared derelict, and we're considered squatters. A non-threat, really, which means the Bishop's people don't care if we live or die."

She picks up her coffee once again, and as if nothing has happened, seats herself on the armchair. I stand up to stretch my legs before sitting down once again.

"Look, Ashen—we need to figure out what to do with you. You're looking for your friend, and chances are, he's in the

Bishop's headquarters. We need to figure out how to get you there."

"Where are these headquarters, exactly?"

"A place called the Palace," Adi says. "That's the very modest name of the Bishop's second home. It's not an *actual* palace, of course. It's the Waldorf Astoria—one of New York's old hotels. It's fortified like crazy, surrounded by razor wire, snipers, laser-equipped drones, you name it. Anyone brought in is basically a prisoner there until the Bishop either deems them worthy, or decides they're not worth his time."

"You're probably right. That's got to be where they took my...friend."

She shrugs. "Sure. Unless they label him a traitor for stealing that drone, in which case they'll probably just kill him."

"They won't," I assure her, attempting to project more confidence than I feel. "His parents..."

I stop, cursing myself for coming so close to saying too much.

"His parents?" Adi asks. But when I don't answer, she sits back in her seat and lets out a low chuckle. "Oh, man. Your *friend* is Finn Davenport. The Duchess's kid. Of course. How did I not figure that out right away?" She turns to Cillian and says, "You know who he is, don't you, Cill?"

He nods, frowning. "Sure. I saw him in one of the videos. He made it abundantly clear how much he hates his mother. I guess we should admire him for that, even if he *is* a Krat."

He says the last word like it's poison, and despite his faint praise, something tells me he would gladly murder Finn if he found himself alone with him.

I glare at him, angry on Finn's behalf. "He's not like that," I say. "He's only an Aristocrat by blood. He believes in justice, freedom, equal rights for all. Anyhow, he and his mother may not have the best relationship, but the Duchess won't let any harm come to him," I add, still not entirely convinced by my own words.

"Oh, I'm sure you're right. It wouldn't do to murder her own child. The Bishop wouldn't approve, for one thing. No, she'll keep her son safe in his Palace, at least until tomorrow evening."

"What's happening tomorrow?"

"Every Friday at the Palace, they hold something called the Choosing Ceremony," Adi says. "It's the official method the Bishop uses for declaring who's allowed to live inside the Moth. One person is selected for residency each week, and their family gets to accompany them. Rumor has it that there are quite a few residences sitting empty in the Moth, but the Bishop only offers them to people who can offer *him* something. People like the King—the ones with influence and power."

I find myself staring blankly at her. "Wait—you're telling me some Aristocrats are actually rejected?" I ask. "Their wealth isn't enough to get them inside? It's the biggest Arcology in the world. There must be enough room for anyone who wants in."

She shakes her head. "The Moth isn't like other Arcologies. It's...not what you might think. It was built for the Wealthies, but when New York's Elite rejected it and the Bishop took over, they say he rebuilt the inside completely. Only a few floors of the three-hundred are residential. The rest are....well..." She trails off, and I'm sure I hear a catch in her voice, like she's getting choked up.

As if looking for help, she glances at Cillian, who says, "We don't know what they are, not exactly. We have suspicions, but the truth is, no one who goes in ever comes out, except for the Bishop and his most trusted Aristocrat allies. So there's no way to find out exactly what's going on inside. All we know is—"

As he's speaking, someone walks into the room—the same young woman who brought us coffee earlier. She pads over to Adi and whispers something in her ear.

"Are you sure?" Adi asks, pulling her chin up to look the girl in the eye.

The young woman hands Adi a small black device, says, "See for yourself," then turns and leaves the room.

Adi flicks a finger over the device. A moment later, a holographic video begins to play above her palm, punctuated by a faint voice making what sounds like an announcement.

From where I'm positioned, I can't quite make out what Adi is seeing or hearing, but she looks stunned when she flicks it off and sets it down.

"What is it?" I'm apprehensive, though I'm not sure why.

"The official competitors for tomorrow evening's Choosing Ceremony have been selected. Your friend Finn's mother is going to be vying for her chance to get into the Behemoth. If she gains entry, her family will go with her."

Go with her? I think, panic inspiring a bead of sweat to dampen my brow. If Finn is forced to move into the Behemoth, and I'm out here…

"You never told me what the Choosing Ceremony is, exactly," I say, trying in vain to keep my voice steady. "Is it some kind of competition?"

"A competition, yes," Adi says. "And I feel I should tell you —it's pretty intense."

Part of me is pleased to hear it. There's little I want more in the world than to see the Duchess brought to her knees.

Maybe she'll lose, in which case Finn won't be sent to the Moth.

That would be a definite win-win for me.

"What is it?" I ask. "Some kind of IQ test?"

"Not exactly," Cillian tells me. "Unless you know of an IQ test where one participant ends up dead."

8

THE TRODDEN

"Dead?" I echo softly.

Fights to the death are nothing new to me. After all, I've participated in a few myself.

But making *Aristocrats* fight is unheard of—particularly when they're high-ranking members of the Directorate.

"You're seriously telling me the Duchess is going to fight for her life?" I stammer, convinced I misheard. "*The* Duchess?"

There is no one on the planet I hate more than that woman. No one I'd rather see lying dead on the ground in a vast pool of her own blood.

But the idea of her being forced into battle is...surreal.

If indeed the Bishop has convinced her to fight, he's more powerful than I've even begun to imagine.

"Yes, that same Duchess," Adi replies. She stares at me for a few seconds before adding, "You look traumatized."

I am, I think. *Because if someone else kills her, I won't get to do it myself.*

"Why would any Aristocrat even agree to this?" I ask. "They're the most powerful people in the world. The Duchess can afford a house in Manhattan, and she isn't the sort of person to put herself in danger willingly. She's always been shielded by the Directorate Guard. What could possibly exist in the Behemoth that's enticing enough to make her risk her life? I mean, even if she wins, it sounds like her family will end up locked inside a building they can never leave."

As I'm speaking, the answer comes to me.

If her family is locked away, it means no one can get to them. Finn will no longer have a chance to rebel against the Directorate, to join forces with the Consortium.

Or to be with me.

"Honestly, it's probably simple curiosity," Cillian says, a tinge of bitterness in his tone. "And power. And...something else. Something none of us knows about. There are things happening on the inside that only the Bishop's closest allies get to see."

"And it may surprise you to hear it, Ashen," Adi interjects, "but the truth is, I'd be willing to risk my own life if there were a chance I could get into that place."

"But why?" I ask, my tone more aggressive than I intend. "I mean, I've been inside the Arc. The Behemoth can't be that different. They're both prisons in their own right."

"What if someone you cared about was locked inside the Moth?" Adi asks quietly. "Would that change your mind?"

I think of Finn then, of the very real possibility that he will end up on the inside.

She's right. If the only way I could ever see him again was to enter the Behemoth and risk getting stuck there, I would take that risk.

But the truth is, it's not only about Finn.

I would probably follow the Duchess to the ends of the earth if it meant I was given the chance to kill her.

"Yes, it would change my mind," I admit. "But right now, there's no one on the inside I care to see. I just want to get Finn and get out of here." I don't mention Merit, if only for his own protection. As obliging as Adi and Cillian seem, there's no point in putting a target on Finn's younger brother.

My words seem to strike something inside Adi, who suddenly looks pained. She sets her feet on the floor, leans forward, and looks me hard in the eye. "There's something in the Behemoth—something that comes with membership to that very exclusive club—that people die for. *Kill* for. Something some Aristocrats will sell their souls to access. But no one on the outside has ever managed to find out what it is."

"Whatever it is, it's not my concern," I say, pushing myself to my feet. "Now, if you don't mind, I've wasted enough time. I need to find Finn before tomorrow evening."

"You'll never get near him as you are now," Cillian warns, his voice tight. "Even if you could get across the bridge into Manhattan, the Bishop's men would kill you before you got within a hundred feet of the Palace."

"I can hide," I say. "Go into stealth mode. They'll never see me. I can slip between them and cross the bridge, and—"

"And?" Adi replies with a derisive snort. "Then what? You think you'll just slip through layers of razor wire into the Palace, then walk into the Choosing Ceremony? Don't get me wrong, that stealth suit of yours is impressive, but I suspect if I took a blade to it, I could slice right through it. You're not invincible."

For a moment, I go quiet. She's not wrong; the suit is many things, but not razor-proof. I would be cut to pieces, that is if the Bishop's men didn't detect my presence and blast me full of bullet holes first.

"But we can help you," Adi says, turning to Cillian with

raised eyebrows, a strange, conspiratorial look on her face.

"Adi..." he says, but she shakes her head.

"No, Cill. I've got it. I've worked out how to get her there." She speaks like she's been pondering this for days, not mere minutes. Her eyes have gone wide to the point where she looks like an entirely different person.

"Adi," Cillian says again.

This time, she approaches him and whispers into his ear for several seconds before backing away to watch for his reaction.

"Fine," he finally says. "I suppose that's the only thing that makes sense."

She nods, clearly excited. "She could pass as one of them, if we got her properly disguised. That's probably why the Bishop..."

She cuts herself off, almost as if she's said too much.

"The Bishop what?" I ask, nervous all of a sudden.

"It's why the Bishop would welcome you with open arms," Cillian says, the words coming quickly. "Adi's right. You're exactly his kind of person. You have a Gift, for one thing."

"*Gift?*" My stomach is growing queasier as the seconds tick by.

"The Bishop," Adi explains, "has a weakness for people with innate skills—genetic or otherwise. Skills like what you did to Cillian and Cormac earlier. That blue blast was amazing."

"Thanks for that, by the way," Cillian says, rubbing his back where he collided with the wall.

"Sorry," I tell him. "But the Surge isn't a natural gift—it was an implant Finn gave me. It's really just nanotech. I can't just extract it and hand it to someone to use themselves."

"Doesn't matter," Adi says. "All we have to do is get you to him so he can see you in action. But to do that, we need to convince his people that you're one of them."

"Okay," I say slowly. "But why are you so eager to get me over there? A minute ago, you seemed to think the idea of me heading to Manhattan was folly."

"No. The idea of you sneaking in as a *Dreg* was folly. But…" Adi throws Cillian another look, but she doesn't answer my question. Instead, she pulls her chin down, her hands tightening into fists at her sides.

"I'll level with you," Cillian says slowly. "If you could get to Manhattan—if you could infiltrate the Behemoth—"

"Whoa…" I reply, holding my hands up. "I was only talking about getting to Finn. I have no intention of setting foot in that Arcology. From what you've told me, I'd never get out again."

"If anyone could get out, it's the Crimson Dreg," Cillian says.

"Would you sit down, Ashen?" Adi's voice has gone quiet, but the words are clear. "Just hear us out. Please?"

She's gone from an authoritative figure to someone shrunken, almost mousy, in a matter of seconds. I know that look—that helpless, shaken, weakened look that comes with being beaten down for weeks or months on end.

Emotional exhaustion.

It's almost as if something has occurred to her in the last minute or so—something she didn't want to confront.

I oblige and seat myself once again, crossing my arms and narrowing my eyes. I've sacrificed a good deal already, sometimes for people who were virtual strangers. I've lost friends and family.

Whatever Adi and Cillian are about to say to me, it had better be good.

"One day a few years ago," Adi tells me, her voice trembling a little, "some men came to the house where I was living at the time. It wasn't uncommon to have spontaneous visits like that; they'd been going from house to house for years. Rumors swirled that they were running random assessments on Dregs."

"Assessments," I repeat. "What kind?"

"Medical," she says. "They sent doctors around—doctors with a flowering tree on their lab coats. It's the Bishop's mark —the symbol, he says, of Life Itself."

I can hear the capital letters in the way she says the words.

She continues. "His doctors examined each and every one of us. They scanned us in every way you can imagine."

With a sickening, sinking feeling, I recall a place called the Evaluation Center in the Bastille—a sort of medical center where young children and teenage girls were tested to determine whether they were worthy to enter the Aristocrats' world.

The children were given to Wealthies to raise, as offerings in exchange for peace.

The young women, too, were given as offerings. Young brides for Aristocrat men in the hopes they would be able to provide them with children.

Is that what's happening here?

"Most of the Trodden—" With that, Adi reaches out and takes Cillian's hand for a moment before letting it go again.

"It's what we call ourselves," he explains. "*Downtrodden.* It's an understatement, really."

"They took our blood. Examined us. Our eyes, ears, skin, all of it. We were scrutinized like livestock about to be auctioned off." Adi offers up a weak smile when she adds, "I didn't pass the test, so they didn't take me."

"Or me," Cillian adds.

"But they took my sister," Adi tells me, and at that, I tighten.

This is the first mention of a sibling, though I'm not entirely sure why I'm surprised. So many of us have family members who were either taken or killed by the Directorate.

"After Stella was tested," she continues, "they told us some men would come for her a few days later. They assured us it was a great honor—she'd been selected as one of the Chosen, as they called them."

She looks away, the playful twinkle that seems to reside permanently in her eyes faded to dullness.

"When they took my sister, she was sixteen. I was fourteen." I can hear the pain in her voice as she speaks, but surprisingly, she lets out a quiet laugh. "The craziest part is that I was jealous of her. Isn't that insane? *Jealous*. Because I thought she was going to get to live in the mysterious, elite Behemoth with some rich family. I thought maybe she'd be some kind of glorified lady's maid and get to dress some woman in pearls and gold, and brush her hair, and possibly even be treated like an adopted daughter. Our parents were dead by then, so all I could think was that Stella would have a family, and I would be alone. It seemed so unfair."

"Why didn't they take you?" I ask, my voice tight. "Did they say?"

She winces, then shakes her head. "They never said a thing to any of us. They rejected more people than they took. Eventually, we heard that the Bishop's Examiners were leaving the city, going all over the region in search of Chosens. Most of the people they tested around here weren't good enough, apparently. We were left in the boroughs to rot. At the time, I was resentful. But I've realized since that we were the lucky ones."

I feel uneasy when I ask, "Your sister—do you know if she's alive?"

"She is," she says with a nod. "If you can call it that. *Alive* is a word I reserve for people who do more than merely exist. My sister is still breathing. She has blood pumping through her veins. But no. She's not *living*."

"So you've had contact with her, then?"

"No. None. Not since the day they took her."

"Then how...?" I begin, but I chastise myself. If she wants to explain, I have no doubt she will.

Adi looks up at Cillian. He gives her a mild shrug and says, "I suppose it couldn't hurt to tell her. We've gone this far."

"The day before my sister was taken," Adi says, looking me in the eye, "Cillian here did something clever."

I raise an eyebrow as I watch and wait for Cillian to explain.

"I used to volunteer at my mother's veterinary clinic," he tells me. "From the age of ten or so. It was still up and running until a few years back, mostly for the sake of the Wealthies who still lived nearby. The richer pet owners often came in asking for ways to monitor and track their cats and dogs. You know, in case any escaped or were taken. There used to be a few companies that developed tech exclusively for pets. Global positioning collars so people wouldn't lose their dogs or cats, that sort of thing."

"Right," I reply. "I remember."

"There was something a little more sophisticated, too," Cillian adds. "It was developed only a year or two before the Blight began to take over our country. A micro-reader that a veterinarian could inject under an animal's skin. It was highly sophisticated, and kept track of their stats. Heart rate, blood pressure, illness, anxiety levels, you name it. With it, a vet could remotely keep tabs on any animal. Some of them even had neuro-reading capabilities to monitor their thought patterns."

With a shudder of horror, I realize what they're describing reminds me of the implant I received in the Arc—the one that warned the Directorate if I was frightened or if my adrenaline was spiking. It was their way of keeping a close eye on their Candidates and making sure we were behaving ourselves.

"Cillian had the smart idea to inject one of the readers into Stella before they took her away," Adi explains. "They'd told us we wouldn't be able to talk to her, so I suppose it was a way to stay connected to her. We didn't tell anyone we were doing it, of course, and it seems they never detected it. Well, it turns out the chip has a powerful signal. It's impressive—it still works, despite the fact that she's miles away from us."

Adi reaches into her pocket and pulls out what looks like an old smartphone. Pressing a few buttons, she shows me the screen, but all I can see are a list of acronyms and numbers which make no sense to me until I consider them for a few seconds.

"BP?" I ask her, my brow furrowing. "Blood pressure?"

She nods. "Her heart rate is on here, too. In theory, I can even track her mood changes. Only..." She lowers her chin and I watch her chest heave slightly.

Cillian lays a gentle hand on her shoulder and says, "Her mood hasn't fluctuated in years. Nothing has. She shows no signs of being awake or asleep. From the information we receive, it seems she's..."

"Comatose," Adi says, her voice cracking under the weight of the word.

I stare at them both for a few seconds, contemplating what to say. Finally, I reply, "How long has she been this way?"

"Since two days after she arrived in the Moth," Adi musters. "For three years now."

"Are you sure the chip is working?" I ask, turning to Cillian. "Maybe…"

But I can see from his expression that he's confident. "There are slight changes in her patterns every now and then. Moments when her heart rate spikes, or she has a brief adrenaline rush. Then…nothing for months. Those spikes wouldn't show up if the chip wasn't working."

"I need to get her out of there," Adi says. "I want her back. I want to give her back the life they've stolen from her."

I look down at my hands, which are tangled together in my lap. I feel for her. I feel for Cillian, who clearly cares deeply for Adi.

But this isn't why I came here.

I tell myself coldly that it's not my problem.

"I can't help you," I say, rising to my feet. "I'm really sorry, but I came here for one reason only, and it doesn't involve getting mixed up in anyone else's lives. If you're looking for a quid pro quo, I'll find my own way to Manhattan."

I'm prepared to say goodbye, walk out the front door, and take my chances.

But to my surprise, Adi takes a deep breath, pulls herself off the chair, and says, "We're going to help you anyhow, Ashen."

"What? Why would you do that?"

"Because I think you're a decent person. I also think you have a chance of getting to your Finn. And once you do, who knows? Maybe you'll find a way to help me get my sister back after all. So come on. We're heading for the Tunnels."

9

THE TUNNELS

I DON'T KNOW what Adi and Cillian have planned for me.

And at this point, I don't care.

It's not that I have no sympathy for Adi. I know all too well what it feels like to lose a sibling, if only temporarily. The last remnants of her family are inside the Behemoth.

But I have no desire to stick around and become a martyr for the Trodden's cause. I've wasted enough time already. If my companions can get me closer to Finn, that's good enough for me.

Striding along quickly, I accompany Adi and Cillian to a mudroom at the back of the large house, where Adi peels back an old, worn rug from the floor to reveal a hatch that I can only assume leads down to a basement or crawl space.

"Should I even ask where we're headed?" I venture as she opens the hatch to reveal rickety wooden stairs that lead into a cobweb-filled void reeking of mildew and filled with a grim, thick darkness.

"Since it's not safe to wander outside," Cillian says, "we use tunnels built under the neighborhoods years ago. We're headed a few blocks away to see a friend. He's the only one in possession of the right materials for your tattoo. Your *mark*, I mean." As he's speaking, he taps the back of his head with his index finger. "We need to make you into a proper Aristocrat. It's the only way to get you into Manhattan."

The thought sends a wave of nausea surging through me. A tattoo, unlike an implant, is permanent. It may be hidden by my hair, but the thought of getting the Aristocrats' symbol inked onto my skin isn't something I relish.

"Isn't there another way?" I ask.

"Not if you want to get over the bridge in one piece," Cillian replies. "The Bishop's people will be looking for it."

Shuddering, I tell myself to think of it as a scar—a badge of honor, a war wound. It's the sacrifice I must make to get Finn and Merit to safety.

With the newfound conviction swelling inside my mind, I take a step onto the unstable stairs to follow Adi. To my relief, when we get to the bottom, she flips a switch and the tunnel lights up with a series of flickering bulbs—enough for us to make our way along without too much risk.

The tunnel itself, its walls gray stone and its floor hard-packed earth, is actually quite clean, not to mention devoid of the rats and other vermin I half expected to encounter.

"We're going to see a guy called Trace who lives close to the bridge," Adi tells me. "He's a genius with tats and cosmetic procedures. He mostly does cover-up work for Dregs who are trying to hide their brands."

When I look confused, Adi stops, turns my way, and says, "You didn't know?"

I shake my head, and she holds up her right hand. At the center of its palm, the flesh is angry red and raised in the pattern of a solid X. From the looks of it, it was burned into her skin with a red-hot piece of iron.

"Wait—the Directorate did this to you?"

She shakes her head and keeps walking. "Not the Directorate. It was the Bishop's people, shortly after they took Stella away. The X is to show I'm an Undesirable. It's how they know not to bother testing me again."

Suddenly, tattoos and microchips don't seem so bad.

"That's sickening," I half-snarl.

"It's the Bishop's way," Adi says. "We've come to see our brands as a symbol of strength. And yes, in case you're wondering—it did hurt like a bitch."

"What about you?" I ask Cillian. "You have one, too?

"Had," he says. Still walking, he holds up his hand, palm-out, to show me. I can see that the skin is slightly raised, but it's covered over by the dark image of a bird in flight. "I had the X, too. But I hated looking at it—the sight always brought back the pain. Trace helped me out a couple of years back."

I only see the bird for a moment, but it's long enough to be reminded of Atticus, Rys's amazing robotic owl drone. I wonder with a shallow sigh if there's any way I'll ever see him again. I almost hope he doesn't come looking for me if I do make it to Manhattan. Something tells me things are even more dangerous on that side of the bridge, and a roving metallic owl would stand out like a sore thumb to a bunch of trigger-happy guards.

After a time, we come to a fork in the tunnel, and Adi leads us to the right. We walk another few hundred feet before she turns again, this time into a shallow alcove where we come to a solid wood door. It's unmarked and unremarkable, which, I suppose, is exactly how you'd want a door to a secret location to look.

Adi knocks in a *tap-tap-tappity-tap-tap* pattern, and after ten seconds or so, I hear the sound of footsteps before someone pulls it open from the other side.

The young man who greets us is tall and lanky, black, scraggly hair hanging down to his shoulders. He's dressed in a leather vest and an off-white shirt that's half hanging out of his torn jeans.

Something about him—his disheveled appearance, his relaxed attitude—is oddly reassuring, and I feel at home as we step into the stairwell that will lead up into his apartment.

We come through a doorway into a bright, sunny kitchen equipped with few luxuries—a coffee maker, a toaster oven, a microwave. The windows are covered in a thick film, and I wonder if they're deliberately dirtied in order to offer the owner some privacy.

"Ashen, this is Trace," Adi says.

"The man nods at me once before turning back to Adi. "Nice to see you. You came because…?"

He speaks with a thick English accent, his tone jovial in spite of his apparent confusion.

"We need a crown for our friend here, and we need it right away."

"Ah. Well, as it so happens, you're in luck." He examines me curiously, his sleepy eyes widening a little as he studies me. "A supplier came by just this morning. I have plenty of compound, so I guess it's one crown, comin' up."

As he gathers his tools, he explains, "The ink for the Krat-Tats contains tiny flecks of gold and diamonds, crushed to a pulp—which isn't quite as smooth as the regular stuff. They say it's to show evidence of wealth. All I know is it means the tats have texture—a raised, uneven surface. But don't you worry; it's nothing to fret about. I'll make it pretty, I promise."

Trace wastes no time in ushering me to a plastic chair in the center of his kitchen and gesturing to me to sit.

"Normally, I'd shave the spot I'm about to ink," he tells me, lifting my hair to choose the best destination for his needle. "But if I do that, they'll know the crown is brand-new. So I need to find...ah, here it is. The perfect bit of skin."

"My hair won't get in your way?"

"Of course it will. But that's part of the challenge, isn't it?" He inhales, then adds, "This will hurt a little. Possibly a lot. Bear with me, it won't take long."

I nod before telling myself to stop moving my head.

I don't care about pain. I just want to get to Finn.

I wait, bracing myself for the agony to come and commanding myself tacitly not to let my discomfort show on my face.

Adi and Cillian seem like reasonable people—and they seem to be on my side. But I've learned never to show weakness, and not to let anyone—even close allies—know my vulnerabilities.

When the needle first pierces my flesh, the sensation isn't as bad as I'd expected. It feels more like pinpricks than an agonizing drilling into nerve endings. And before too many minutes have passed, Trace says, "There. All done," and turns away from me to grab something from his kitchen table. A moment later, he hands me a small glass container with a screw-on lid. "Salve, for quick healing. Apply it now and every time you think of it. It will age the tat quickly and kill any redness in your skin."

"Do I really need to be that thorough?"

He lowers his chin and throws me a dubious look. "They'll check you at the bridge. That is, if they don't shoot you first.

You need to convince them you're not a Dreg posing as one of 'em. Trust me—you need to be thorough."

"I know what you're thinking," Adi tells me. "And I know you want to get to your friend, but if you want to do that, you'll need to convince the world you're someone entirely different from the real you. Which means we have more work to do."

"What exactly are we talking about?" I ask, attempting and no doubt failing to hide my impatience. "How much longer do I have to wait before I can head to Manhattan?"

"We'll get you to the bridge first thing tomorrow morning."

"Tomorrow? Why wait that long? Can't I go tonight?"

Cillian shakes his head, throwing Adi a look I can't quite read. "Tonight isn't possible. The bridge will be swarming with soldiers."

"There's a Hanging in Brooklyn tonight," Trace explains. "That's what your friends here aren't saying. It's a weekly ritual, a murder to remind us Dregs we could be next." With that, he looks knowingly at Adi and Cillian. "It's probably wise for us to remember that today, of all days."

"Are they hanging a Dreg?" I ask.

Trace lets out a cynical laugh. "No. They're killing one of their own."

My mouth drops open with shock. I know about the Choosing Ceremony, but that sounds like an exclusive affair. The hanging sounds public. "They kill Wealthies out in the open?"

Adi nods. "It's a huge spectator sport. Thousands of people come to watch. But when the Hangings occur, they shut everything down—which means there's no chance of crossing the bridges."

"The best hope we have," Cillian adds with a nod, "is to finish preparing you and get you to Manhattan tomorrow morning. Which means we should head over to Shar's place."

I don't know who—or what—Shar is, but at this point, I couldn't care less.

"I'm in your hands," I tell them. "Help me get across that bridge tomorrow, whatever you have to do. Pierce me, brand me, whatever. Just get me to Manhattan before it's too late."

10

PLANS

As Adi and Cillian guide me down another series of grim tunnels, my mind turns once again to thoughts of Finn.

The Duchess made the mistake of punishing him once. If she were in the Arc, she might do it again, if only to make a spectacle of her traitorous son. But she wouldn't dare do such a thing here, not when she's most likely hoping to make a good impression on the Bishop. She'll want to present the Davenport family as a bastion of perfection. Power, wealth, beauty, all wrapped up in a tidy, close-knit, affectionate package.

The Duchess is probably going on right now about how saving Finn from the King's fallen drone was the greatest relief of her life. I can just imagine her telling the Bishop about her ordeal: "Thank God he's safe from that wretched Ashen Spencer. That girl is the devil herself, always trying to corrupt my son and turn him against the Directorate. It's a blessing that Finn is free of her influence at last!"

As we slog our way through the dank tunnels, I find myself wondering if the Bishop is the sort of man who would buy into the Duchess's lies. Is he the kind to fall prey to her beauty and faux-charm?

Something tells me the answer is a resounding no.

Though I know it's a terrible idea, I still want to meet the Bishop with a desperation that doesn't feel entirely healthy. To look him in the eye and see what it is that elevated him to a position of power above the Directorate, above even the man who lorded over hundreds of thousands in the Arc—the one I know as the King.

As we advance, my hand strays to the back of my head and I gently touch the bandage that Trace adhered to the place where he tattooed my scalp. I am marked now. I'm a step closer to becoming one of them—one of the Elite. And soon, I'll even *look* like one.

Now, I just have to learn to act like one.

The thought of it sends a shudder of disgust through me.

"We're almost there," Adi calls back over her shoulder, tearing my mind away from its torment. "Shar's shop is only a block or so away. She'll get you fitted for a few outfits. Something casual, something formal, and, if all goes well, by the time we step out, you'll look like someone else entirely."

"Fine." I nod impatiently. "So what's your plan? How will I get across the bridge when the time comes?"

Adi looks sideways at Cillian. "We still have a few kinks to work out, but we do have something in mind."

"Aren't there old subway tunnels leading from Brooklyn— I mean *Broken*—into Manhattan?" I ask hopefully. "That seems like the simplest route."

Cillian turns back to me. "The subway tunnels were sealed up years ago. There's no getting inside them anymore—not even for the Bishop's people. There are two ways across the river: by boat or on foot. The last person who tried to cross by boat…"

"Exploded," Adi says curtly. "It wasn't pretty. The guards didn't exactly ask questions first and shoot later, either. Suffice it to say the river is off-limits."

Holy crap.

"Let's just get your transition to Krat completed first, then we can talk strategy," Adi says. "One step at a time, okay?"

"Fine," I say again, but the truth is, I'm chomping at the bit. I want—*need*—to know Finn is all right. I need to get him away from his beast of a mother before she has a chance to destroy his life.

When we climb a set of rickety stairs up to an unmarked metal door and Adi raps in a distinct pattern of knocks, a tall woman with chin-length white hair cut into a tidy bob opens the door. She's dressed in a black suit with a black shirt and tie. Her eyes, too, are so dark that I can't distinguish her pupils from her irises.

"Adi, Cillian. How nice to see you," she says in a satin-smooth voice.

Something about her is regal, elegant, and she carries herself with all the pride of a member of a true Royal Family —if there is such a thing in the world anymore.

"And who is this?" she asks, eyeing me with intense scrutiny as we emerge from the stairwell into what appears to be a large walk-in closet with a false back.

"Someone who needs to get into the Bishop's good graces," Adi tells her with a knowing smirk. "She needs a look that's suitable for a Wealthy. Top priority is a dress fit for the Choosing Ceremony tomorrow night, just in case she manages to get in."

"I see," the woman says. She looks me up and down once before saying, "I'm Shar, by the way."

"I'm A—" I begin, but I stop when I see Cillian take an involuntary step forward. *Right. Don't say your name.* "I'm..."

"Her name is Ana Miller," Cillian says with a strange, unwavering certainty. When he and Adi exchange a look, I can tell without asking that he didn't simply invent this name on the spot. This is part of their plan...which I'm realizing is far more sophisticated than I knew.

"*Ana,*" Shar says skeptically, but she smiles and welcomes me into the room, which is darkly elegant. "Let's get you fitted with a new face, shall we?"

"What?" I snap reflexively.

"Before you freak out," Cillian interjects, pulling a small device from his pocket, "It's simpler than whatever you're thinking. No one is going to butcher you or slice you up. It's a lot easier than all that." Holding up the little silver device—a circle, covered in small dots of various colors, he asks, "Have you ever seen one of these?"

"It looks like the Disruptors we used in the Arc," I tell him. "A device for overriding the Directorate's systems—except this one has more buttons."

"This is called an Activator," he tells me. "You use it with what's called a Holo-Veil—a facial modification system only used by the wealthiest residents of this city."

"How did you get your hands on it, then?"

Cillian glances at Adi before replying, "It was...a gift."

I'm about to inquire further when he adds, "The Activator is only used for the initial programming stages. After that, you'll use pre-programmed voice commands to alter your appearance."

"The Aristocrats back home wear masks," I reply. "This seems…a lot more complicated."

"The Krats around here change their faces as often as their clothing," Adi explains. "Holo-Veils may be pricey, but they are easy to use. They're highly realistic simulators of facial features. They're less risky than plastic surgery, and less obtrusive than masks. At first, the Krats only used them to tweak their features, to hide the occasional wrinkle or gray hair—I'm sure you know the Wealthies have a disdain for aging that's almost pathological. But now, it's like there's a competition to see who can make themselves into the most beautiful, most youthful, most near-perfect."

"What Adi is telling you," Cillian says, stepping in front of me, "is that we're about to give you the same kind of absolute control over your own appearance." As I watch with my eyebrows raised, he says, *"Activate Red."*

For a moment, I almost wonder if I've been drugged. His face has begun to morph in front of me in strange, subtle ways. His eyes lighten, his jaw narrows, his lips fill out, his nose shrinks a little. His hair changes from black to a deep, rich red.

He's utterly different from the young man who was speaking to me a moment ago—he's more polished now, almost to the point of disconcerting perfection. His eyes are piercing and intense, his skin glowing with an almost other-worldly iridescence. He reminds me of the movie stars who were famous when I was younger, and I find myself realizing with a jolt of discomfort that despite his seeming perfection, I'm not entirely sure which version of him is the real one.

He keeps talking, his altered lips moving naturally and eerily convincingly. "The device detects your facial structure, right down to the subtleties of your skull's shape, and creates a high-end hologram that hovers just above the skin and alters you to look like whatever it is that you've customized for yourself. You can change anything from your skin tone to your face shape to eye and hair color, provided it all fits the basic shape of your skull."

"Won't I look…weird?" I ask. "Like, won't I stand out if I create a new face?"

Adi lets out a laugh. "I promise you, not a single Aristocrat over thirty is walking around Manhattan with their *actual* face. They all spend the entirety of their lives attempting to resemble twenty-three-year-olds. Of course, in your case, we'll be aging you instead of making you look younger. We don't want them knowing you're under twenty; they'd become immediately suspicious."

"Don't forget, you still have to convince the powers that be that you're worthy of entry into Manhattan," Cillian warns me. "It won't exactly be easy."

"Gee, thanks," I say sarcastically.

He smirks. "I didn't mean it as a disparaging remark. The guards might be on the lookout for you, now that they've taken Finn. You need to look like someone completely new. Which means we need to alter your eyes, your hair, all of it."

When he mentions my hair, my breath catches. *They aren't going to cut it off, are they?*

I'm not vain by any means, but still, I can't quite fathom losing it.

If it's what you have to do to get to Finn, it's a small price to pay.

I shoot Adi a look of slight terror, but she gives me a reassuring nod and we follow Shar into a large room that lights up to reveal a floor to ceiling mirror on every conceivable surface.

Shar walks over and presses a finger into the center of one

mirror, which flies open like a cupboard door to reveal what look like a thousand small devices like the one Cillian just used to alter his face.

Shar picks one up and hands it to me before opening a drawer below the display case and removing a small white package, which she peels open. Inside is a tiny, clear circle that almost looks like a small, flat contact lens.

"May I?" she asks, laying the device on the tip of her finger and reaching for my face.

"I have no idea what you're about to do," I tell her. "But I suppose you may."

She takes my chin gently between her fingers and turns my face away from her, pulling my dark hair from behind my left ear. She presses the small device into the patch of bare skin behind my ear, holding it there until I feel a strange, quick pin prick of pain.

"Ouch," I mutter under my breath.

"Just securing the Source," she tells me. "It's the control center for the Holo-Veil. It reads your facial structure, hair color, genetic make-up, all of it."

"I see."

"Now...would you like to be a blond or a redhead? I think brown and black are too close to what you have at the moment."

"I..."

"Blond," Adi says without waiting for my answer. "Make her strikingly different. There should be no similarities to what she is now."

"Fine. We'll narrow her nose and cheekbones, alter her chin a little. Lighter brows, green eyes. Let me just program the Remote."

She carries the small handheld device over to a hovering

holo-screen at the room's far end, and I find myself wondering how Brooklyn's Dregs have managed to get their hands on such advanced tech in their homes and workplaces. Back in the Mire, with our sporadic electricity, the notion of screens and programming systems was all but unheard of.

Then again, it sounds like the Bishop enjoys watching a certain amount of chaos flourish in New York...which means granting Dregs a little power.

Though I've never met him, I suspect I already know what kind of man he is. He probably derives pleasure from knowing his enemies pose a potential danger to him and to his friends. He craves the fighting, the constant mayhem. It distracts the world around him from whatever havoc he's wreaking behind the scenes.

And I have no doubt he wants people like Adi and Cillian to be well armed so it's more satisfying to catch and torture them.

Over at the screen, Shar moves her fingers rapidly through the air, flicking images this way and that until a composite picture begins to take shape—the face of a young woman.

She looks nothing like me, yet there's something oddly familiar about her.

"Come see, Ana," she says, gesturing to me to approach. As I obey, she adds, "We can't alter your actual skeleton, of course, but we can build something new on top of it. Have a look at your new incarnation."

I stare at the screen for a moment before Shar turns to me, takes my shoulders, and faces me toward one of the mirrored walls.

It's only then that I realize the woman in the reflection before me is the same as the one I was just looking at on the screen.

I stare at my new self. There's no denying that she is—I mean *I am*—beautiful. I'm perfect in the same disconcerting way as the new version of Cillian. My skin has the faintest shimmer to it, a sort of vague electrical field that betrays the lie that is my new face. But unless I were to look extremely closely, I would probably never notice it.

My eyelashes seem to have grown longer and darker, my shapely brows arching perfectly over eyes the color of emeralds. My lips have grown fuller beneath a narrow nose that's neither too big nor too small.

I should be pleased. This Ana person is what I always thought I wanted to look like when I was younger. She exemplifies the ideal of female beauty that stared out at me from so many old magazines and billboards—something unachievable until this moment.

But now that I see her, all I can think of is an unnatural mask, something inhuman and alien.

Wearing this face will be tantamount to lying my way through life, and it feels sickeningly wrong.

On the other hand, it might just keep me alive for a few more days.

11

SHAR

As ADI and Cillian sit together in the small area at the front of the shop, Shar spends the next hour tending to my every need.

She plies me with coffee, pastries, and chocolate.

"I don't know where you got all of this, but I'm grateful," I say as I take a bite of a chocolate croissant.

Shar explains as she measures every inch of my body that "Brooklyn is like London back in the days of the Blitz. The shops and cafés are open—but if you venture into one, you have to be prepared to run for your life at the first sign of trouble."

I want to ask her how they live like this. Then I remember what Kel, my mother, and I lived through for years in the Mire. Near-starvation. No material possessions. Having to hike into the mountains to acquire potable water.

We have all suffered at the enemy's hands.

Just in different ways.

Shar has me try on various garments as I stare at my

strange new face and hair in the mirror, disconcerted at how convinced I am that I've waltzed into a surreal dream.

I almost don't notice the pants, shoes, boots, or skirts that I try on, elegant as they are. It's not until Shar shows me the dress she's selected for the Choosing Ceremony that I finally manage to pull my mind away from my shocking new appearance.

The dress is unbelievably beautiful, a sort of deep turquoise that brings out the green that's found its way into my eyes. The skirt is made up of layer upon layer of flowing silk, and there's so much fabric that I feel like I could conceal an entire army beneath it.

"This will make a statement at the Choosing," Shar says as she zips it up. "It's like it was tailor-made for you. I must say, I'm very pleased that I won't have to alter it."

"There's no guarantee that I'll be invited to the Choosing," I tell her. The truth is, there's no guarantee that I'll make it across the bridge alive, for that matter. And even if I do, who's to say I'll get to meet the Bishop? Even with my new identity, I'm still far from anyone important, just some unknown Aristocrat.

"The second the Bishop lays eyes on you, you'll receive your invitation," Shar assures me. "How could he possibly resist?"

"Have you met him?" I ask, expecting the answer to be a resounding no.

"Of course I have, darling," she replies with an exaggerated flick of her hair.

I turn to look into her eyes, trying to figure out if she's joking. "Really?"

"I've tailored garments for him—and for a lot of the other Krats. They cross the river regularly. I like to think it's because they know I'm better at my craft than anyone in stuffy old Manhattan."

I hesitate for only a second before asking, "What's he like?"

"The Bishop?" Shar smiles mysteriously. "He's unlike anyone you've ever met. Oh, you'd expect him to be one of them—a cold, snobbish Krat, just like the rest. But there's something...I don't know, *endearing* about him. Something that invites you in and makes you want to stay. He has a charisma that can't be taught." Her expression changes when she adds, "That's not to say he's a good man. He's responsible for some of the most despicable acts I've ever seen or heard of. I'm convinced he gets away with it because no one can manage to stay angry with him for more than a millisecond. I have no idea how he does it—how he manages to seem so charming and terrifying simultaneously. Given all the things he's done..."

"What *has* he done, exactly?" I'm almost afraid to ask the question, but part of me wants to know what I'm about to walk into.

"He's a murderer, plain and simple," Shar says. "A cold-blooded killer." She leans in close, looking toward Adi and Cillian, who are still chatting by the shop's front window. "But the truth is, I think he's doing a lot worse things than killing."

"What's worse than killing?"

Shar backs away, putting her hands on her hips when she says, "Ana—or whatever your name is—I suspect you already know the answer to that question."

I stare at her, trying to work out what she's talking about.

But I know perfectly well that she's right.

There are far worse things than being killed.

I've seen the haunted look on the faces of those the Directorate has wronged. My mother, who lost her husband and soulmate in the earliest days of the Blight. My friend Kyra, who trained alongside me in the Arc. Peric, who found his long-lost parents, only to lose them again within a matter of mere days.

I've even seen the light leave my own eyes over time, hope slowly bleeding from my veins, replaced with a cold, numb cynicism.

I think of Adi's sister then, trapped inside the Behemoth, both alive and dead at once. My heart hurts for her, for Adi.

I remember with horrid clarity what it felt like when Kel went missing after my mother was killed.

Forcing my mind away from the thought for fear that I'll burst into tears, I turn to the mirror, focusing once again on Shar's beautiful dress.

"This may sound odd, but could I see what it looks like with my own face?" I ask her, feeling oddly self-conscious. "I know I won't be able to show myself to anyone, but…"

"Of course," she tells me with a strange sympathy in her voice. She picks up the remote device from the tabletop next to me. "You can either hit the first three buttons in a row or use the voice command, 'Revert to Original.'"

I nod, then speak the three words.

"Well done," Shar says, taking me by the shoulders as I try to grow accustomed to the strangeness of seeing myself alter so abruptly. A swell of relief hits when I look into my own eyes, reassured to know I'm still in here somewhere.

The imperfections that mar my natural face cry out to me now, reminders that I am indeed human. Every pore and hint of discoloration in my skin seems oddly amplified, as if I see myself through a magnifying lens now. But odd as it may seem, I feel like I'm learning for the first time to appreciate the face that I've lived with since I was born.

I can almost hear Finn's voice when I look into my eyes, aware that, as imperfect as my features may be, this one is the face he loves. These are the eyes he looks into when we speak. This is the skin his fingers caress—fingers that make me tremble with pleasure each time I feel their touch.

The artificial face, beautiful though it may be, is that of an intruder, a stranger. Someone who hasn't lived the life I have, who hasn't suffered the trials and tribulations of the girl called Ashen Spencer.

Sighing, I say the words, "Activate Ana Miller," and transform into my blond self. Immediately, I'm confronted by the young woman who hopes to meet and charm the Bishop. The woman who, with any luck, will succeed and, by some miracle, manage to whisk Finn and Merit away from Manhattan.

But the more I stare into her eyes, the more I understand she is someone I don't know, someone I've never had the opportunity to be.

Someone I would never *dare* to be.

I realize with a smile that part of me is looking forward to play-acting a new identity.

"Thank you for all of this," I tell Shar. "Really. You may be helping me to save a couple of lives."

"I have my reasons, and I'm afraid they're more than mere generosity," she says with a chuckle. "I don't know if the others told you…"

I look over my shoulder to see Adi and Cillian seated on small leather chairs, their heads close together as they converse in low whispers, shooting the occasional glance our way.

"Told me what?"

"My son," Shar says. "He was taken into the Moth several years ago. Many others were too, of course. And like them, he never returned. Whatever they're doing with him and so many others in there, it can't be good. I just want my boy back."

I look away, biting my lip. I don't know what to tell her. The truth is too cruel.

Your son is probably dead. And even if he's alive, you'll probably never see him again.

"Do you have any idea why he was taken? Did the Bishop's people say anything?"

"No," Shar says with a shrug. "All I know is they say there are over a hundred thousand Dregs on the inside. I know Adi's sister is in there, too. I want to know what's happening to our loved ones."

"You said you work for Krats sometimes. Can't they tell you anything? They must know something."

She shakes her head and whispers, "The Krats who live in Manhattan don't have information about the place...and anyone who does refuses to share, beyond the bare minimum. All they know is that something huge is going down in that place." She gets choked up as she adds, "I just want to know my son is all right. He's all I have in this world. I need to know he's alive."

I'm not sure what overtakes me when I say, "I promise you —if I end up inside that place, I'll find out what's going on. I'll do everything I can to get your son back to you, and to get Adi's sister back, too."

Stupid, Ashen. So stupid. You can't make promises like that— you can't even promise you'll be alive in two days.

But I've seen so much death, so much pain. So many families torn apart by what the Directorate has inflicted on all of us.

I'm so very tired of watching cruelty win.

"Thank you, A—Ana," Shar says, and for a second, I wonder if she knows what my real name is. "Something tells me you may well be instrumental in helping me to get my son back home."

I offer her a weak smile and add, "I've failed many people. My own mother. Some of my friends, too. I could easily fail you."

But she just shakes her head, puts a hand on my shoulder, and says, "No matter what happens, you won't have failed. If you only knew how rare it was to meet someone who cares. That in itself is a sort of miracle." When I shoot her a confused look, she lets out a quiet laugh and adds, "It's not that the world is filled with unfeeling monsters. It's only that the people who survived the last few years are exhausted, mentally and physically. This city is a mess, filled with corrupt individuals, spies, traitors, and angry rebels. Sometimes you don't know which is which until it's too late."

"What are Adi and Cillian?" I ask softly enough that they can't hear me. *Rebels? Spies? Or traitors?*

"They're survivors," she says. "All of the Trodden are. They walk around like sad corpses waiting either for the winds to shift, or for their lives to end." She peers over at them before saying, "They could leave this place, you know. Cillian has no family here, and none in the Moth. His people are dead. But he's so loyal to Adi that he'll never leave her side. And she'll never leave, not as long as her sister remains alive."

"I understand."

As I'm speaking, I peer over to see that Adi and Cillian have turned to stare out the window. At first, they look like they're panicking quietly, but very quickly, they both press their faces to the glass, seemingly fascinated by something on the street outside.

"What is it?" Shar calls out. "Scorps?"

"No. I think it's a...drone of some other kind?" Adi says, her tone full of confusion. "But not like any I've seen before. I mean, I guess it could be a real owl, but..."

Owl?

Without thinking, I spring over to the front window and press my hands to the glass only to see Atticus perched atop a lamp post, his bright blue eyes staring directly at me.

12

A FRIENDLY FACE

"Atticus!" I cry as I leap over to the shop's front door and try to push it open. But it doesn't budge.

"Wait—you *know* the drone?" Cillian asks.

"Very well," I reply, turning back to Shar. "Please—I need to talk to him."

She looks skeptical and vaguely untrusting, but when I throw her a pleading look, she relents and strides over to the door, pressing her thumb into a small panel to its left.

"Quickly, now," she says. "Keep an eye out for Scorps."

I leap outside and hold an arm out, and Atticus comes in for a landing, wrapping his metallic talons around my flesh with extraordinary gentleness. Scanning the area to make sure we're not being watched, I speak softly.

"Are you in there, Rys?" I ask, searching for my old friend.

The others watch through the window as I make my way over to a nearby bench and seat myself, warily watching the sky. Atticus flaps over to the end of the bench and perches on the armrest.

"I'm here," Rys's comforting voice replies. "But are you,

Ash? I mean, I know that's you—I've been tracking you since you left the drone. But damn, you do *not* look like yourself."

"Wait—you've been tracking me?"

"I…" He sounds like he swallows before continuing. "Okay, fine. I put tracking devices in your uniforms. Yours and Finn's both. It seemed like a good idea."

"It was," I laugh. "Though I would probably have yelled at you for it at the time."

"I know. That's why I didn't tell you. So, what's up with the fancy face?"

I sigh. "It's my new identity. It's kind of a long story."

"I can guess most of it," he says. "You're in Brooklyn. Finn's in Manhattan. I'm assuming that's not by choice."

"So you've seen where he is?" I ask, my heart beating suddenly faster.

"Sure. He's in the old Waldorf. Man, I had no idea New York had become so fragmented. Everything we'd heard was wrong—about the Behemoth and New York's Aristocracy. I thought they'd all moved inside the Arcology, but…"

"But you were misinformed, as was I," I reply. "It's crazy here. And I can't get to Finn, at least not yet. We're planning to make a move tomorrow morning."

"We?" Rys says. "Oh, right. Your new friends."

He doesn't sound convinced, and I can't say I blame him. All he knows is that I've been locked inside a house almost since my arrival here.

I look toward the shop, where Adi and Cillian are still watching me, though from the looks of it they're not attempting to eavesdrop.

"Sort of," I reply. "I'm not entirely sure I can trust them, but then, I'm not sure I'll ever trust anyone again."

"If they want you to go into Manhattan, you definitely

can't trust them. I've been seeing things, Ash. It's far from safe over there."

"It wasn't their idea," I retort. "I need to get to Finn."

"Do you even know where he is?"

"You just said he's in the Waldorf."

"No. I mean do you know whose place that is?"

I push my newly blond hair behind my ear when I say, "Yeah. I know about the Bishop."

"So you know he's terrifying. The guy is a mystery, wrapped in an enigma, wrapped in some handsome exterior that is apparently so seductive that no one ever dares to challenge him."

I nod, staring into Atticus's eyes. "And in spite of all that, I'm hoping to meet him tomorrow."

"What?" Rys all but shrieks. "Ash, that's insane. The guy makes the Duchess look like a teddy bear. He's a total psycho."

"He can't be worse than she is," I reply, though I'm not entirely convinced by my own words. "Anyhow, he has Finn, so I don't have a choice."

Rys goes silent for a few seconds before replying, "You don't know what you'll run into over there. From what I can gather, most of New York's Directorate lives in that area. They'll kill you, even if the Bishop doesn't."

"They wouldn't kill one of their own," I say with a tight smile, pointing toward my face. "Why exactly do you think I look like this?"

"Fine, then. Do the usual crazy Ashen Spencer thing. I'd try to stop you, but I know there's nothing I could possibly say to make you rethink this. Just know I've taken a look at the Waldorf Astoria—the Bishop's headquarters. I won't be able to get you inside. The place is guarded by an entire army."

"Then I'll have to get *myself* inside," I say with a chuckle, though Rys's warning sends a chill along my flesh. I've never known him to shy away from a challenge.

"Ash…"

"Don't worry," I tell him. "Either I'll get in, or I'll be killed. Either way, tomorrow will be an exciting day."

"Maybe you should wait. I can commandeer another Air-Wing. I can be there tomorrow. I'll land outside the city, and—"

"No," I snap. "No way. I need you to watch over me from afar, not jump into the fire with me. I want to get Finn and Merit and get the hell out of here. Having another conspicuous person around won't help anything."

"Fine, then," he replies, and I can hear the pout in his voice. "Oh—speaking of conspicuous, I want to show you something."

"All right," I reply, shifting my gaze to Atticus's silver belly, where a screen occasionally materializes to display video footage.

But instead, Atticus vanishes entirely.

I lean forward, reaching a hand out into the air above the armrest, and my fingers meet the sensation of cold metal.

"He's…cloaked?" I ask, recoiling in shock. "That's new, isn't it?"

"Finn helped me out a few days back," Rys says as Atticus reappears. "We covered him in a composite that has the same cloaking effect as your uniforms. Pretty amazing, huh? It's how I got him into the city without those freaky flying Scorpions pursuing him."

"So you've seen them."

"God, yes. They're awful. And Atticus isn't equipped to take them out. They would've taken him down in seconds if they'd detected him."

"Then promise me you'll keep him out of sight," I say, reaching out to stroke the owl's head. "I need all the friends I can get in this town, and if something happened to him, I think I'd lose my mind."

"I will," Rys promises. "If only because I need to keep an eye on you during this insane venture you have planned tomorrow, you lunatic. In the meantime, I'll make sure to keep track of you—*if* that's all right with your friends."

"It's fine with us," Adi says from behind me.

I twist around to see her standing outside the shop with Cillian. My first instinct is to tell them to go back inside and leave me alone with Atticus, but I think better of it.

"Adi, Cillian, this is Rys. An old friend. The voice, I mean. The owl is Atticus."

"Hello, Rys," Adi says.

"Hello." Atticus's head turns toward Adi, his eyes glowing brighter than ever as Rys asks, "Tell me, do you understand the risk you're putting Ash in tomorrow by sending her into the lion's den?"

Adi tenses and looks at Cillian before saying, "I have some idea. She's putting herself in a great deal of danger."

"And you're going to help her do that?"

"At her request, yes."

"Tell me, what's in it for you?"

"Rys!" I snap, annoyed that he's just risked alienating the only allies I have in this town.

"It's all right," Adi replies. "What's in it for me, owl-man, is the hope that your friend here will help me get my sister back. She's inside the Behemoth, but we have no way to contact her, to make sure she's all right. All we know is that she's alive."

"What if Ash doesn't help you?"

"Then I'm back where I started," Adi says with a shrug. "So

are the rest of us. But there are thousands and thousands of us on the outside with family members locked in that place. We're not the only ones likely to suffer if the Bishop keeps them there."

"What do you mean?"

"I mean that I think he's up to something—something huge. Something bigger than we can possibly imagine. I think whatever he's doing in there is going to affect the future of humanity, but I'm not sure I mean that in a good way."

Rys goes quiet, seemingly processing her words.

"What is it, Rys?" I ask him. "Have you heard something?"

"Not exactly," he says ominously. "But I think she's right."

Just then, Cillian grabs Adi's arm, says, "Be quiet!" and presses a finger to his lips. At first, I think he's simply trying to prevent us from speaking ill of the Bishop.

But then I hear it. A faint, crescendoing buzz.

A drone—or *many* of them—flying somewhere overhead.

The shop's door bursts open and Shar gestures wildly for us to get inside.

"*Flutters,*" she hisses under her breath as I scurry inside, Atticus flapping along behind me. "They're even worse than Scorps. They're controlled by the Directorate, and they'll incinerate you if you're in the wrong place at the wrong time. All of you, into the tunnel. *Now.*"

Shar darts ahead of us and opens the back of the closet once again, and we pile, along with Atticus, into the darkness of the stairwell. When I turn to see if she's coming with us, Shar shoves a canvas rucksack into my hands and shakes her head.

"Your new clothing is inside," she says. "All ready to go. Cillian will help you with your Holo-Veil."

"But..." I protest. "You should come with us. If they find out what you've..."

"It's all right," she says with a wave of her hand. "It'll be fine. Trust me."

"We have to go," Adi insists, grabbing my arm and dragging me down the stairs as Atticus follows close behind. "Come on!"

Reluctantly, I turn and pursue her and Cillian to the base of the stairs as the door behind us closes, sealing us off from Shar.

"Will she be all right?" I ask.

"She's survived this long," Adi says. "And she has friends in high places. She'll be okay."

I take her word for it and follow her, clutching Shar's bag in my arms as we make our way back down the tunnel toward Adi's and Cillian's home.

When we climb out of the tunnel into the house and emerge in the mudroom, Rys's voice announces that he's going to send Atticus outside to soak up some solar charge and do a little reconnaissance work. "I'll check on your friend's shop to make sure she's all right," he promises me. "And I'll keep an eye on you from a safe distance."

"We'll be at the Hanging tonight," Adi tells him. "At the riverside. Keep yourself out of sight—there will be a lot of Scorps there."

"A Hanging?" Atticus's blue eyes turn briefly red so that he almost looks angry. "Are you sure that's a good idea?" Rys asks. "You're already putting Ash in enough danger, don't you think? Why risk being seen by the Directorate and this Bishop person?"

"Because she needs to see what sort of man the Bishop is," Adi retorts. "She needs to know what that beast does to people who don't fit his definition of 'desirable.' Maybe then she'll understand why we need—" Her voice seems on the verge of breaking, and she stops talking.

I look at her with sympathy, my heart aching for her. "I don't doubt what he is," I assure her. "But you have to understand that I have to think about the people back home. We may have taken the Arc, but our homes are destroyed. Those who don't have residences inside the Arc live in neighborhoods surrounded by eighty-foot high walls. I have to help them, too."

"I get it," Adi says, holding up a hand. "I'm telling you right now, though, that you can do all the work in the world to rebuild your homes, your neighborhoods. Rebuild your houses. Get schools and stores open again. But whatever the Bishop has planned will uproot any hopes you have of returning to a normal world."

"Our world will never be normal," I retort, my voice aggressive. "Do you think I don't know that, after everything I've seen? Everything I've done? Do you think I ever expected to be forced to kill people before I hit the age of eighteen? How 'normal' do you really think I can ever be?"

That seems to silence her for a few seconds before she speaks again.

"I'm not going to pressure you, Ashen. I intend to keep my promise—we'll do what we can to get you into Manhattan. In the meantime, come with us tonight. We'll make sure you have a new appearance—the face of another Dreg, so you won't have to worry about being seen. But maybe when you've had a taste of the Bishop, you'll see what we're all up against."

"I will come," I tell her. *But not for the reasons you think.* As curious as I am about the Bishop, it's not him that I care about.

All I want is to get to Finn and his brother, and escape this city in one piece.

13

THE HANGING

IN PREPARATION TO attend the Hanging, Adi lends me some of her clothing—an old, comfortable pair of jeans, a gray t-shirt and a black hoodie. Cillian helps me program a new appearance into my Holo-Veil's control, and I choose one with olive skin, dark brown eyes, round cheeks and thin lips. My hair remains dark as usual, but I can't imagine anyone—even Finn —would recognize me like this.

Cillian and Adi feed me a meal of canned chicken soup as the other inhabitants of the house prepare to head out as well, their eyes occasionally landing curiously on me.

"Can I ask you something?" I venture when we're nearly done eating. Cillian and Adi look at each other, then at me.

"Go ahead," Adi says.

"Do you all trust each other? It all seems so casual, the way everyone wanders in and out of this place."

"You're wondering if someone will turn us in one of these days," Adi says. "If one of our people will tell the powers that be there are Trodden members living here. Is that it?"

I peer out the back window toward the small yard and the

backs of the houses beyond. "Well, you're not exactly hiding yourselves. It just seems like you'd be easy to spot."

The two of them go silent for a moment, then Adi finally inhales a deep breath and says, "They know we're here. They even know we're armed. But the Bishop is a calculating, clever man, and he has his reasons for everything he does—or doesn't—choose to do. If the Directorate or the Bishop want to come for us, they will. Until then, we'll live our lives as the rejects we are."

Her last words hit me hard.

She's just described how my life was for so long in the Mire. The life of a reject—someone deemed unworthy of entry into the Arc until I became "useful" to the Directorate. And even then, they didn't fully accept me into their Elite society. We Dregs were never good enough, never wealthy enough. We were nothing to them but fodder for their own amusement.

"It's time," Adi says as I ponder how much we have in common. "Let's go watch a Hanging, shall we?"

Once outside, Adi and Cillian guide me down several darkened streets, padding along behind other strolling groups of people who look both exhausted and curious at once.

Cillian, seeing the wary look on my face, explains that we don't have to worry about Scorps or Flutters tonight. "The Bishop and the Directorate encourage us to attend the Hangings," he tells me. "So there's no risk from them as long as we head home immediately afterwards."

"How kind of them," I say under my breath.

It doesn't take long before we reach the park that overlooks Brooklyn Bridge, the imposing landmark that has now become a sort of extended roadblock for anyone attempting to enter Manhattan from Brooklyn.

I can see from a distance that the bridge is crawling with soldiers and armored vehicles. Whether they're the Directorate's or the Bishop's, I have no idea.

Huge spotlights positioned every fifty or so feet move slowly about, illuminating the area we're in as well as the surface of the East River. Looking, I suppose, for anyone foolish enough to attempt a crossing.

Some distance away to the east are the remnants of what looks like it used to be another bridge. I'm staring at the crumbling mess of steel and concrete when Adi says, "That's the old Manhattan Bridge. The Bishop's people bombed it a few years back. They've severely limited the number of places where people can cross into Manhattan."

As we move toward a makeshift stadium set up presumably for the sole purpose of watching public executions, Scorpion drones fly over our heads in small V-shaped groups. But for once, they don't make me want to cower in fear.

But the armed guards stationed every few feet are another story entirely.

I'm not wearing my silver uniform, which means I'm unable to disappear if I should want to. And as I stare at the guards, high-powered rifles slung over their shoulders, their presence reminds me that tonight is nothing but a temporary ceasefire between Dregs and Wealthies, a brief respite from the certainty of death.

A powerful jolt of energy crackles its way through my body, and I remind myself that I still have a daunting weapon of my own at my disposal. Should I need to use the Surge, I will.

K. A. RILEY

There must be two or three thousand people gathered in this place, eager to witness the killing that's about to unfold. Most of them, as far as I can tell, are Dregs like Adi, Cillian, and me.

I can only assume they're here for the grim satisfaction of watching one of the Elite breathe his or her last. I can't deny there's some malicious, deep-seated part of me that wants to see it for myself.

Still, whoever is about to be killed, I remind myself, is a human being. I don't know them. They've never done anything to me. And there is no reason for me to revel in their demise. The second I learn to enjoy watching them suffer, I become the inhuman monster I despise.

Adi guides us to a bench high in a section of metal bleachers set up to look out across the river toward Manhattan's once beautiful skyline, marred now by the looming presence of the Behemoth. I stare into the distance for a moment at the sky's hues of purple and orange as the sun dips below the horizon. But my eyes shift quickly to what looks like a large platform that's being wheeled out by a group of men in uniform.

The gallows is gruesomely designed to look like some sort of demented offspring of the Behemoth. It's not made of wood and nails, but metal and glass, jagged shards jutting up here and there as if in violent threat. At its center is a large platform over which a hangman's noose is suspended. The noose isn't crafted of rope, but something else entirely.

"Steel chains," Adi tells me. "Each link has small spikes on it, so it will not only strangle the victim but slice into them, as well."

I flinch at the thought. Even for the Directorate's particular brand of viciousness, this seems extreme.

As I'm struggling to pull my eyes away from the sadistic contraption, a holo-screen flares to life in the air above the gallows, zooming in on the noose. I can see it clearly now, its individual links punctuated by what look like tiny, jagged pieces of razor blade.

My eyes scan the gathering crowd. I know on a rational level that no one will recognize me—that my face and hair are not those of the Crimson Dreg that so many have seen via the videos that were projected in the Arc. But I still cower inside the hoodie Adi lent me, trying to hide my face among its shadows.

Atop the bleachers across from where we're sitting is a sort of boxed-in area that looks like high-security seating designed to accommodate the most important of the spectators. As I watch, a stream of well-dressed people parade out and take their seats, their eyes focusing instantly on the gallows below.

I wonder as I stare at them how many of their faces are their own, and how many are Holo-Veils like the one I'm wearing. There's an eerie similarity between all of the wealthy women—the same eyebrows, lips, cheekbones. It's as if they've each used the same filter to airbrush their features into something "desirable."

The men, too, look like virtual clones, just different enough to distinguish one from the other. But each has a full head of thick hair, a strong jaw, and just the right amount of stubble.

Among the Dregs, the opposite is true. Each person in our section is so different from the next, you almost wouldn't know we're the same species. I spot anything from shaved heads to waist-length hair. Some are dressed in jeans and jackets, others in the solemn formal attire one might wear to a funeral.

After a few minutes, the accused is unceremoniously paraded out toward the gallows. It's a man, dressed neatly in a pressed white shirt, dark gray trousers, and a pair of polished leather shoes.

"What did he do?" I ask Adi, turning her way as a shiver traces its way along my skin. The evening is cold and damp, and the sea of bodies doesn't seem to be helping to keep the chill at bay.

"Not sure," she says with a shrug. "Could've been anything from looking at the Bishop's lover the wrong way to embezzling."

"Lover?" The second the word leaves my mouth, I regret asking. But Adi nods up toward the top of the Wealthies' section of the bleachers, where I spot a tent-shaped roof covering several seats at the very top.

Under the tent are several figures. At the center I see a man and a woman, both elegantly dressed and important-looking.

"That's the happy couple," Adi says. "No one knows who she is—they say she's new in town. They've only been together a few weeks."

I stare up at the woman, fascinated and curious to know what sort attracts a man like the Bishop. I'm distracted when, out of the corner of my eye, I see a flurry of movement as more figures approach their seating area.

"It looks like they brought a few guests with them tonight," Cillian says, leaning toward us.

At first, I can't make out much about any of the figures. But as if in answer to my silent request, the holo-screen above the gallows switches from its view of the accused to the Bishop himself.

As the camera zooms in on the face of a young man, I find my jaw dropping. He's striking in a way I wasn't entirely prepared for.

Long, dark brown hair that's slightly unruly and begs to be played with. A square jaw sprinkled with a coating of dark stubble.

If I had to choose two words to describe my first impression of him, it would be "devilishly handsome." I've never quite understood what that term meant, not really. Not until this very moment. There's a sort of impish malice in his face —it's hard to tell if he's having fun at others' expense or is simply an impartial observer with a twisted smile on his lips.

Either way, something about him simultaneously draws me in and repels me.

"So?" Adi asks, leaning toward me. "What do you think of him?"

"I can't believe that's him," I blurt out, stunned. "I mean, I know you said he was young, but..."

Adi nods. "I know. Crazy, right?" She seems oddly casual about it. "A lot of people speculate about his real age. I mean, the guy walks around like he's been through several world wars, for God's sake. He seems to know everything."

"He's wearing a Holo-Veil, right?" I ask. "I mean, no one is *that* good-looking."

"That's the thing," Adi whispers. "He's not veiled. He prides himself on showing his actual face. I mean, I guess if most people looked that good, they wouldn't hide behind a Holo-Veil, either."

"But..." I say, searching for the question I want to ask, but it doesn't come.

"No one knows how he became so powerful, if that's what you're trying to figure out," Adi continues. "There's speculation, of course. Lots of it. All I can tell you is that he could probably charm a rattlesnake into submission."

"A handsome monster," I reply. He's beautiful almost beyond words, and I'm finally starting to understand his mysterious allure. His is an infuriating, almost unfair sort of beauty.

He reminds me, ironically enough, of Finn, who has features so utterly perfect that when I look at him, it's hard to imagine being angry with him for any sustained period of time. One glance his way, and any ice that's formed around my heart melts instantly.

But unlike Finn, something about the Bishop feels... wicked. There's an aura about him as he looks down at the crowd, as he turns to the beautiful woman to his right, that makes me think he would be an incredibly difficult man to trust.

"Why do they call him the Bishop?" I ask quietly. "I assume it's not some hold-over from the days of Catholicism." He's wearing a navy blue, tailored suit with a white shirt whose collar is undone at the neck. Hardly the garb of an actual bishop.

"No one seems to know," Cillian tells me. "He's not religious or anything, as far as anyone knows. Some say it has to do with chess. Bishops are vital to the game. Sneaky, underhanded. Inexperienced players frequently underestimate them —but in some ways, they're almost as powerful as the queen. The bishop is a killer, but a quiet one who hides in the shadows, waiting to strike."

"He doesn't look so quiet to me," I say. "He's about the most conspicuous person I've ever seen."

"Yes," Adi says, "but what you see on the surface is only a tiny fraction of what he is. His beauty is nothing next to his capacity for cruelty."

As I stare at the screen, I almost want to let out a cry as the camera finally pans away from the Bishop's face. I realize with a shock that I've already grown addicted to something about him, even from this great distance. The man is like a dangerously tempting drug, and his impact frightens me.

But as the camera moves away from him, I let out a loud gasp as a renewed sense of reality hits me like a freight train.

As quickly as it came, the feeling of being drugged leaves me, and I simply feel sick.

Seated to the Bishop's left is the Duchess.

14

IN PLAIN SIGHT

LOOKING FOR CONFIRMATION, I pull my eyes from the enormous screen floating over the gallows to the seats high in the stands.

There she is.

The Duchess, in all her glory.

And she's not alone. To one side of her is her husband the Duke, and to the other is Merit. Sweet, ten-year-old Merit.

Why the hell would they bring him to a public killing?

In the Arc, Merit was shielded from the goings-on of the Directorate. He never came to the Trials, never saw what happened to people like me. I want to be sick, seeing him here. It seems like an act of brutality to force him to witness a killing.

I want to call out to him, to warn him...that is, until my eyes land on a figure who's striding in to take a seat next to his brother. When he sits, he takes Merit's hand in his own and leans in to say something to him, his eyes locking on the gallows.

Finn.

My heart hammers in my chest, adrenaline compelling me to sprint over to his section and leap up the stairs two at a time until I can take him in my arms.

Except for the inconvenient fact that there are hundreds of feet of razor-wire-covered fencing and fifty or more guards between him and me.

My breath coming shallow and fast, I tell myself I could take the guards out. I could use the Surge to blast my way through them and make my way to Finn.

No.

The guards are strategically scattered in front of the crowd. If I hurled my weapon at them, I would risk killing innocent Dregs in the process—not to mention that I'd risk Finn's and Merit's lives, too.

I command myself to be calm, to have patience. It's madness to think it's only been a matter of a day or so since I watched Finn being dragged away from the Air-Wing. It feels like weeks, or even *months,* of separation.

The worst part is that he doesn't even know I'm here. And even if he did, he wouldn't recognize me. Not in this stranger's face.

Still, I'm relieved to see him, to know he's unharmed and reunited with his brother. That was, after all, his greatest wish.

I have to figure out how to get them both away from this forsaken city.

I look around frantically, trying to figure out if there's any way at all that I could signal him. Atticus must be somewhere close by, perched high on a tree branch or soaring overhead. Maybe he could cause a diversion, and mass panic would ensue. If he could get the crowd agitated enough, I might be able to slip through the security checkpoints.

But even as I contemplate it, I spot a familiar sight that warns me not to so much as contemplate any foolishness. One that sends a frisson of terror along my skin.

Two guards are parading in front of the crowd, large rifles slung over their shoulders. Padding along at their sides are large, mechanical cats made of gleaming silver steel. Each is the size of a large panther.

I've seen those cats before, in the service of the King's Guard in the Arc. Rys told me some time ago that the King had exported them to New York to offer them up as gifts, bribery to worm his way into Manhattan society. If chaos erupts, I have absolutely no doubt those cats will leap into the crowd and start tearing people apart.

I pull my eyes once again to the Duchess. She may be some distance away, but I can still make out the lines of her face. Her chin, as always, is held high as she looks down at the gallows. I have no doubt she's waiting impatiently to watch the pending act of malice.

But something in her body language is different from her normal, casual loathsomeness. Even from so far away, I can see a tension in her, a discomfort. It's almost as though…

She's afraid.

I never would have thought it possible, but yes—she's frightened of something. What is it? The Bishop? The battle she'll be fighting tomorrow?

I've never imagined that woman capable of fear. She's too confident, too convinced of her own superiority.

If she's scared of the Bishop, he must be a mighty adversary, indeed.

"Those people…are they—?" Adi asks quietly.

I'd all but forgotten I was sitting with her and Cillian.

Since I laid my eyes on Finn, my mind has been a mess of failed strategies and futile plans.

I nod. "That's Finn and his family. The Duke, the Duchess. Merit. But why would the Bishop bring them?"

She shrugs. "The Duchess sounds like a wild card, and the Bishop doesn't like ambitious, powerful Krats around. I suspect this is a *keep your friends close and your enemies closer* situation."

"Where will he take them after the Hanging?"

"Why? You're not contemplating going after them, are you?"

"Just answer the question," I say, my eyes pleading.

"He'll bring them back to the Palace to let the Duchess prepare for her battle tomorrow. If he wants her to win, he'll probably fill her in on who and what she's up against."

"Do you know who she's fighting?"

Adi shakes her head. "No idea. What's her skill?"

I freeze for a second, a horrific vision filling my mind of the moment when the Duchess wrapped her white-hot hand around Peric's throat, melting his flesh with nothing but her touch.

"She grows very hot," I say, though the words are too simplistic to describe the horror of the Duchess's power. "It's like she's made of molten lava, as if she's about to explode. She...hurts people in a way that's agonizing."

Something breaks in my voice, and Adi reaches a hand out and lays it on my arm only for a moment as she says, "I'm sorry." I can tell without asking that she knows what I've seen.

"Her husband is probably the one the Bishop wants," I say, stiffening under Adi's touch. I don't like showing weakness, particularly to someone I don't know very well. I started the day as Adi's captive, and as honest as she seems, I can't entirely bring myself to relax in her presence. "And Finn is a genius. He would be of great value to someone like the Bishop, if it's great minds he's looking for."

"It's more than just great minds," she says softly.

"It's about to start," Cillian interrupts in a whisper, and I look toward the area below us to see the steel gallows rising from its position at ground-level to an enormous height. I notice with a gasp that there's nothing support the structure— no Conveyor, no mechanism lifting it from the ground

"It's a Mag-lift," Adi explains. "They say the interior of the Moth is full of them. I don't know if it's true, but if so, it's impressive."

I watch, my jaw almost dropping when a large man in a black hood, dressed like a medieval executioner, strides out to another, smaller platform that's still on the ground. When he's positioned at its center, it begins an ascent to the height of the gallows, triumphant, dramatic music blaring through the speakers. The effect is chilling, the bizarre spectacle almost complete as the audience begins cheering and calling for the death to come.

I watch as hundreds of Dregs pound their fists in the air, crying, "Kill the Krat! Kill the Krat!" in practiced unison. A vindictive, cruel chant that sends needle-thin shards of ice crashing through my bloodstream. I remember all too well hearing the Arc's Aristocrats calling for the murder of Dregs —the bloodlust in their voices. The desire for suffering.

I suppose it goes both ways.

When the two platforms have connected, the hooded man —who must be close to seven feet tall—strides toward the accused. Despite the cold wind whipping at his fabric mask, the executioner is shirtless and glistening with sweat.

Adding to the spectacle, I think.

Once again, the Bishop appears on the massive holo-screen above the gallows. He rises to his feet, his face larger than life in all its strange perfection, and calls out a name.

"Soren McNamara!"

The crowd goes silent, and I watch as the accused turns to look over at the man who just spoke.

"You stand convicted of conspiring to overthrow the Directorate and to assassinate me. You are also guilty of fraud, of theft, of mutiny—to name only a few of your crimes. Your sins are many, and they are *significant.*"

The camera focuses back on the accused, who opens his mouth as if to plead his case. Standing next to the gigantic, silent executioner, he looks like a mouse.

When he fails to speak, the screen shows the Bishop once again as he holds up his hand and laughs. "I don't want your plea. I don't need to hear your defense. You know as well as I do that you are guilty and will soon be hanged by the neck for all to see." He turns to look down at the crowd, addressing all of us. "Not one of you has the capacity to conceal a crime from me. I see all. I see the truth, and I see lies. Let this man's fate be a lesson to you all, whether you are rich or poor, powerful or weak. I am not here to torment you. I am here for the good of you all, and the sooner you realize it, the better your lives will be."

The strange, short speech, coming from anyone else, would seem like utter madness. He speaks of himself as though he's some sort of living god.

No one sees all. No one is that powerful.

But something in the way the Bishop speaks feels terrifyingly final, like there's an absolute truth in his words that I can't bring myself to dispute...not even in my own mind.

K. A. RILEY

Without another word, the Bishop nods once toward the executioner.

The camera zooms in on the gigantic man as he extracts something from his waistband and holds it up to catch the light. I gasp when I spot what looks like a small, gleaming blade in his hand.

"This is supposed to be a hanging," I say under my breath. "What is he…"

The question is answered before I finish forming the words, even as the chant erupts again.

"Kill the Krat! Kill the Krat!"

A wave of nausea assaults me when the executioner stabs the accused in a series of rapid, violent thrusts, leaving angry red slashes along his crisp shirt.

The slashes quickly swell to horrifying, grotesque stains.

But instead of slumping to the ground, the accused man simply looks shocked. To my horror, the executioner seems to have hit with surgical precision, missing all vital organs despite at least seven separate stab wounds.

"Kill!"

Moving quickly, the executioner pulls the metal noose around the man's neck, grabs him by the arms, and stands back to watch as the floor opens under Soren McNamara. The accused falls rapidly, the camera following him as his legs thrash wildly, the blood pouring out both from the stab wounds and from the fresh slashes to his neck.

I realize with horror that we're witnessing a desperate race between his blood and his breath, and I find myself wishing him a swift death for his sake.

The truth is, though, I want it for my *own* sake. My throat catches, and I find myself pushing down a sob for the man who was brave enough to attempt to tear down the Directorate from his seat of privilege.

Whoever Soren McNamara was, he wasn't all bad.

I want to weep, to think. But I don't have the luxury of time to sit and absorb what just happened. The second the Hanging is over, the Dregs begin to disperse, slipping away like rats fleeing a deluge.

"Anyone caught here in an hour will be imprisoned, or worse," Adi explains quietly, taking my arm as I glance up toward Finn and the rest of his family, who are already accompanying the Bishop out of their box seats and toward a nearby exit. "We need to get you back to the house before we draw attention to ourselves."

I nod, though my eyes are still locked on the Davenport family. I'm still wondering if there's a way to get to them—a way to intercept them before they climb into whatever vehicle brought them here. But my hope fades as I see a swarm of guards, along with their robot cats, surround the small party of VIPs.

I'm about to surrender to Adi's plea to accompany her when the Bishop stops, turns, and looks in our direction.

I stop breathing, my body frozen.

Even from such a massive distance, I'm convinced that he's looking straight into my eyes.

No. He can't be. It's a ridiculous thought; he's too far away. Not to mention that there are still hundreds of people between me and him.

But there's something strange in the way his eyes are boring into me. Something that draws me to him in a way that feels like a violation.

Against my will, I find myself longing for tomorrow to come. Aching to put on the exquisite dress Shar gifted me, to ensconce myself in my new identity, and to meet the man in person. As much as I hate myself for it, I feel an aching need to find out exactly what it is about the Bishop that is so daunting and engaging at once.

As I watch him turn away, my breath returns to my chest. Just as quickly as the wild moment of desire surged through me, it's gone.

I ask myself how the hell he managed to draw me in like that. I wonder silently if Finn, too, has fallen under his spell. I can only imagine how overwhelming it must feel to sit so close to him, to be able to look him in the eye. I tell myself Finn is wily and clever, and unlikely to fall into any trap.

But the Bishop is more than a mere trap. He's something far darker, far more dangerous. His allure isn't physical, exactly. It's something more. An addictive substance that floats on the air and infiltrates the mind like a virus.

"That man scares me," I say softly.

"He scares us all," Adi replies as she takes me by the arm and guides me down the steps and toward the nearest street. "Trust me. We know his power."

"Power," I repeat as I stay close to her and Cillian, winding our way between swiftly moving bodies. "That's it, isn't it? It's a power, plain and simple. Like the Surge, or the Duchess's ability to conjure heat."

"They say he can bend anyone to his will," Cillian says, "so long as they're in his presence. But he's capable of a lot more than that. He can convince pretty much anyone to sell their soul. He's a freak of nature."

"I'm not sure nature has anything to do with it," I say, my voice tremulous. "But it is terrifying."

"Yet you still can't wait to meet him," Cillian says bitterly, his eyes on me as we duck into a narrow alley.

"I didn't say that," I retort.

"You didn't have to. It was written all over your face back there. You were like a dog staring at a meat-covered bone." He laughs, his expression softening. "It's all right. We all look like that the first time we see him. He's like a vice, something incredibly pleasant that we know is bad for our brains, our bodies, our souls. Just...be careful tomorrow, if you do manage to get anywhere near him. If he senses you're hiding something, he will do everything he can to get the truth out of you."

"He won't," I promise. There's too much at stake for me to let him in on any secrets.

"You say that now...but you'll see soon enough. Resisting him isn't exactly easy."

15

ENEMY HANDS

I SUPPOSE it's a little ironic that I'm about to spend the night on the very bed where I was tied down only a few hours ago. But at least the bonds are gone. Not to mention that the door remains unlocked, which I know because I tested it a few minutes ago.

As I lie down on the bed, I think about the day's events. About Adi and Cillian and the strange menagerie of silent lurkers who move about this half-ruined house like ghosts.

My mind settles when my thoughts shift to Finn, to the sight of his beautiful face earlier this evening, so focused on the spectacle unfolding before us all. I wonder with a sinking feeling what it must have been like for him to be forced into his mother's presence again—to have to spend time next to the woman who pitted him against me, who, for her own personal satisfaction, risked the life of her own son.

More desperately than ever, I want to go to him. To put my arms around him, to talk to him, make sure he's all right. He's been through so much in the last several months, his mind tortured by his mother, his father, the very blood that runs through his veins.

And through it all, he's remained strong, protective. I love him more than ever, and all I want in this moment is to know I'll feel his lips on mine again.

I remember reading once that love—or what we *perceive* as love—the mad, passionate kind that sends butterflies flitting through stomachs—is a sort of addiction. My love for Finn is still in the chemical stages, I know. I crave him. I dream and fantasize about his eyes, his lips, his touch. If we're fortunate enough to still be together ten years from now, the dreams will likely have faded to something more domestic and tame, though I can't entirely imagine it. I can't quite fathom taking him for granted. He excites me, energizes me, gives me strength every single day.

I comfort myself with the thought that being close to Merit is probably granting *him* strength now.

If I survive my risky venture, I'll get to see them both tomorrow.

It's a big *if.*

On the way home from the Hanging, Cillian, Adi, and I talk a little more about their plan for the morning. They don't tell me much, only that it's one that requires a massive amount of trust on my part. Under any other circumstance, I would refuse to take part. Ashen Spencer trying to pass herself off as an Aristocrat seems like folly.

But there's something else luring me across the bridge to Manhattan, and as it untangles itself I curse myself for it. In spite of every instinct inside me railing against the idea, I feel a strange, insidious need to meet the Bishop in person.

An argument has been raging inside me, my reasonable

side telling the other half of me that the idea is preposterous, foolhardy, dangerous.

But my emotional side can't stop thinking about that strange man—about the way he stared across the chasm between us tonight and looked right into my eyes. It felt like a summons, a call to my soul…

And I want to know why.

As I drift to sleep, my mind reels with half-dreams of tomorrow. The challenge I'll face in the morning, the part I'll be playing with every ounce of dramatic skill that I possess.

I know I may not make it through the day.

But I will fight like hell to make my way to Finn. If I die, at least I'll die knowing I tried.

In the morning, Adi wakes me up with a whisper of my name.

"Ashen. It's time."

"Time for what?" I spit, disoriented as I shoot up to a sitting position. I can't quite remember where I am, how I got here.

Then it comes to me like an assault on my mind.

Oh, God. This is really happening.

"You all right?" she asks.

I nod. "I just need to wake up properly," I moan, rubbing my eyes. "Remind me again why I'm doing this?"

Adi chuckles. "Because you want to get to Finn and Merit. You want to save them."

"I can't save them," I say, looking at her. It seems my confidence from the previous night has disappeared with the rising of the sun. "Can I?"

She sucks in her lower lip for a few seconds before smiling. "Who knows? Maybe you can. All I know is that staying here in Broken won't help anything. You won't be happy until you get to Finn."

"True," I reply, pulling myself out of the bed. "I'm ready. Tell me your plan."

Adi tosses me a dressing gown then guides me to the kitchen, where she hands me a muffin, pours me a cup of coffee, and says, "We're going to turn you back into Ana. Face, hair, everything but your clothing. Then Cillian and I will escort you to a spot about a block and a half from the barricade at this end of the bridge."

She chuckles a little as she hands me my coffee. I sit down at the small kitchen table and spot a large backpack sitting on the nearby window seat.

"Your clothes are in there. Everything you'll need, but nothing incriminating. Nothing to tie you to your true identity."

Nodding, I take a sip. "Okay."

"I'll lend you some clothes to wear this morning. You need to look like you're trying to disguise yourself as a Dreg, but not entirely pulling it off."

"A Dreg disguised as an Aristocrat disguised as a Dreg. I get it."

Adi grabs my arm, and flips it over, pointing to the scar on my wrist from where I sliced the Directorate's implant out long ago. "This here is a giveaway that you were in the Arc. We'll have to disguise it with a small, fresh wound. Not a bad one—just enough so it's not obvious that you removed an implant a while ago."

"Do whatever you need to." I take another sip. "So, are you going to tell me about Ana Miller? Who am I, exactly? I don't know anything about my supposed life."

"An Aristocrat from the midwest," Adi tells me. "One who disappeared some time ago. You were born and raised in Evanston, Illinois."

I gawk at her, surprised. "Couldn't I pretend to be someone from the Arc? At least I know that place. I could—" But even as I speak, the answer hits me like a slap to the face.

Of course I can't. The Duchess knew the identity of every Aristocrat in the Arc. She would know I was lying the second she spoke to me.

I need to show up as someone obscure—someone no one here knows. It's the only way to ensure they won't figure out I'm lying.

Adi takes a step toward me. "There was recent unrest in Chicago—the beginnings of a rebellion. It was spreading fast, so you made your way east thanks to a series of bribed Dregs and helpful Krats who were only too happy to take your money. You don't know their names—they tried to keep it all on the down low. Got it?"

"Sounds simple enough," I say.

As I'm speaking, Cillian walks in, looks at Adi with raised brows, and says, "Have you told her the fun part yet?"

Adi shakes her head with a rueful grimace.

"What fun part?"

Adi winces as she says, "I'm...sort of going to need to stab you. And I'm not talking about a little cut on your wrist. I'm talking about a proper wound."

My eyes widen, my fight or flight instinct kicking in. I have to grab hold of the table to convince myself not to get up and run out the back door.

"I'm not sure I understand," I reply, my voice tight. "Why, exactly?"

"The only way to get you across the bridge into

Manhattan," Cillian explains, "is to convince the Bishop's guards you're fleeing for your life, and that you're an Aristocrat in need of help. It's a little hard to do that if you just wander up and tell them, "Hi, my name is Ana and I waltzed straight through Brooklyn without a single Dreg going after me, even though I'm carrying a pack full of expensive clothes and wearing an even more expensive Holo-Veil."

My heart sinks. He's right. There's no disputing it. I need to be running *from* something, not just *toward* the Behemoth. Otherwise our plan will seem as transparent as glass.

"Well, I guess there's a silver lining to all this," I say with a bitter snicker. "Acting has never been my strong suit. But if you stab me I definitely won't have to fake it."

"That's the spirit!" Cillian replies with a laugh that does little to hearten me. "Don't worry, Ashen. Adi knows more about human anatomy than most people. She won't hit an artery or major organ. You just need a wound that's convincing enough to fool the guards."

"Make it as convincing as you like, but I need to survive long enough to see Finn. Dying of a voluntary stab wound wouldn't exactly be the glorious demise either of us was hoping for."

"You'll survive," Adi assures me. "You'll need a couple of stitches at the most—and you'll be fine by the time the Choosing Ceremony begins, I promise. Besides, no one has better doctors on hand than the Bishop."

I've always had a horror of knife wounds, despite the fact that I've used a blade to inflict a few of my own. There's something so invasive, so violating about the thought of a blade slicing through flesh.

I suppose that's why sadists prefer knives to guns. There's

something purely visceral about that particular act of violence. The thought makes me cringe.

But Adi is right—if I'm going to pretend to be seeking asylum in Manhattan, I need to put on a thorough act. I saw the crowd chanting last night, thirsting for the blood of a Krat. There's no way the residents of Brooklyn would let a Wealthy wander her way through this place unscathed.

When we've finished eating, I change into the clothing Adi has provided—a pair of jeans, a black t-shirt, a gray sweater, and some old sneakers—and activate my Holo-Veil before grabbing the rucksack Shar gave me, which contains all my new clothing. When I look in the mirror, I almost want to wave hello to Ana Miller, the pretty, blond stranger with the glowing skin and sparkling personality.

Adi is dressed in jeans and a hoodie, as is Cillian.

I fold my silver uniform and leave it on the bed, sad to part with such a trusty old friend.

When Adi asks if I'm ready, I nod. "As ready as I'll ever be. Let's get it over with."

We leave the house through the back door to begin our trudge toward Brooklyn Bridge.

"The bridge is guarded on both sides by the Directorate Guard and the Bishop's men," Cillian tells me. "It's also monitored by drones, as you saw last night. Which means the stabbing will have to take place in a blind spot, but close enough to the checkpoint that you can make your way over to the guards without taking unnecessary risks."

"Like bleeding out, you mean?"

He gives me a sheepish nod. "Kind of."

I pull my eyes up to see Atticus flying high overhead, just far enough away to seem as if he's not entirely with us, but close enough to keep his electronic eyes on me.

"I have to tell him about the plan," I say as the realization hits. "Rys will freak out if he sees you hurting me, and I can't guarantee you won't end up fighting off a robot owl who's trying to peck your eyes out."

Cillian whispers something to Adi before she nods assent. "Fine," she says, looking around to see if we're being watched. "Just make it quick."

I gesture to Atticus, who flaps down and lands on my arm. As quickly as I can, I explain to Rys what's about to happen, topping it off with "Don't worry. I'll be fine," despite the fact that it feels like a lie.

"Ash," Rys says, "This is insanity. There are other ways to get to Finn, surely. I could send Atticus in—he could..."

But he knows there's no way to finish that sentence. Even an army of drones probably couldn't find their way into the Palace without being blown to pieces.

"You know as well as I do that this is the only way," I tell him. "It will be all right."

"But you—"

I cut him off with a gesture of my hand. "I'm only telling you so Atticus doesn't try anything. He needs to stay stealthed and quiet. Anything else will put me in a lot more danger than a little knife wound."

Rys goes quiet for a few seconds before I hear a sigh, then he says, "You're a lunatic. You know that, right?"

"Absolutely. Now, do I have a promise you'll keep Atticus safe?" I ask, stroking my fingers over the owl's head. "Keep him invisible, at least until I get where I need to go."

"Promise," Rys says grudgingly. "But for the record, I freaking hate this."

"Noted."

RISKY BUSINESS

WHEN ADI, Cillian, and I reach our destination, Adi checks me over quickly as she gives me a few final instructions.

"You'll stagger—or whatever you choose—toward the bridge. Tell them your name, and if you have to, say you want to talk to the Bishop."

"Really? What could I possibly have to say to him?"

"It doesn't matter," Adi says, glancing at Cillian. "If they believe you are who you say, they'll bring you to him."

My eyes widen a little. I'm not sure why Ana Miller would merit such attention from the guy who allegedly runs New York.

"You guys are playing with fire," I say. "We all are. You know that, right?"

"Fire isn't always bad," Adi says, pulling up her dark hood and reaching into her pocket to extract a small folding knife. She pulls me into an alcove at the side of a red brick building and says, "We need to cut your wrist here, now, away from surveillance cameras. Nothing deep. Like I said, it's just a way to keep them from noticing your scar."

I nod, wincing, and hold my arm out, averting my eyes. "Make it quick, please," I plead quietly.

"You know, you're pretty squeamish for the leader of a massive rebellion," Adi chuckles.

"A rebellion where I didn't have to do any stabbing," I reply. "The Quiet War, remember? Silent and simple."

"Silent is good." Adi takes my wrist and says, "Okay, on three. One...Two..."

As she says, "Two," I feel a sudden jolt of pain shoot up my arm and I stupidly look down to see the knife tearing into my skin, just enough to rip through the scar tissue that's already there, and leave a bloody but shallow wound.

I watch as the cuff of my borrowed sweater turns deep red. When I put my hand down, the blood trickles down my wrist into my palm.

"Are you all right?" Cillian asks.

"Never better," I say through gritted teeth, feeling the color draining from my face. "That hurt."

"The worst is yet to come," Adi says with a sheepish grin.

"Thanks for the reminder."

We skulk around corners until we're only a block or so from the bridge. There, Adi and Cillian, their hoods pulled high around their faces, take me by both arms and drag me into broad daylight until I'm visible to the guards standing on high alert.

I pretend to struggle against their grip, waiting until I catch the eye of one of the guards, then pull myself free and begin to run.

That's when Adi grabs me again, yanks me backwards, and presses the knife deep into my side.

The blade pierces my flesh, the grim attack surprisingly quiet.

The sensation isn't altogether what I expected—it's more like a deep pressure than a slice. It's when she pulls the blade out and the sting of it assaults me viciously that I let out a sharp, involuntary cry.

"I'm really sorry," she whispers into my ear, then turns to flee once I've yanked myself free again. Watching her only for a moment, I turn and stumble my way toward the bridge, the rucksack suddenly an impossible weight on my back.

I fall forward, my eyes landing on the guard, positioned in front of a gate that's set up to block any traffic that might attempt to cross the bridge. When he and his partner spot me coming, the guards raise their guns in unison. But one of them, stepping forward, holds up a hand. Through my narrow-eyed wince, I see a symbol on his uniform, but it's not the Directorate rose that I've come to expect.

It's a pretty, flowering tree.

"Who are you?" he asks as he scrutinizes my too-perfect face. Turning to his partner, he says, "She's veiled. Must be one of us."

"My name is Ana Miller," I announce through gasping breaths, glancing back over my shoulder with a fear that isn't entirely contrived. "I'm an Aristocrat—I traveled here from Illinois. I was...trying to make my way..." I gesture down to my left side, where the wound has bled through my shirt and sweater. "Those Dregs...they attacked me..."

Instead of showing any sympathy, the guard lifts my shirt to eye the stab wound in my side. Once he's convinced it's real, he grabs me by my shoulder, spins me around, and rifles through my hair until he locates the tattoo Trace gifted me.

I've been applying the salve he gave me every time I think of it, but I still hold my breath, terrified the guard will announce that it's fake.

But instead, he says, "She has the mark."

"I need to see the Bishop," I sputter as I press a hand into my aching side.

As if he's said it a hundred times, the guard drones, "You'll see him soon enough, Miss. But right now, you need medical attention. Even if you didn't, there's no way we'd let you near him like that. You're covered in blood, for God's sake. You probably won't be able to speak to him until at least tomorrow."

My heart sinks. Is this guy seriously telling me I may have done all this for nothing?

Tomorrow will be too late, I want to scream. *Tomorrow may as well be next year!*

"But I need to see him! It's very important. I—I have information for him."

"You may well. But like I said, you're not seeing him in this condition," the guard tells me, lifting my shirt a little again, as if to remind me I'm still bleeding. I look down to see a red stain at my side, which is enough to make me go dizzy with disgust.

"Please..." I plead.

With a roll of his eyes, the guard pulls his left wrist to his mouth and says, "Boss, we have an Aristocrat here. Veiled and marked. Needs medical attention."

A voice on the other end tells him to bring me across the bridge. I glance warily over my shoulder, taking note of the crowd of Dregs who have gathered some distance away to watch the spectacle. I can't help but wonder if they're enjoying the sight of a frightened, wounded Aristocrat fleeing for her life.

They look angry, almost resentful that they weren't the ones to get their hands on me.

On a few faces, I read a distinct message:

Had I been the one with the knife, you wouldn't have survived, Krat.

I want to call out, to assure them that I'm one of them.

But then I remember who Ana Miller is.

Or rather, who she's *supposed* to be.

I narrow my eyes and raise my chin high, turning to follow two of the guards on a painful trek over to a small military truck with an open back. With one of the men's help, I climb in, take a seat on a hard, cold bench, pressing my head back and letting out a groan.

When we've driven to the other side of the bridge and the guards have helped me to climb down, I find that there's another vehicle awaiting us—small and white, with strange, transparent wheels. The driver leaps out, takes my backpack, and lays it in the trunk before offering to help me into the back seat, but I gesture to my blood-soaked clothing.

"I'll stain the upholstery," I warn him miserably. "Do you have a blanket or something? A towel?"

"Don't worry about it," he replies. "This isn't exactly the first time I'll have blood stains in my vehicle."

He's jovial and young, wearing a gray tartan cap that looks like something out of an old movie. Nothing about him particularly screams "Aristocrat," but then again, if he's a driver, maybe he's a Dreg who's risen through society's ranks to earn a trusted spot in Manhattan.

"Thanks," I tell him, and I mean it. As clean as the wound in my side is, it still stings, and the last thing I want to worry about right now is how to avoid dripping blood onto immaculate white upholstery.

"Are you all right, Miss?" the driver asks when I'm sealed

inside the vehicle and he's climbed into the driver's seat. "You still with me?"

"Mostly," I tell him with a weak attempt at a smile. "Where are we going?"

"Well…normally, I'd take you to a hospital. But for some reason, the Bishop gave me strict instructions to bring you to the medical center inside his residence. You know, the place they call the Palace."

"The Palace," I whisper. "I'm going to the Palace."

"What's that?"

"Nothing at all."

I sit back, press my head into the headrest, and in spite of everything, I smile.

THE PALACE

DESPITE THE PAIN in my side, I want to sing.

It's happening. We're going to see the Bishop—which means there's a chance I'll see Finn.

And there's a chance we'll make it out of this city in one piece.

Still, as the driver speeds along Manhattan's mostly deserted streets, I try to force the happy thought from my mind. After all, I'm *supposed* to be upset and afraid. I've just suffered a trauma, after all. A brutal attack by a cruel enemy.

"What exactly happened to you, then?" the driver finally asks. But before I can reply, he adds, "It was those damned Dregs, wasn't it? Pretty thing like you could get killed just for showing up in those monsters' territory. Everything about you *screams* Aristocrat. It's clear you don't belong there. I'm shocked, to tell you the truth, that you even made it to the bridge."

I nod, watching his eyes in the rearview mirror. There's something kind about him.

Which, for some reason, makes me want to trust him less.

"I know," I tell him. "I was stupid to try and find my way here on foot. It's just...the driver who brought me to New York..." I think fast before coming up with a suitable lie. "Her vehicle broke down some distance away. She's an Aristocrat, so of course she's rich, but there was no way to get it fixed quickly enough. I was desperate to get to Manhattan to attend tonight's Choosing Ceremony. So I made my way across Brooklyn as carefully as I could yesterday. I had to sleep on the street, then made a dash for the bridge this morning. It was only in the last few blocks that I ran into a couple of them, and, well...you can see what they did."

"You took quite a risk," the driver says with a hint of admiration in his voice. "Someone like you should know better than to wander through a Dreg Zone. Those parasites would eat you alive."

Parasites.

Okay, so maybe he's not so kind, after all.

"You don't have to tell me," I reply weakly, looking down at my blood-soaked clothing. "Who knows what else they might have done if I hadn't gotten away?"

"Well, you're safe now, Miss..."

"Ana," I reply. "Ana Miller."

"My name's Harry. I'm a part-time driver for the Bishop. Occasional Medic."

"Nice to meet you," I tell him, though at this point, I don't mean it in the least. I wait a few seconds before asking, "What's it like, working for the Bishop?"

I pull my chin down shyly when Harry eyes me in the mirror. "All the ladies want to know about him," he says. "And quite a few of the men, too. Not that I'm surprised. There's something about him, isn't there?"

I'm irritated that he hasn't answered my question, but I nod.

"He's...interesting," he finally says. "He's the most charismatic man I've ever met. Charming beyond belief. Benevolent in ways most people don't know."

"Benevolent? Really?" I nearly choke. Nothing I've seen about the young man who presided over a brutal killing last night seems benevolent to me.

"Were you at the Hanging last night?" Harry asks, reading my mind.

"I watched from a distance," I tell him, hastening to add, "That man—the accused—he deserved what he got if he betrayed the Directorate."

"You're so right. And his death served as a warning for anyone who might be stupid enough to cross the Bishop in future. He's such a powerful man. A god among insects. I've even heard—" He slams his mouth shut, seeming to realize he was about to divulge something he shouldn't. "Let's just say he's not to be trifled with."

I nod again, pulling my eyes to the window and watching immaculate glass buildings go by as we make our way toward the Palace. "There was a family with him last night at the Hanging," I say as casually as I can. "Do you know anything about them?"

I pull my gaze back to the mirror and see Harry narrow his eyes for a second before speaking again. "I don't, not really. Just that they're very important, for some reason." He inhales before adding, "The family's oldest son was quite handsome, they say. I heard some girls talking about him."

"Oh?" I ask, amused. "I hadn't noticed him."

"Well, maybe you'll run into him at the Palace."

"Maybe."

We arrive at our destination a few minutes later. The vehicle pulls into a steeply descending driveway, and Harry waits as a door opens up to reveal a bright underground garage.

He drives down and parks, pressing a button on the dashboard and telling me to wait a moment. Seconds later, a woman and a man dressed in white scrubs come running toward us from a distant corner of the garage, as though they've been waiting in the shadows for our arrival.

The woman, a black bag in hand—a medical kit of some kind, I assume—opens the door on my side and looks me in the eye.

"How many wounds?" she asks, her tone hurried.

"Two," I tell her, trying to sound more panicked than I feel. "A small cut on my wrist and a larger one on my abdomen…I was stabbed."

"Let's see the stab wound first," she says, holding up a light to shine at my stomach.

When I lift my shirt, her companion opens the medical bag, removes something that looks like a moist cloth, and gently presses it to the bloody wound.

But when he pulls it away, the woman looks confused.

"Strange," she says. "Harry—did *you* see the knife wound?"

"No," the driver replies, slipping out of the vehicle, "but the guard on the bridge did. Told me it was deep."

"It may have been, but now it's…" The woman stops there.

I look down, curious as to why she seems puzzled, and immediately, I understand.

Most of the blood is gone.

But so is the wound.

All that's left is a thin, light-colored line, like an old scar that's healed over the course of several years.

"I don't get it," I tell them, genuinely shocked and confused. "She stabbed that blade right into my side...I can...I can still feel the pain."

"I'm sure she did," the woman says, taking my wrist in her hand. My fingers are still covered in dried blood, but as the woman eyes my wrist, she shakes her head. "This one is sealed, too," she says. "Freshly. But yes, it's completely closed up."

Pulling her eyes to mine, she asks me, "Has this ever happened to you before? This...rapid healing?"

I shake my head. "Never. I don't get it. Why would I...?"

It's an honest question. I'm as baffled as they are.

But instead of replying, the woman throws a look at Harry, who quickly climbs back into the vehicle and turns on some kind of communication device. He speaks a few words I can't make out before climbing out again and looking at me with a smile.

"The Bishop wants to see you, Miss Miller."

It takes me a second to realize he's addressing me before I gasp, "What? Right now?"

"Right now," he nods.

"Why?"

The question comes out more sharply than intended. The truth is, I'm not mentally prepared for this. My head is reeling with a baffling hit of everything that's just happened, and now I'm expected to go stand in front of the man in charge of the Behemoth and all of New York City—and convince him my name is Ana Miller, that I'm an Aristocrat from Evanston, Illinois?

"I'd watch my tone if I were you," Harry chastises, his former friendliness fading fast. But he softens after a moment and adds, "Look—the Bishop doesn't like insolence from anyone—not even Aristocrats. Point is, you have something he wants. That makes you valuable. Besides, I thought you *wanted* to meet him. I figured I was doing you a favor by telling him what's going on." With that, he gestures toward the angry stain on my sweater.

"I get it. I do—it's just..." I look down at my sullied clothing. "I would have liked to get cleaned up first."

"You will have an opportunity to clean up, of course," the woman says. "We'll take you to a suite and give you clothes to change into—unless there's something in your pack you wish to wear. Don't worry, you'll have a little time to adjust to the new surroundings. A few minutes, at the very least."

"Thank you," I say gratefully, but the truth is, I want to throw up.

I'd expected my first encounter with the Bishop to be at tonight's party, in front of witnesses. Not like this. Not one-on-one, and not mere minutes after I've discovered I have the power to heal almost instantaneously from a deep knife wound.

If I wasn't already in shock from Adi's attack, the news of my strange gift would be enough to throw my mind into a state of chaos.

At this point, my brain and body feel like they've been through a blender.

I'm about to ask another question when the woman asks me to follow her.

She brings me to a set of elevators at the far side of the parking garage, and when a set of sliding doors opens, I follow her on board. The elevator is old-fashioned, with brass casings around the door and the buttons. It moves painfully slowly, but eventually the bell dings and we exit into an elegant hallway with a dark red carpet and an impressive assortment of what look like original oil paintings hung along the walls.

My calm escort, who is starting to remind me eerily of the Arc's Chaperons, brings me to room 3008. She unlocks the door with a press of the inside of her wrist and guides me into a large living area inside.

"The Bishop stays in the penthouse," she informs me. "This is a Guest Level. Only you and a few others are staying here at the moment."

"Anyone exciting?" I ask.

"Depends on what you consider exciting," she replies with what sounds like a snuffle. "They're all Aristocrats—people the Bishop is curious about. He likes to keep a close eye on anyone intriguing, which, I suppose, is why you're here." She nods toward a door at the room's far end and says, "That's the bedroom. You should find some clothes in various sizes and anything else you need in the closet and dresser. You have fifteen minutes to prepare yourself. I'll be back in a few minutes to bring you up to the penthouse."

I nod, thanking her before reminding myself that I probably shouldn't be *too* obliging and thankful. A real Aristocrat would probably be demanding and difficult. As the medic leaves, I call out, "I'd like some water sent to the suite. And maybe a croissant or two. Please let someone know."

"Of course," the woman replies, tightening as she speaks, and as she closes the door behind her, I smile to myself.

It's kind of fun to be a demanding ass.

I make a vow to put on a convincing show for the Bishop as I head into the bedroom and rifle through the closet, which is teeming with clothing suitable for someone of every build and stature. For a moment, I contemplate slipping into one of the elegant dresses on display, but instead, I reach in and grab a white blouse and a pair of neatly folded jeans sitting on a shelf to the right of the closet.

Slipping out of my clothes, I step over to the en-suite bathroom to clean myself up, remembering when I see my reflection that I don't need to worry about hair or makeup. My Holo-Veil is permanently in a state of perfection.

Staring into the mirror, I move my face to the left and the right, eyeing my strange new features and wondering if there's any chance the technology could fail while I'm talking to the Bishop. Pushing its limits, I toss my hair back over my shoulders in one sweeping gesture. It still has its usual length and weight, but its illusion of light color stuns me. I feel like I'm inhabiting someone else's body as I live this strange, bold lie.

I stand back, gawking at myself for a moment in my underwear and bra, realizing how exposed I am.

I can see all, the Bishop said at the Hanging. That was his warning to all inhabitants of New York.

The thought that he might have his eyes on me even now sends an uncomfortable shiver along my skin, and I grab the shirt and jeans and pull them on quickly. I head back into the bedroom for socks, shoes, and a hair clip, pulling my hair back to enhance my artificial face.

When I'm ready, I leave the bedroom to stride over to one of the living room's windows, peering out over the nearby rooftops. It's then that I see Atticus flapping down to land on a ledge on the building opposite the one I'm in.

With a sigh of relief, I think, *Thank God Rys knows where I am.*

I watch Atticus as his eyes flash red once before he disappears into his stealth mode.

Good boy.

K. A. RILEY

I'm still staring out the window when a knock sounds at the door, startling me.

I call out, "Who is it?"

"Security, Miss," a man's voice says. "I've brought you a visitor."

"Visitor?" I reply, confused. I'm supposed to go up to the penthouse to meet the Bishop. I don't have time for visitors. Unless...

No, I think. *It couldn't be Finn.*

Could it?

I pat my hair nervously, striding over to pull the door open.

But the man on the other side is the farthest possible thing from the boy I love.

"Hello, Ana," he says. "It's so nice to meet you."

18

THE BISHOP

My legs are shaking.

The Bishop's presence terrifies me, though I'm not entirely sure why.

I may not be wearing Finn's silver uniform. I may not have my dagger at my side. But I'm still strong. I still have the Surge at my disposal.

If he tries anything, I can always kill him.

But when I look at him, something tells me this man—this strange, grinning creature with perfect white teeth, exquisite skin, and eyes that invite me in like a sparkling pool on a hot summer's day—does not intend to hurt me.

At least, not right now.

The security guard who knocked on my door turns to leave, which only heightens my sense of unease.

I offer up a smile—one that twitches and hesitates before finally curling my lips into something vaguely resembling an appropriate configuration. I remind myself that this Ana person, unlike me, is an Aristocrat. She was raised with

129

money and power. She should be haughty. A little snooty, even.

Stop acting like a terrified kitten, Ash.

"Nice to meet you, too," I finally reply, ironing out my voice to a smooth lilt as I shuffle from one foot to the other in an attempt to seem flirtatious rather than petrified. "I've heard so much about the famous Bishop."

"Oh?" he asks, taking a step closer. His chin is down, his eyes laser-focused—I can see now that they're dark blue with a golden ring at their center—and something tells me he's scrutinizing me. I wonder with a shock of horror if he can somehow see beyond the Holo-Veil to assess my features, my true bone structure.

I take in his scent as he nears me. It's decidedly masculine, but there's something else about it, too. Pine. Moss. The outdoors.

The mountains.

He smells like home. The very air around him *tastes* like home, like comfort.

"What exactly have you heard?" he asks, distracting me from the surprising realization.

There's a quiet menace in his tone, but he still smiles that charming, sweet smile of his, his eyes sparkling unnaturally bright. As I peruse his features, I take in his lips which are full and pink, almost pouty, and I find myself wondering how many women have fantasized about kissing him.

This *is your power,* I think. *Your face, your voice. That devastatingly intimidating gaze of yours. You scare people into submission, make them fear disappointing you.*

It must hurt to disappoint a god.

I can't begin to imagine what it would feel like to wield such a weapon.

Staring at him, I manage to hold onto the grin I've forced onto my lips. "Only that you're brilliant. And that you've earned the respect of every Aristocrat and Dreg in this city, which is saying something."

"I believe you mean I've earned their resentment and disgust," he says with a laugh. "Come, sit down on the couch with me. You must be tired after your ordeal."

We stride over and seat ourselves, him at one end of the couch, one leg crossed over the other, his arms spread across the back. I tuck myself into the other corner, all but cowering, trying to shield myself from his strange, powerful energy. I have no idea what it is about this man that makes me fearful as a kitten in a den full of vipers, but I'm determined to figure it out.

I just need a little time.

"I hope you don't mind my asking," he says politely. "But my people told me you were stabbed?"

"I was," I tell him with a too-enthusiastic nod. "By a Dreg."

Reminding myself who I'm meant to be, I try my best to utter the last word with a hint of disdain.

Gesturing to my torso, I say, "The wound is—was—here."

"But it's gone," he says knowingly. "Healed, from what I understand."

I nod, unsure how to respond.

"May I see?" he asks.

The question throws me. He...wants me to lift up my shirt?

The thought of it feels utterly inappropriate and far too intimate. He's no medic, after all. Yet I can't fathom saying no to him.

"I...really? Are you sure?"

"Look, Ana, I'll be blunt," he says, his smile fading fast. "My people told me what happened. At first..." He stops talking and laughs, and I find myself laughing too, more out of discomfort than mirth. "At first, I thought you might have lied about the injury to gain entry to Manhattan. I know, it sounds ridiculous, doesn't it?"

This time, I laugh for real. If he only knew how much the wound hurt, how terrified I was that Adi might accidentally hit a vital organ. It may have been planned from beginning to end, but there was nothing fake about it.

"It was very, very real," I tell him, wiping away a tear. "It hurt like hell."

"I'm sure it did. I even spoke to Reynaud, my man at the bridge—the one who saw the wound when it had just been inflicted. Excellent soldier, that one. He thought you'd need several stitches, if not surgery." He looks down to my stomach again. "Please—may I see?"

My smile fades and I nod, turning his way and pulling my shirt up to reveal the place where Adi stabbed me.

The Bishop slips closer and stares at my abdomen, which is enough to make me feel woefully self-conscious. Then, to my horror, he runs a fingertip along the narrow trace of a line where the wound used to be.

"Incredible," he says.

I tremble. I can feel a strange, unnerving power in his touch, though what sort, I can't say. All I know is that in this moment, I suspect I would do anything he asked of me. And the thought frightens me to my core.

"You told them this has never happened before, correct?" the Bishop asks, his finger still on my skin. "This quick-healing of yours?"

"That's right," I reply. "Never. It was a shock, to put it mildly. I still have a scar on my chin from where I fell out of a tree and cut my face as a kid. I never thought I'd manage to heal like *this*."

"Mmm-hmm." He finally pulls his hand away, but now he moves it to my chin, cupping it in his fingers. I try not to shudder when his eyes lock on mine and he says, "No scar now, though. Not with that Holo-Veil covering your face. I would love to know what you look like under there, Ana. Veils are convenient, but they do occasionally fill me with frustration, I'll admit." He pulls back, sighs, and adds, "But I understand. Privacy. Vanity. We Aristocrats like to keep a few secrets, don't we?"

I nod, pulling my eyes away from his. "Believe me, I look much better this way. You wouldn't want to see my actual face."

"I don't know. I can see your bone structure despite your Veil. I can tell you're beautiful. Still, I won't ask you to show your true self to me, at least not yet." He reaches out and lays a hand on my arm, drawing my eyes back to his, and I wonder for a moment if any woman has ever rejected him. "There is something I would like from you—if you're willing to give it."

"What's that?"

"A sample of your blood."

My throat tightens and I nearly choke on the air I've just inhaled.

Why does he want my blood? Is he going to look through some huge Aristocrat database and figure out if I'm actually who I say I am?

If he does, the game is over. I'm as good as dead.

"Of course. But...may I ask why?" My voice is far too mousy for my liking.

The Bishop smiles, easing closer still so that I can feel the heat of his breath on my skin when he whispers, "I want to know where this power of yours comes from. I want to study it. What you have…it could help so many people, Ana. So many who are suffering. I'm sure you understand."

There's something almost vampiric in the way he speaks the words. Something that makes me feel as though he wants to take possession of my body, my mind.

For the first time, I feel like I fully understand what it is about him that's so alluring. He's deeply dangerous. Threatening. Powerful in a way that makes me want to get close to him for the shelter his strength provides, rather than risk being his enemy.

I'm filled with a deep certainty that his protection would be more valuable than all the money in the world.

I turn to him, aware that my face is still a mere few inches from his own. My lips curl up as I stare into his eyes. "You can have anything you want," I tell him, forcing myself to play my role even as I wish myself a million miles away. *You're too dangerous. Too charming. Too smooth.*

It's not…

Natural.

"Thank you, Ana. I will have my people come to you to extract a sample."

With that, he pushes himself to his feet.

"There's something I want to ask of *you*," I tell him before he has a chance to leave.

"Oh yes? What's that?" he replies, and I can see him tensing as the words come, as though he's unaccustomed to being asked for anything.

"The Choosing Ceremony tonight. I would like to attend, if it's all right."

He turns to look down at me, his dark hair falling about his face. He combs it back with his hand and says, "Of course.

I would be delighted if you would come. The event begins at seven p.m. in the Grand Ballroom." As he stares at me, he adds, "There's more to you than meets the eye, isn't there? Perhaps a little morbid curiosity combined with a little sadism?"

No sadism, I think. *Only a desire to find the boy I love and get him and his brother as far from you as possible.*

"Curiosity, for sure," I reply. "I'm curious about many things. There's...even a part of me that wants to see the inside of the Behemoth. Am I out of line for admitting that to you?"

I have no idea why I said that. None. What was I thinking?

I don't want to see the Behemoth.

Ever.

The Bishop eyes me in a way I can't entirely read. His eyes narrow, his lips twisting uncertainly before settling into another smile. "Many people would like to see the inside of that incredible structure," he tells me. "But few are invited in. However, if you prove as...valuable...as I suspect you will, I will issue you an invitation myself."

"Thank you," I say, rising to my feet and stepping toward him. "I must admit, I was frightened in Brooklyn. I thought... well, let's just say those Dregs really wanted me dead."

The Bishop steps back to me and cups my chin in his fingers again, lifting my face. His eyes seem different now. I could swear they were blue a minute ago, but now, they're a dark brown. Almost black. "I would not let anyone hurt you," he assures me, "Unless you wronged me, that is."

"I wouldn't wrong you," I promise. "Never."

"Good," he replies, dropping his hand to his side and backing away, leaving a trail of searing heat along my skin. "Wear something beautiful for me, Ana. I have high hopes for you."

With that, he finally leaves me alone in the suite, closing the door gently behind him. My breath is trapped in my chest, and I find myself falling back onto the couch, sinking into the cushions as my heart races far too fast, hammering as if it's making a concerted effort to escape my body.

My mind reels as I try to grasp at the threads of the conversation we just had. I find myself wishing more than ever that I could talk to Finn—or at least that I could open the window and let Atticus into the suite with me. I could ask Rys why he thinks the Bishop wants my blood. What if...what if he figures out that I'm Ashen Spencer, a rebel Dreg from Sector Eight?

Stop. Stop. Stop.

You're freaking out over hypothetical situations.

You're here to get Merit and Finn away from this place. If you're lucky, you can do it tonight, long before anyone has taken your blood.

But my hopes are quickly dashed when a knock sounds at the door.

When I stride over to look through the peephole, I recognize the woman on the other side—she's the Medic who first noticed my wounds had healed.

I let her in, and she says coldly, "I'm here for the sample."

"Sample?"

"Your blood," she drones, as if my inability to figure that out means I'm an absolute idiot.

"Oh, right," I tell her, cursing under my breath. "Sure. Of course."

We sit down at a small table by the window and she asks me to roll up my sleeve. As I do so, I ask, "Do you know what the Bishop intends to do with this?"

"Analyze it," she tells me.

It doesn't exactly answer my question, though.

"Analyze it how? Is he going to compare it to anything?"

She sighs. "Our specialists will isolate whatever it is that helps you to heal. They'll extract it and attempt to generate a formula that can work for other humans. I'm sure you know something of the Bishop's methods."

I hesitate for a few seconds before saying, "Not exactly. I mean, I've heard rumors, but…"

The woman looks at me, a surprised expression in her eyes. "That's right. You're not from around here." She leans in and says, "It's a miracle, what's happening in the Behemoth. It will change the future of humanity for the better. I know some people aren't too happy about the Bishop's work, but trust me when I say he is going to save our entire species."

"How?"

"By ridding the world of all its ills," she says with a strange shrug, as if it's the most obvious answer in the world.

As I watch her take the sample and leave, a chill makes its way through my bloodstream. Ridding the world of all its ills should sound like a good thing, a moment of massive progress for humans everywhere.

So why do the words terrify me almost as much as the Bishop does?

19

WAITING

THE CLOCK on the console table by the suite's door reads three o'clock. The Ceremony, the Bishop said, is at seven, down in the Grand Ballroom, which I can only assume is on the first floor.

I contemplate venturing downstairs to take a look, but when I poke my head out into the corridor, I see armed guards stationed every fifty or so feet as if just waiting for fools like me to dare venture out of our temporary prisons.

Stir-crazy and feeling trapped, I explore the suite, which I have to admit is more than a little luxurious with its combination of antique and modern furniture and a hardwood floor polished to a pristine, warm shine. In the bedroom is a large sleigh bed, its perfect white linens accented by a tidily folded pile of fluffy towels.

Is this what it feels like to be a member of the Elite? To be doted on and coddled, offered every comfort known to humanity? With a wince, I confess to myself once again that I could get used to it.

Except for one thing: what distinguishes me from most

Aristocrats is that I would never want any of it, not if such luxuries came at the expense of a single other person's well-being.

Opening the rucksack that Shar gave me, I extract the cleverly rolled-up gown—the turquoise beauty that I'm to wear tonight. I wonder with a shiver of delight what Finn will think of it...before remembering that he won't recognize me, even if he stares right at me.

I glance around once again, searching for possible cameras, micro-drones, anything that the Bishop might be using to monitor my suite. But aside from the full-length mirror leaning against the wall, which I pull away to make sure there's no secret compartment concealed behind it, I see no sign of planted surveillance equipment. I even go so far as to run my fingers under lampshades and tabletops, as well as under my bed frame.

After a time, I surrender to the notion that maybe the Bishop isn't quite as evil as some Aristocrats I've known. He *is* charming. Warm, even. In fact, his most disconcerting characteristic is the simple fact that he's so damned young.

How does anyone who's only a few years older than I am manage to wield so much power?

I tell myself not to think too hard about it. My mind is meant to be focused on Finn, on our mission. Tonight, I need to find him before the Ceremony—to figure out if there's a way we can both make it out of here with Merit in tow. Maybe if we made our way back to Brooklyn...

I realize with a slump of my shoulders that I never came up with a plan to get back there, never even talked to Adi and Cillian about the possibility. It's almost as if I didn't think there was a chance I'd survive this day.

Yet here I am. Not only very much alive, but I've actually

met the Bishop. I'm a few hours from a possible encounter with Finn.

He and I will find a way.

We always do.

Holding the turquoise dress before me in front of the full-length mirror, I find myself staring not at the garment itself, but at my wrist, at the place where Adi cut into my flesh. Not only is the wound she inflicted healed, but the scar that was there previously seems to have disappeared, as well. My body has learned to heal itself on a level deeper than simple flesh wounds, and I have no idea how or why.

Not that I'm complaining. It could come in very handy in a fight if my opponent were to draw blood.

A knock at the door interrupts my moment of thought. I head over to open it, expecting to come face to face with another of the Bishop's servants.

Instead, to my utter shock, the person standing in the hallway is Finn.

VISITOR

"F—" I breathe.

But I immediately inhale a breath, remembering that I'm not supposed to know him. I'm not Ashen Spencer; I don't even *look* like her. Worst of all, the guards are still in position down the hall, so I can't even grab him and pull him close to whisper the truth. I can't touch him, kiss him, tell him how much I've missed him.

I close my eyes for a second and tell myself I've never met this young man in my life. That I need to act accordingly.

"Hello," I stammer, opening my eyes. "Can I help you?"

"I..." Finn stares at me, a flicker in his eyes as if for a moment he's taken aback. "Uh...my name is Finn Davenport. My family is staying down the hall, and we heard there was someone new in this suite." He leans in a little when he adds, "The truth is, I wanted to know..."

He stops, seemingly searching for the next words.

"Yes?" I say.

"A friend of mine flew into the city with me," he says. "And

I don't know where she is. More than a friend, really. Much more."

I have to fight back the smile that wants to slip its way over my lips as he keeps talking.

"Since you're new in town, I wondered if maybe you'd seen her or heard something." He runs a hand through his hair and bites his lip. "Look, I really hope I'm not disturbing you."

"Not at all," I tell him with the smile that I've given up trying to subdue. "Would you like to come in?"

I stare at him, wondering what he'll do. Accept the invitation from a strange young woman to enter her hotel room? Or...

Finn glances up the hall toward his suite's door before shaking his head. "I...don't think so," he says. "It wouldn't be right. I..."

He stops short of saying anything about a girlfriend, but I know he's thinking it. Then again, *boyfriend* and *girlfriend* aren't exactly terms we use for one another; they seem too light, too trivial, after all we've been through.

"It wouldn't be right," he repeats. But instead of leaving, he looks at me awkwardly for a moment before adding, "I'm really sorry—this may sound weird, but there's something so familiar about you. I can't put my finger on it, but..."

"Do you know anything about surveillance in our suites, Finn?" I ask him. *Complete non-sequitur, I know.*

"Uh..." he replies with a chuckle, glancing around. "Given that the Bishop owns this building, I imagine it's pretty thorough. But I have yet to see a single camera or micro-drone, now that you mention it. Why do you ask?"

"No reason," I say with a shrug and another smile. "I'm just curious. So—your family..." I'm not sure how to ask the next question without giving away what I know. *Is your mother still giving Satan lessons in How To Be Evil? Is your father still spineless? Is your little brother all right? Have they hurt you?*

"Your family," I repeat. "They're Aristocrats, then?"

He nods. "We're from the Arc, out west. I..." He stops speaking, stares at me, and says, "Your voice..."

I bite my lip. Of *course*. There's nothing disguising my voice. It's just as it always was. I mean, it's never been particularly remarkable, but to Finn's ear, it must be jarring to hear it coming from someone else's face.

He looks into my eyes, this time with a deep understanding infiltrating every inch of his face. "Actually," he says, "I've changed my mind. I *will* come in, if the invitation still stands."

With another tight smile, I back up and gesture to him to enter, afraid to utter another word until we're inside.

"Could I have a quick tour?" Finn asks as I close the door behind him, his voice full of hidden meaning. "Of the suite, I mean? I'd love to see how different it is from ours. The Bishop's people have really done amazing things with this building."

"They have," I agree. "Is it true that it used to be a hotel?"

He nods. "The Waldorf," he says absently as he heads for the window and looks out. Atticus is once again visible, perched across the way as if showing himself deliberately to Finn, who grins, the owl's presence confirming what he already suspected.

Finn walks around the living room, commenting casually on the artwork, the furniture. He peeks his head into the bedroom before saying, "Do you mind if I look at the bathroom?"

"Of course not," I tell him, careful to keep my distance in case of curious, intrusive eyes. "Be my guest."

I watch him head in, but only a few seconds pass before he calls out, "I didn't catch your name."

"Ana," I call back, expecting him to re-emerge.

But he doesn't come back out.

"Ana," he repeats. "Hey—you should see the door in here. This hook looks loose."

I step through the bedroom into the bathroom, and Finn immediately closes the door behind me, grabbing me by both shoulders.

"There *is* surveillance in this place—a lot of it, hidden away in the walls and ceilings," he whispers. "I heard my parents talking. But they said there's a setting in the bathrooms. The surveillance shuts itself down for a few minutes after the door closes before it comes on again."

"Oh," I say. "I—"

I'm still not completely sure he's figured out who I am, that is until I feel his grip loosen on my shoulders, his hands moving down to my waist. From the look in his eyes, he's seriously considering kissing me. "Ash," he says so quietly that I'm not entirely sure I didn't imagine it. "That *is* you, isn't it?"

I nod faintly, turning to face the back of the door, my fingers reaching for the hook. "You're right," I say loudly, in case anyone is listening via the microphones in the next room. "It *is* loose."

I reach back and take his hand momentarily in mine, squeezing. It's all I can do not to spin around and throw my arms around his neck, press my lips to his, and savor the kiss I've been aching for ever since the Air-Wing landed in Brooklyn.

"I suppose maintenance could fix that," he says, pressing himself close behind me and whispering, "I was so worried about you. I wanted to get out of this place, to come find you. I tried more than once."

"It's okay," I reply quietly. "I came here for you—which was quite an ordeal. I had to get tattooed, even." With that, I laugh, turning to look at him.

"Tattooed?" he asks, a confused look on his face.

"Apparently it's a thing for Aristocrats," I shrug.

"Um, no, it's not," he tells me, his brow furrowing. "I've never heard of an Aristocrat getting inked."

"Maybe it's not in the Arc, but it seems to be here," I offer.

He stares at me with a skeptical glint in his eye, and I add, "Look—all I know is the guards at the bridge checked me for it. When they saw it, they decided I was an Aristocrat. It's the only reason I managed to get into Manhattan."

"I believe you," he says. "Whatever it took to get you here, I'm grateful. I don't care if you have a million tattoos. I'm just glad you're safe."

A second later, his lips are on mine, kissing me tenderly, needfully, as if it's been a year instead of a day since we were last together.

He pulls back, letting out a little laugh. "It's so strange, seeing you like this," he says, slipping a finger over my cheek. "I miss your face."

"I miss it, too," I tell him. "Once we're out of here, I can take this thing off. Shut it down for good."

At that, his expression goes solemn. "You know my mother is going to fight tonight, right?" he asks, drawing my mind in a new direction.

"Yes," I tell him. "I take it you know what happens if she wins."

"It's the Behemoth for all of us," he says quietly. "Yeah. I've heard."

"We can't let that happen," I tell him. "We didn't come here to get trapped inside a new Arcology—we came to get your brother."

"We may not have a choice, Ash. We're *already* trapped. I don't like it any more than you do, but it's the truth. If either of us tries to leave the Palace, we're as good as dead. I had to surrender my silver uniform when they took me, and I suspect you don't have yours, either. It's not like we can stealth our way out of here. I told you, I've tried getting out. I wanted to get to you so badly—"

"What happened when you tried?"

He clams up for a moment, clenches his jaw, then says, "The place is guarded like nobody's business. I couldn't even get on the elevator without two armed guards stopping me every time I took a step in their direction. But I did manage to slip by them late last night, after we'd come back from the Hanging. Everyone was exhausted, and the place was quiet. I actually thought I had a chance to go hunting for you."

I wait, watching his eyes as a deep pain seems to build behind them.

"What is it, Finn? What happened?"

"They stopped me in one of the stairwells as I was making my way down. Two armed guards. They brought me to him."

"Him. You mean the Bishop."

He nods.

I reach for him, taking hold of his hand and bringing it to my lips. "What did he do to you?" I ask, recalling the strange, awful hold the Bishop had over me while I was in his presence. If he hurt Finn...

"Nothing, not exactly," he says. "But he told me he knew how to hurt me deeply. That he knows how much I care about Merit.

That he wouldn't hesitate to use my brother as a weapon, as well as anyone else I care about. He told me that while my mother was his 'champion' for tonight, I'm the prize...whatever that means. Ash—I'm so sorry. But I couldn't leave. I couldn't risk him hurting Merit. Not even if it meant a chance at getting to you."

"It's all right," I tell him. "I'm here now. And trust me—if you end up in the Behemoth, I'm coming too."

"Damn right you are."

As we stand there, locked in each other's arms, I let out a deep, throaty sigh of surrender.

A possible venture into yet another terrifying Arcology isn't what I signed up for. But at least I'm safe, I'm with Finn, and Merit is safe, too.

Things could be worse.

"The good news," Finn says, "is that I heard my parents talking. It sounds like there's something going on inside the Behemoth—something incredible. Huge medical advancements the likes of which none of us has ever seen. The Bishop hinted at it, too. He said he wants me to be part of it. And my father. He said he could use our expertise." He pulls back and looks into my eyes. "Don't get me wrong—I would far rather get in an Air-Wing and fly back home with you than stay here. But if we *are* forced to stay, it sounds like we could become part of something extraordinary."

I stare at him, my heart swelling with affection and fear at once.

"What are you thinking?" he asks.

I smile. "I'm thinking you're a glass-half-full guy at heart, aren't you? Here I've been railing against the idea of ever seeing the inside of that monstrosity, swearing I'd never willingly enter it. And you're okay with marching right in, because there may be something in that place that could help make the world a better place."

"I'm not always so optimistic. And I'm not sure what to think of the Bishop, not really. But I heard my father talking to someone—apparently, the Behemoth has some incredible bio-tech facilities. So if—*if*—we get stuck here, I intend to find out what's going on."

"I can tell you it's not all good," I tell him. I fill him in quickly about Adi's sister, about Shar's son. Dregs disappearing, stolen from their former lives never to be heard from again. "The Bishop's people may be working on something extraordinary, but from the sounds of it, it's costing people their lives. Not to mention that if we end up in there, we may never be able to leave."

"We'll be okay," Finn says in a resolute tone. "Ash, we'll find a way out. The Bishop comes and goes all the time."

Surrendering, I drape my hands around Finn's neck and say, "I would go to the ends of the earth with you. I just want to make sure I can see Kel again. You understand, right?"

He nods. "Of course, Ash. And I promise—we'll get back to Kel. I'm just glad he's in good hands."

He's right. Kel is in *great* hands, even, with Kurt and Illian watching over him, as well as Kyra. He's surrounded by friends and protectors.

If Finn and I can find some way to infiltrate the Bishop's project, to help make the world a better place…I suppose it's worth delaying our trip back home.

"Listen," he says, "you'll be at the Choosing Ceremony tonight?"

"Yes."

"Good. When I see you there, I'm going to hit on you. I'll

stay by your side as much as I can. If my mother thinks I'm flirting with an Aristocrat, so much the better. I—"

Suddenly, he stops talking. We both hear it then—a strange, quiet buzz from somewhere in the far corner of the marble-inlaid shower. A micro-drone—one that looks like a wasp—is crawling through a tiny hole in the grout.

Thinking fast, I pull the door open, laughing as if Finn's just said something uproariously funny, and head back through to the living room.

"It was so good to meet you," I tell him in my politely reserved Ana voice, all too aware that we're still being watched. "I was afraid I'd be all alone in this place. I'm essentially on my own here in New York." I look him flirtatiously in the eye, almost *hoping* the Bishop has his eyes on us. "I didn't know I'd find such handsome Aristocrats in this town, but here we are."

"Well, thank you," Finn says with a comical puffing of his chest. "I'll see you at the ceremony tonight?"

"I'm looking forward to it," I reply as he opens the door and steps through.

I slip into the corridor after him and turn toward the two armed guards at the end of the hall, watching Finn's every move as he makes his way to his family's suite.

I'm certain in that moment that Finn is right.

There is no escaping this place.

21

PREPARATIONS

As SEVEN O'CLOCK APPROACHES, a knock sounds at my door.

I rush over to open it, hoping to see Finn's face once again. But this time, it's a woman dressed in a purple uniform. She's tall and stone-faced, her expression somewhat grim when she says, "I was sent to give you directions to the Grand Ballroom. Simply turn right out of your suite and take the elevator at the end of the hall. There is no need to press buttons; it will take you directly to the location. The festivities begin in a few minutes, but the brawl begins at eight o'clock."

"Thank you," I tell her, doing my best to mirror her chilly demeanor. "I'll get ready to head down, then."

She lifts her chin and looks down at me as if trying to figure out which parts of me are real. I wonder with tension overtaking my body if my disguise is really that transparent. Then again, I suppose it doesn't matter. From the sounds of it, nearly everyone I'll see tonight will be coated in the same kind of fake veneer.

I wouldn't be surprised, in fact, to learn the Bishop is nothing more than a homely man in multiple holographic layers—though I didn't spot any evidence of a Holo-Veil when I spoke to him. None of the strange, translucent appearance I noticed in my own face or Cillian's, or that occasional sparkle of light piercing through to reveal another, more solid layer beneath.

When the woman has left, I head to the bedroom to put on the turquoise dress. I find myself staring in the mirror as I hold up the beautiful garment Shar gave me—at my odd face, my jarringly different hair color. I wonder for a moment if Finn liked what he saw—if there was anything in this face that appealed to him more than my usual appearance.

In a moment of annoying insecurity that feels like a pestering gnat, I ask myself if it's possible to be jealous of someone who doesn't actually exist.

Ash, you idiot.

Of course he was attracted to the blonde.

*She's **you**.*

I shake my head and laugh at myself before slipping into the dress, enjoying the way its skirt flows in aqua-colored waves as I move through the suite. Seating myself on a chair in the living room, I pull on a pair of silk shoes Shar provided and stand up to assess the entire picture in the full-length mirror.

"Not bad," I say out loud as I scrutinize my fake face. "Though I still think I prefer the original."

The corridor is empty when I head out, and I walk past the Davenports' suite, wondering if they've already made their way down to the Ballroom. Knowing the Duchess, they arrived early so she could position herself strategically to watch everyone enter, her eyes locked on each attendee like a predator assessing potential prey to sort the weak from the strong.

As I ponder the thought, my mind swirls with violent fantasies. *What would I do if I had the privilege of fighting her this evening? How satisfying would it be to end her once and for all?*

The world would be a better place without her—a fact that probably even *she* knows.

But I remind myself I'm not attending the Choosing Ceremony to revel in anyone's death—not even hers. The only reason I want to attend in the first place is to try and extract Finn and Merit from this fortress and to flee before we all find ourselves trapped in a prison we can never escape.

My stride is quick and long as I approach the elevator, and the two armed guards split apart to let me on. As I step inside, I remind myself for the hundredth time to sink fully into my Ana persona. Tonight, I need to be a powerful, wealthy Elite. I must be charming, intriguing...but invisible enough so that the Bishop doesn't take further notice of me. One false move, one stupid utterance, and it's game over.

It would be all too easy to accidentally give myself away, to destroy everything in one fell swoop.

As the elevator begins its slow descent, my stomach lurches in a tangle of excitement and fear. I'm all too aware that whatever happens tonight will determine Finn's and my futures, and yet I must force myself to remain relaxed, composed, calm.

When the elevator comes to a stop and its doors split open, I find myself staring out directly at a ballroom teeming with elegant guests. Women in flowing dresses slip effortlessly from one person to the next, smiling and laughing as they greet one another. The men wear suits of many colors, unburdened by the rules that normally dictate black tuxedos and starched shirts. All told, it's a happy, pleasant display and the beginning of an undeniably festive night.

It's a stark contrast to the Aristocrat gatherings in the Arc, which always involved a level of shadiness and deceit, the guests concealed behind their stiff, solid masks as they schemed and connived.

Then again, I think, scanning the unrealistically young-looking crowd, *everyone I see is masked in their own way.*

As I slip forward, my eyes moving from one veiled face to the next, I feel a hand press into my back and slip slowly downward. I inhale sharply, telling myself not to react overtly to Finn's touch. *Just savor it, Ash. Enjoy it for the few seconds you can.*

But when a pair of lips moves to my ear and utters the words, "Hello, Ana," I quickly realize it's not Finn who's touching me.

22

THE BALLROOM

"Enjoying yourself?" the Bishop asks. His hand is still on my back, and he offers no indication that he intends to remove it. It's an oddly possessive gesture on his part, and I tell myself I need to pull away, rude as it may seem.

But for some reason, I can't find the strength. It's as if the merest contact from his fingertips is enough to take control of some deep part of me and coerce my body and mind into acquiescence.

Some people say he could charm a rattlesnake into submission.

There's more to him than good looks or a smooth voice. I can all but taste it on the air around me right now—a pleasant, bliss-inducing mist that I can neither see nor touch, yet I'm convinced of its existence.

How is he doing this to me?

"I just arrived," I finally say. "The place looks incredible."

"Welcome to the Choosing," he replies. "I hope it proves an interesting evening for you."

"Thank you. I'm sure it will. I'm honored to be here."

His stare twists its way into my mind, and I find myself

shuffling uncomfortably from one foot to the other, wishing the floor would open up and swallow me whole. I want to escape this odd, pleasant discomfort. I want to escape *him*.

"You look absolutely exquisite, by the way," he finally says. "That's a very beautiful dress. Tell me—is it one of Shar's creations?"

My heart leaps into my throat. How could he possibly know about Shar? Has he been watching me this whole time?

Then I remember that Shar said she's met him, that she often tailors clothing for the Aristocrats in Manhattan society, and I relax slightly.

"Yes, it is," I tell him. "It was in her shop. I was amazed to find it fit perfectly."

"I see. Well, it suits you brilliantly. It really brings out your eyes."

My fake *eyes, you mean. To go along with my fake hair, fake lips, fake everything.*

A sudden desire assaults me, compelling me to show him the real me. But I quash the destructive urge, telling myself it's just some sort of Bishop-induced madness.

"Thank you again," I say shyly, pulling my chin down in an attempt to look bashful when the truth is, I simply feel hideously self-conscious. My voice—the voice that's supposed to belong to a confident, privileged Aristocrat—is starting to tremble now, to betray my true nature.

I don't like what he's doing to my mind. I don't like him standing so close.

Yet I'm powerless to stop him.

"Oh—by the way," the Bishop says with a knowing grin, as if he's laughing behind his eyes at my discomfort, "your blood sample is now in our lab. I suspect the results will be fascinating. I look forward to studying them."

There's a strange insinuation in the final sentence that makes me nervous, but I simply nod and say, "I hope you get what you need," as I force myself to stare into his eyes, to prove to him that I'm not afraid.

Even if I can't prove it to myself.

A strange, fleeting memory comes to me then of a quiz I took many years ago, when the internet was still accessible in the Mire. The quiz asked "Can you spot the difference between an actual human and a person generated by Artificial Intelligence?"

I wasn't sure at first that I could, but soon discovered there was something eerie and off-putting about the A.I.'s creations. They were too symmetrical, too close to perfection. They didn't look entirely human, yet they looked oddly, indisputably *real.*

It occurs to me as I stare at the Bishop that he has the same strange, unfathomable quality. He looks like a combination of all the most beautiful men I've ever imagined, all somehow funneled into one perfect specimen.

The notion is preposterous, though. The Bishop *is* human. I can feel the heat of his skin when he touches me, feel his warm breath on the surface of my flesh. And as much as I search him for signs of a Holo-Veil, I still don't see any.

How do you even exist? I wonder as I assess his face.

"What are you thinking, Ana?" he asks softly as his eyes lock on my own.

To my horror, I find myself not just answering, but blathering a response with absolute, unfaltering honesty.

"You remind me of pastries I've seen in the most elegant bake shops—delicacies that look so beautiful that you hardly dare eat them, as if they'd kill you with their sweetness if you so much as took a bite."

He pulls his face slightly sideways and narrows his eyes at me for the briefest moment before he lets out a jovial laugh. "My goodness. That might just be the greatest compliment I've ever received."

The thing is, I didn't mean it as a compliment. He feels sweet to the point of toxicity, like a beautiful, brightly colored lizard whose skin is coated in a potent poison. And the more time I spend in his presence, the more dangerous he seems.

But even with that knowledge, I'm finding it hard to pull my eyes away from him. I feel myself falling under his spell over and over again with each word out of his mouth, each breath he takes. Endorphins rush through my system as though my own mind is betraying me. But as handsome as he is, as silver-tongued, I'm acutely aware that the attraction isn't a physical one. It seems as though my mind has fallen into a sort of fascinated, obsessive love with the very notion of him —one that I know is unhealthy, that makes me want to flee for my life.

Yet I am physically incapable of running.

I suspect, in fact, that this entire city is under his spell. Even Adi and Cillian, the self-declared "Trodden," seem to respect him in their own grudging way.

Perhaps his greatest power is the ability to persuade the world to overlook his cruelty and malice just long enough for it to flourish.

"Someone is quite taken with you, it seems," the Bishop says, tearing me out of my thoughts. He nods toward Finn, who's watching us from some distance away.

I don't have to guess what's going through his mind. I've seen that tension in his body before, that concern on his brow. He's in protective mode. Bracing himself, ready to sprint across the room if the man who runs New York City should even so much as threaten to hurt me in any way.

I offer Finn an almost imperceptible nod, telling him to hold on.

I'm safe...for now.

"You've met young Mr. Davenport, have you?" the Bishop asks me.

I'd almost forgotten he doesn't know who I really am.

"Yes, I...I met him earlier," I reply with a slight smile. "He came by my suite to say hello."

"Ah. Good for him."

"It was...nice to talk to someone. He seems like a nice young man."

"He is," the Bishop says, clapping his hands together. "Well, as much as I'd hate to be parted from you, perhaps you should go speak to Mr. Davenport. He's probably nervous about his mother's battle royale tonight—and about certain other developments. I'm sure he'd appreciate your company, if only to take his mind off things."

"You may be right," I say with a smile. *What did he mean by developments?* "But...may I ask what exactly happens tonight? I mean, I know there's a fight, but of course I've never actually witnessed a Choosing Ceremony. They're quite legendary, as you can imagine."

The Bishop cocks his head to the side, his ever-morphing smile shifting once again, this time to something mischievous. "It's quite simple, really. The Duchess will fight an opponent I've selected for her. If she wins, she will be granted a residence in the Behemoth, along with her family."

"And if she loses?" I ask, returning his mischievous smile. This time, it's sincere. I'm envisioning the Duchess on her knees, begging for her life.

The Bishop's lips twitch almost sadistically when he says, "I believe you already know the answer to that question. This is a fight to the death, Ana."

I have to make an effort to contain myself when I reply, "I've heard." *Interesting to hear it from the horse's mouth, though.*

The Bishop lets out a quiet chuckle, then adds, "What you may not know is that her whole family will be punished, as well."

A swell of nausea hits me then, and once again, I try to conceal my emotions behind the shield that is my Holo-Veil. "Punished?"

"You didn't know?" He leans in close when he says, "They, too, will die."

I pull back, my eyes darting to Finn, who's still watching us from afar. Suddenly I'm panicking, shaking, horrified, and I know perfectly well that the Holo-Veil isn't nearly powerful enough to conceal the intensity of my reaction.

"Die?" I repeat, forcing my eyes back up to the Bishop's. "But...isn't there a young boy in their family? Finn said he has a younger brother."

"He does indeed." He's still leaning in close, speaking in a conspiratorial tone. "But don't you worry that lovely head of yours, Ana. The Duchess will win. I'm so confident of it, in fact, that I've already sent their youngest to the Behemoth, along with his father. Merit and the Duke are currently settling into the residence I've prepared for them."

"What?" I spit the word out before I have a chance to stop myself.

Oh, God.

The reaction was far too aggressive. Rude, even. Completely inappropriate for someone who should be an indifferent guest.

"You seem surprised. You've taken a personal interest in the Davenports, have you?"

"I'm sorry," I reply with an awkwardly forced chuckle. "It's just that...I would have thought you'd wait until the fight was over to—"

"You should know by now that I do things as I wish to do them, Miss Miller," the Bishop says, his tone suddenly icy cold. "Tonight's result will be based on a simple fact: the Davenports are of great value to me, while the Duchess's opponent is not. Therefore, I am invested in her victory. Do you take issue with that?"

I stare blankly at him, torn up inside. The sudden chill in his tone is one I can feel in the marrow of my bones, an injury inflicted with nothing more than a few well-placed syllables.

"I don't take issue with it at all," I say. "I'm very glad to hear Finn's brother and father are safe. I'm sure they'll be happy in their new home."

"Good. I would hate to find that you and I are on opposing sides." Once again, the Bishop's voice is smooth as silk and he presses close to me—so close that I can feel his warm breath on my cheekbone once again. "As I told you earlier, I am very much hoping to welcome *you* to the Behemoth very soon."

I stare blankly at him, unsure whether to be grateful or horrified. At this point, I'm not sure I have any choice but to accept his strange offer.

"Don't worry," he laughs. "There will be no death match for you. You may not yet understand why, but I think you and I could be of great use to one another."

He utters the final sentence with all the weight of the Behemoth itself. The words somehow manage to be terrifying and oddly flattering at once, and I can't decide whether to feel pleased or petrified.

Once again, he's inspired a strange, profound desire in me. Not a desire for him—even a man as charming as he is couldn't begin to threaten my loyalty to Finn—but a desire for the unseen, the unknown.

This morning, the thought of walking into the Behemoth was abhorrent to me.

But right now, staring into this man's ever changing eyes… it's my heart's greatest desire.

Under any other circumstance, I would push away the strange craving and reject the ache that's beginning to throb in my mind—the burning need to understand who this man is, and what lies inside the Behemoth.

But tonight, Finn will probably be escorted to that strange, mysterious place.

And all I want is to follow him.

23

THE CHOOSING

WHEN THE BISHOP has finally stepped away to speak to someone on the other side of the ballroom, I stride over to Finn, a careful smile plastered on the face I'm wearing like a shield.

Looking incredible in a dark gray suit with a gun-metal blue tie, Finn smiles back at me as I approach. But in his eyes, I see a deep worry that wasn't there this afternoon.

"It's nice to see you again, Ana," he says, glancing around cautiously. "I must say, that's quite a dress."

"Thank you," I reply, looking around to see if any of the Bishop's people are close by. "I'm very fortunate to have found a tailor who could supply it at short notice."

"Agreed." He leans in close and whispers, "The Bishop has sent Merit and my father to the Behemoth. I feel like it's my fault."

"Your fault? Why?"

"I told you earlier—he threatened to hurt Merit because of my escape attempt. Maybe this is his way of doing exactly that."

I shake my head. "I don't think that's it." The smile is still plastered to my fake lips as I glance around to make sure no one can hear us. "The Bishop told me he's certain your mother will win tonight, which means you were all going to end up there anyhow."

Finn looks both disappointed and relieved to hear the news. He lets out a breath and extends a hand to me. "Let's dance," he says, and when I nod, he guides me out onto the floor with the other couples who are twirling around to the sound of an invisible orchestra booming through unseen speakers.

We begin spinning to the music's rhythm, just as we did on an evening that seems so long ago now, the Introduction Ceremony on my first night in the Arc. I still remember the feeling of hope and promise that radiated through my soul as I looked into his eyes, scarcely believing Finn was real. The plans I had for the future. For my mother, for Kel. The feeling that maybe my life would turn out to be filled with wonder and beauty, after years spent struggling to survive.

But now, with the very real possibility that Finn and I will soon find ourselves prisoners in yet another Arcology...all I feel is dread.

We sink into one another, our bodies entwined tightly with the realization that our futures are once again uncertain.

"We need to stay together," Finn says. "I've lost you before. I'm not losing you again. We need to find a way to get you into the Behemoth, too."

"Agreed," I reply with a sigh. "I suppose I have good news, then."

"What's that?"

I tell him as quickly and quietly as I can about the Bishop's offer of a residence inside.

"That's weird," Finn says. "Isn't it?"

I laugh and tell him I'm not sure if I should be offended. "You don't think I deserve an invitation?"

"Of course you do. You deserve the entire world," he says, his tone so sincere that it makes me quiver with affection for him. "But as I understand it, the Bishop doesn't do that unless you have something to offer that he can't possibly resist. I mean, look—he's making my mother, the freaking *Duchess*, of all people—fight for her life. He only let the King inside because the freaking guy gave him most of his family's belongings, which amount to a huge fortune."

"Well, he seems to think I have something he wants," I reply, pondering it for a moment before a thought occurs to me. "Tell me something. Did his people take your blood when they brought you to the Palace?"

He nods. "They did the same to everyone in my family. It seems like regular protocol. Why?"

I look around once again before determining that it's safe to say, "Something happened, Finn. Something I didn't tell you about earlier. And the Bishop knows about it."

"What are you talking about?" Finn asks in a whisper, his voice tight. "He doesn't know about the Surge, does he?"

I shake my head. "No, it's something else. I had a stab wound. It was deep, but…"

He pulls back, looking horrified. "What? Why didn't you tell me about this?"

"Because you would have freaked out like you're doing right now," I say with a laugh. "It's okay, really. Let me finish."

"Someone stabbed you," he hisses. "Tell me who it was. I'll kill them."

"It's a long story, but for the record, it was completely consensual. It was the only way to convince the guards I was desperate to get across the bridge. But the stabbing was hardly the most shocking part of my day. I healed, Finn. Almost immediately, like the wound was never there in the first place."

The tension slowly leaves his body and he finally smiles. A warm, happy grin that fills me with hope. "It seems you have a gift," he says. "I couldn't be happier to hear it, Ash. If you knew how often I worry about you. How sick I was when we got separated, not knowing what had happened to you..." He reaches a hand to my face, but pulls it back, slipping it around my waist as we continue dancing. "Damn it. I want to kiss you so badly it hurts."

"Me, too," I whisper into his ear. A few seconds later, I ask, "Do you think the Bishop wants to study me or something? Is that why he wants me in the Behemoth?"

"Maybe," Finn nods. "He probably wants to figure out what's making you tick. His researchers, from what I understand, have been studying cellular regeneration."

"I don't really know what that means," I laugh.

"It has to do with cells re-growing. It's all tied in to aging, healing, fighting illness, you name it. Rapid healing is just part of the whole picture. If you healed that quickly from a stab wound, it means your cells have developed the capacity to regenerate much faster than most. I can see why someone like the Bishop would put a huge value on you for that alone —but..."

"But what?"

He shakes his head. "Nothing," he says. "I just hope he doesn't use you. If he lays a hand on you, Ash, I swear to God..." The growl in his voice is tinged with an almost feral possessiveness.

"If he lays a hand on me, he'll have a close encounter with

the Surge," I reply. "Don't worry. I'm not about to let him hurt me."

"Good. But I saw how he put his hand on you earlier. I also saw how he looked at you. I mean, I know the guy is a living god, but it doesn't mean I don't sort of want to break his perfectly-sculpted jaw."

I want to laugh, but I stifle it, terrified that I'll draw looks from the crowd. "Careful, now," I whisper. "We aren't supposed to know each other this well. We're supposed to—"

Before I can finish my thought, a bell clangs somewhere at the far end of the room.

Murmurs erupt from all around us, and I look around to see a sea of faces—most of which are no doubt mere Holo-Veils like mine—revealing myriad expressions from worry to excitement to absolute jubilance.

"It is time for the Choosing," the Bishop's voice says, though I'm not entirely sure where it's coming from. "The brawl begins in a few minutes. So let us move away from the center of the floor to allow the Ring to materialize."

"Ring?" I ask quietly.

My question is answered when the crowd moves back toward the room's walls. The floor begins to split open, only to reveal a dirt floor underneath the exquisite marble tile we were all dancing on a moment ago.

"Eugenia Davenport," the Bishop's voice booms, "Are you prepared to fight?"

My breath catches when I see the Duchess step toward the dirt-floored arena, slipping between members of New York's Elite. She's dressed in a long, dark purple gown, fitted to her narrow physique like a well-tailored glove.

As she steps onto the soft surface of the Ring, she pulls her high-heeled shoes off, an act that might seem comical under almost any other circumstance. Right now, though, it feels like a gruesome challenge.

"Of course I'm prepared," she says, and when I peer down at her hands, I see that they're balled into fists, her veins and knuckles already throbbing orange-red with a simmering, expectant heat.

The Bishop strides toward her, the crowd parting to let him through. To my horror, when he reaches her, he turns and fixes his gaze on me.

For a moment, I'm convinced he's going to force me to fight her.

Oh, God.

Has he discovered who I really am?

Is this some sadistic ploy on his part?

But he simply smiles at me before moving his eyes to a man standing at the far end of the large room. I turn to assess him, relieved and curious at once.

The man is wearing a dark suit, his hair streaked with gray, his lips pulled down in a scowl. His shoulders are broad, as is his chest.

He looks as if he could stop a freight train with a well-placed fist.

"Maurice Blanchard," the Bishop calls out. "You came to me some time ago, requesting your chance to enter the Behemoth. I have decided that tonight is your chance."

The man called Maurice nods his head, his scowl turning into a smile. I can tell what he's thinking:

I'll have the Duchess dead on the ground in a matter of seconds.

I want to warn him. To tell him not to underestimate her. *Don't be a fool.*

But then I remember what happens to Finn and his brother if the Duchess loses.

A woman to Maurice's right grabs his arm, her features wrenched into a tormented howl. But he pulls away, snapping something at her that I can't quite hear.

She must be his wife. And she knows she'll be killed if he loses tonight. It's no wonder she's devastated.

He locks his eyes on the Duchess, a malevolent grin crinkling the corners of his eyes.

"He's not going to stand a chance against her," I tell Finn quietly. "He's all brawn and confidence. He has no idea she'll burn him alive."

"I'm not so sure about that," he replies. "The Bishop is smart. He wouldn't select someone who had no defense against a person like my mother. It would make for a dull fight."

"Do you know who this Maurice person is?"

Finn shakes his head. "No. But we're about to find out."

As Maurice steps into the ring, pulling off his suit jacket and cufflinks and rolling up his sleeves, the Bishop turns to face the crowd.

"My friends," he says, turning slowly to take in each person in the room, "Welcome to the Choosing Ceremony. You know by now how this works. Two enter the ring, one comes out. The winner is invited to dwell within the Behemoth and is granted access to our secrets, to all that goes on inside that magnificent structure. The loser...well, I don't need to tell you."

With that, he chuckles, and the crowd follows suit with a series of sycophantic guffaws.

Turning to Maurice, the Bishop gestures and says, "Here we have a man with special gifts. A talented individual whom I've been saving for weeks for someone worthy. Maurice is from the Arcology in Houston. He found it a little claustrophobic, and so he brought his lovely wife to New York some time ago. And I, for one, am very glad he did. I very much look forward to watching him in action this evening."

When the Bishop has finished talking, the Duchess steps forward, her dress trailing on the ground, and I can't help but think how confident she looks. Whereas Maurice looks like he's prepared to go several rounds in a boxing match, she looks as if she's not even worried about chipping a fingernail.

"The Duchess," the Bishop says, gesturing to her with a wave of his hand, "is a special woman. Not only because of her particular ability, but because of her *very* gifted family." With that, he turns to look at Finn, a greedy, possessive glint in his eye.

A deep, frightening understanding infiltrates my mind then. He intends to take ownership of them. To what end, I don't know.

As nervous as I've ever been, I press closer to Finn as the Bishop pulls his eyes to the two opponents. His tone is menacing and powerful when he asks, "Are you ready?"

When they both nod, he backs away, stepping out of the Ring and crossing his arms over his chest.

"Proceed, then. And please—don't make it too quick."

24

THE BOUT

I DON'T EXACTLY KNOW what I'm expecting to see.

A slow dance, perhaps—the Duchess gliding around the fighting ring in her elegant evening gown, bare feet and all. The man called Maurice circling her like a carnivorous creature staring down its next meal.

There's something so undignified about the concept of watching two Aristocrats murder each other in cold blood before this crowd of polished onlookers that the concept seems outlandish.

But when Maurice charges at the Duchess, ramming himself shoulder-first into her narrow, fragile-looking torso, it's clear that he's not even remotely concerned about dignity. He's a ram charging its rival, not for simple dominance, but for his very survival.

The Duchess, caught off guard, tumbles backwards in an almost hilarious display of flailing limbs, hitting the ground hard and tearing her expensive dress in the process. With a strange, feral growl, she pushes herself to her feet, chin lowered, eyes locked on the man who just insulted her.

I stare at Maurice, whose hard features quickly shift from a look of pure determination to utter fear as he registers the look in his opponent's eye.

"He should have killed her with the first blow," I say under my breath.

To his credit, he was obeying orders—starting the fight with a hit that wouldn't end the Duchess, but knock the wind out of her. But now, he's simply weaponized her via an act of humiliation.

Nothing is more valuable to the Duchess than the projection of power, and Maurice just robbed her of it. There's no way in hell she'll let him do that to her again. The only questions are how quickly she'll murder him...and if he has more tricks up his sleeve than simple brute force.

Because if that's all he has, he's as good as dead already.

As the Duchess steps slowly toward him, Maurice pulls something from his pocket. Not a gun—those aren't allowed —but something small and silver. At first, I wonder if it's a switchblade or some other kind of knife. But when the man slips a finger over it, some kind of armor slips over his entire body, a sort of translucent mesh that's both glittery and fine, as if it's made of little more than twinkling particles of air.

"An Aegis," Finn whispers.

"Like yours?" I ask. Finn's ability to create shimmer-walls and near-invisible shields is extraordinary, and until this moment, I've never seen anyone else do it.

"Yes," Finn says. "But his isn't internal. Someone has designed that device for him. He must have known what my mother might do to him." He sounds impressed, though we both know the shield will do little against the Duchess's incredible and horrifying gift.

The Duchess moves closer, pushing her mussed-up hair

away from her face. Her chest is heaving, her eyes narrowed. I've seen her angry before. I've seen vindictive expressions on her face—and malice.

But I've never seen her this enraged.

She thrusts a hand out in front of her, hurling a fireball through the air that hits Maurice square in the chest, breaking through the Aegis in one intense explosion of heat and light. It scalds his clothing, but doesn't manage to penetrate the fabric.

The Aegis just saved his life. Whether it will offer any more protection, I can't say.

He stumbles back a few steps, but he manages to right himself and step toward her again.

This time, the Duchess shoves both hands out and two more fireballs, searing with white-hot intensity, slam into his chest and stomach. This time, Maurice falls to the ground. I hear a fizzling, crackling sound, then the smell of burning flesh meets my horrified nose.

Even with two scorching wounds in his torso, Maurice somehow pulls himself to his feet, lowers his chin, and narrows his eyes at the Duchess. I can see from the tension in his jaw that he's trying to mask his pain, which must be excruciating.

My gaze moves to the Bishop, who's watching with rapt fascination, his hand combing its way through his long hair. But unlike those around him, he doesn't simply seem entertained.

Something in his eyes tells me he's studying the two opponents, assessing them. *Judging* them.

I wonder if he's changing his mind about Maurice. Maybe a man who can withstand such devastating attacks is worthy of a place in the Behemoth, after all.

When Maurice has inhaled a few deep, pained breaths, he lunges at the Duchess again. But this time, it isn't with the speed of a normal human. He sweeps across the ring so fast that my mind can't register it. One instant he's in one place, and the next, he's on her, his hands around her throat, shoving her to the ground.

It's easy to see that she, too, was taken by surprise. Her eyes bulge, her hands grasping at his wrists as he squeezes the life out of her.

A jolt of envy hits me as I watch the man come so close to ending her.

I wanted so badly to do that myself.

Gasps meet my ears, as well as a smattering of polite applause. Those who came to see a proper brawl are getting what they wished for. Still, I get the impression the crowd wants more. They're aching for something spectacular, like the magnificent finale of a fireworks display.

And the Duchess, determined to live another day, gives them what they want.

FIRE

WITH MAURICE'S fingers still wrapped around her neck, the Duchess's skin glows and crackles red, orange, then white, splitting apart then coming back together like a living, breathing entity all its own.

Her opponent screams in pain and pulls his hands away, leaping off her as he curses at the air like it's wronged him somehow. I glance over at his wife, whose face is buried in her hands.

She knows there's no way he'll win this battle. Which means her life, too, will end tonight.

You're right, I think. *And I'm sorry for you.*

Finn seems to be thinking the same thing as he turns my way and says, "When they take us away, I won't be able to communicate with you. You should find a way out. Get your-self back out west, back to the Arc where you'll be safe."

"No. We have to get you out of here," I whisper with a quiet shake of my head, desperately, looking around for an exit. But every way out is guarded by several large, daunting men under the Bishop's control, as if he's already predicted any attempts at escape.

"You know as well as I do that's not going to happen," Finn says. "I need to get to Merit. It's the whole reason we came here. Look—do what you can to let Rys know via Atticus what's happened. See if he can find a way in or out of the Behemoth. Maybe..."

He stops himself. We both know there's no simple solution to our current dilemma. Either we both make our way inside and take our chances, or we go our separate ways.

Neither is ideal, to put it mildly.

"I'll find a way in," I say. "I'll make sure he invites me like he said he would."

Finn shakes his head. "You don't want to do that, Ash. I have a feeling..."

When he doesn't finish, I whisper, "A feeling that what?" and turn to look up at him.

I feel a sudden pressure on my arm. Finn's fingers are digging into my skin, signaling me that something is wrong. I look over to see the Bishop staring at me, his eyes bright and piercing.

A sudden, terrifying realization hits me:

He knows what we're saying.

I'm not sure if he's able to read our lips, our expressions, or our minds. All I am sure of is that he knows too much.

Next to him, his lover is staring at me, too, a strange, knowing look in her eye. For the briefest instant, I'm convinced I detect a shake of her head, a warning of some sort, before she turns her attention back to the Duchess and Maurice.

The bout is still raging. Both opponents are pulling their

punches, circling each other like cats about to pounce. Each wants to end it, but neither is willing to land the death-blow quite yet.

After a minute or so, Maurice leaps at the Duchess. He slams into her, punches her in the stomach, sends her crashing to the ground. By now, her dress is streaked with dirt, torn in various places, her hair a disheveled disaster.

But she still looks oddly dignified and unfazed, as if she's simply biding her time as she awaits the moment when she'll strike the final blow.

By now, it must be a full half hour since the bout began. Every Aristocrat in this place has had an opportunity to see the Duchess up close, and I'm beginning to wonder if she wants to imprint her face on their memories, to make sure they know exactly who she is...and how powerful.

For good measure, she pauses in place as Maurice's chest heaves. He's exhausted, the flesh of his hands red, torn, and bloodied from his attacks on her lava-hot skin.

The Duchess turns to face the crowd, her eyes locking on each audience member's in turn. When they come to mine, I force myself to stare back, challenging rather than recoiling from her. She doesn't know who I am, I tell myself. I'm just a pretty stranger.

Yet there's something in her look that feels familiar, accusing.

Hateful.

"Here we go," Finn says under his breath. Maurice is running at his mother again, and this time he sends her reeling back into the crowd before she strides back into the arena.

Another insult.

Her skin flares up, glowing alternating blue and orange. And when she turns to face him, her eyes have begun to do the same, giving her a terrifying, demonic look.

"Enough!" she calls out irritably, like she's simply been tolerating his nonsense this entire time.

She issues Maurice a final glare before summoning an enormous fireball.

He tries to move out of the way, but this time, the Duchess's conjured projectile is unbelievably fast, shooting toward him like a flaming missile.

It assaults him square in the chest, and his jaw flies open even as his body hurtles through the air then hits the ground at his wife's feet, his entire torso smoking black, his shirt burned to nothing but soot.

I want to pull my eyes away, but I know better. The Bishop is still standing across from us, still looking at me. He's studying me, trying to figure me out. And I refuse to show weakness.

Drawing my eyes to the Duchess's victim, I bear witness to what she's done to him. A broad, black hole has been burned into his chest, so cavernous that I can see his ribs protruding. The scent of burning meat fills the room, and gasps fill the air.

Maurice lies there, unmoving, his eyes staring up at the ceiling. And without a word being uttered, the crowd understands that he's breathed his last.

After a few seconds, a wail of torment erupts from the woman who is now his widow. I watch her with sympathy as she falls to her knees, cradling his head. It's then that I remind myself of a hard truth:

These people are the Wealthy. They are so-called Aristocrats.

They *choose* to be here, to fight for the right to enter the Behemoth. Not because they have to, but because they truly believe it grants them some kind of superiority over the rest of society.

The man called Maurice wasn't forced to fight tonight. He chose it out of sheer greed.

It's a choice no Dreg has ever had the luxury of making.

I glance at Finn, reality hitting me like a freight train.

In a few minutes, he and his mother will be taken away to join Merit and his father in the Behemoth, and there's not a damned thing I can do about it.

The departure comes sooner than I expect when the Bishop steps into the Ring, claps his hands once, and says, "Eugenia and Finn Davenport, you have been granted entry into the Behemoth. You will be provided with a residence fit for a king and queen. You will never want to leave the paradise you discover there—and through your contributions, you will help to make this world a better place than you've ever imagined."

With that, he summons the Duchess, who's now shrouded in a dark velvet cloak. As I watch helplessly, a guard strides over and takes hold of Finn's arm. I almost reach for him as he's pulled away, but remember that I'm not Ashen.

I'm Ana Miller, a virtual stranger. Someone who only met Finn today for the first time.

All I can do is watch helplessly as the guards take him from me, and wonder when I'll see him again.

When the Bishop's men guide him over to his mother, the Bishop, taking his lover by the hand, turns to the crowd and says, "Please, enjoy your evening. I will be back soon."

I watch Finn and the Duchess leave, escorted by the Bishop's men. The Bishop and his lover follow close behind.

As the audience watches, three men march over to Maurice's body and, in spite of the fact that his widow is still holding his head and weeping, they pick him up and take him away. Seconds later, the marble floor seals up over the blood-stained dirt of the fighting arena, and all evidence of what just occurred disappears.

When they're gone, I find myself standing in a ballroom filled with people. Yet I feel entirely alone.

I head over to a long table where dozens of champagne flutes are positioned in wait of desperate hands and grab one. I don't suppose anyone has a problem with me consuming alcohol; I'm supposed to be over twenty, after all. Not that anyone around here cares one iota about drinking age.

I sip the champagne nervously, my eyes scanning the room, and spot someone approaching from my right. I turn to see the Bishop's lover stepping up next to me. She's tall and lean, elegantly dressed in a long, red silk gown that fits every curve like a glove. Her hair is dark like mine normally is, her skin bronze, her eyes the same turquoise shade as my dress.

I stiffen, expecting hostility from the strange woman.

"Your name is Ana, isn't it?" she asks quietly, taking a glass of champagne and downing it in one quick swig. She has a thick accent—French, I think—which takes me by surprise.

I nod. "It is." I glance toward the far door and add, "I thought you went with the others."

"I was going to, but told the Bishop I'd like to mingle a little while he escorts his new tenants to the Behemoth." She frowns as she overlooks the room, leaning in and saying, "I hate these things. So many despicable people all gathered in one place."

Then she grabs another champagne flute, swigs it as if seeking courage. "Your name isn't really Ana," she whispers.

"It's Ashen Spencer. You come from the Mire, near the Arc. You are the one they call the Crimson Dreg."

Terrified, I meet her gaze.

My hand shakes, my heart pounding as I set my glass down on the table and say, "I think you have me confused with someone else. My name is Ana."

She doesn't look angry or accusing. Instead, she stares back at me almost with an intimacy, a conspiratorial look in her eye.

"I'm someone you're going to be glad to have in your corner very soon. The Bishop knows me as Naeva. I am no ally to the Bishop or the Directorate. I despise them all."

I pull back, shocked. "How did you…?" I begin, unsure how to even ask the question.

She reveals her left wrist, which is tattooed with a symbol I can't quite place. It looks a little like an ornate letter S. "This is the symbol of the Aristocracy in Paris," she says. "A disguise, much like yours. My backstory is simple: I came here recently. The Bishop took a liking to me, just as he's taken a liking to you. When he finds a woman—or anyone, for that matter— interesting, he tends to take them under his wing, and as you can imagine, he's very persuasive." She glances toward the door at the far end of the ballroom. "In fact, it's why he wanted the Duchess inside the Behemoth. Much safer to have her under lock and key."

"Does he have *you* under lock and key?"

With a laugh, she says, "No. Not exactly. I'm new blood, and he's still trying to work out what to make of me. We only met two weeks ago, so right now, he's trying to decide if he can trust me. He has a certain way of assessing people, you see. He knows things he shouldn't about all of us. He…sees things. It's one of the gifts he's snatched for himself."

I look around nervously again. What she's saying makes sense—I suppose it's why I felt like he was able to hear Finn and me earlier. Maybe it's just that he has a way of *seeming* all-knowing and powerful. A projected sense of strength and intellect that few people possess.

I whisper, "Do you think he can hear this conversation? I mean, are there micro-drones in this room, or hidden microphones, or…"

She shakes her head. "He uses them, of course—but he prefers not to. Cameras and drones can be hacked into by undesirables. The Bishop's methods are unhackable."

"And what exactly are his ways?"

She taps her temple with a perfectly manicured fingertip. "He does it with his mind. He reads people just as you or I would read a book."

Nausea swells in my belly. I thought as much, but was hoping I was merely being paranoid.

"Does he know who I really am?" I whisper as a man brushes against my arm and excuses himself while he reaches for a glass. Naeva waits for him to move off before replying.

"All I can tell you is he knows you're not Ana from Evanston, Illinois. And after your blood test, he will know with absolute certainty you're no Aristocrat."

I find myself hunting the room for potential escape routes again, but Naeva reaches a hand out and presses her fingers into my arm to calm me. "It's all right," she says. "You want into the Behemoth, don't you?"

I nod. "I mean, I didn't think so, but things have changed. I have to get to Finn and his brother. I—"

I raise my eyebrows when she says, "Yes, I know. You want to free them from the shackles of their parents." As my jaw hangs open, she presses closer to me and whispers, "Well, I have good and bad news. The good is that you'll be in the Moth sooner than you expected—and you won't have to fight for it. The bad news is that you won't have a choice in the matter."

26

THE LOVER

"Be prepared, Ashen," Naeva tells me, reading my dumbfounded expression. "He'll come for you tonight when you're asleep. Or else his men will. They'll force your Holo-Veil off, and there will be no more hiding from those eyes of his."

I start to reply, but she shakes her head. "Just listen to me. It's all right—he's not going to hurt you. You're too valuable to him. The Bishop is many things, but he's not stupid. He doesn't destroy items of extraordinary value."

"What is he planning to do to me?"

That's when her expression alters, turning grim before she forces a reassuring smile onto her lips. "I'm not sure. But I'm going to do my best to keep you safe, Ashen."

I'm not afraid. If the Bishop wants to abduct me in the night, so be it. I'm already a prisoner here in the Palace; I may as well be one in the Behemoth.

"Who are you really, Naeva?"

She shakes her head. "My real name—my real purpose here—they're things I'd rather keep secret for now. There is a great deal at risk. I was sent to New York because I have a particular skill, one that the Bishop finds irresistible…and one that allows me to get close to him without arousing suspicion."

"What is it?"

"He can't read me like he can everyone else," she says. "I'm a closed book to him, and I intrigue him for that reason. He wants my trust, my loyalty, and hopes to use me to gain power overseas. He believes he can use me for his own purposes, and he intends to. But I have my own plans, and the truth is, I need help. I am alone inside the Behemoth. Consider me a rebellion of one."

"You're a spy," I say, breathless.

"I am more than a spy. I am a fly in the ointment. I have seen some of what goes on in that monstrous place, and I intend to do something about it."

"What *does* go on?" I ask as quietly as I can. "What's the big mystery?"

She shakes her head. "It's not one I can utter here. There's too much risk. Let's just say you need to see it for yourself. And soon, if all goes well, you will. I intend to take you under my wing. You will see what I can do, what we can do *together*. I have weaponry at my disposal, but in order to use it, I will need to do more than merely charm the Bishop. Your arrival, and that of Finn Davenport—well, let's just say you might be the two puzzle pieces I need."

"I don't know what you mean," I say, aching for more details. "I…

I'm cut off when one of the Bishop's men approaches and stops in front of Naeva. "The Bishop has asked me to bring you to his quarters," he tells her, eyeing me only for a second. "Immediately."

"Of course," Naeva purrs, shooting me a last glance. "I look forward to our next encounter. I'll be keeping an eye out for you...Ana."

That night, there's no chance of sleep.

I lie in bed, dressed in a pair of jeans and a t-shirt, telling myself I'm ready for whatever is to come.

As my mind reels with the evening's events, I think of Naeva, wondering why the Bishop summoned her so abruptly, terrified that he's in the process of punishing her for speaking to me.

I tell myself the guard showing up to summon her was pure coincidence, and that I'm worrying over nothing. The only thing I should be concerned about is the fact that the Bishop's men will probably come soon.

I stare at the ceiling, Naeva's words racing around inside my mind.

They'll force your Holo-Veil off, and there will be no more hiding...

I bite at my lip, realizing that when he discovers the truth, I'll be putting the Trodden in danger. People like Adi, Cillian, and all their allies. They gave me shelter. They were part of the scheme to get me to Manhattan.

What will the Bishop do to them if he finds out?

Whoever Naeva is—whatever power she may have over the Bishop—something tells me it won't be enough to prevent him from hurting the people I've met since my arrival in New York.

Only one thing is certain:

There's no hope of a single minute's rest tonight.

There is some part of me that's actually eager for the moment the Bishop's men burst through the door and take me. The sooner I get to the Moth, the sooner I can see Finn.

On the other hand, if the Bishop discovers who I am, it's likely I'll never be allowed to see Finn or anyone again.

Yet for some reason, as I lie here, a sense of profound calm starts to wend its way through my body and mind. I'm almost looking forward to my next face-to-face with the Bishop.

I've lost it completely.

Or maybe I haven't. Maybe I simply want to free Finn again. I want to find out what happened to Adi's sister, Shar's son, and so many others. I want to see what makes that place so profoundly mysterious, what secrets lie hidden behind its walls of glass and steel.

Most disconcertingly of all…

I want to figure out what it is about the Bishop that makes him so utterly irresistible.

It must be four in the morning when I finally hear a series of loud footsteps coming down the hall, followed by something scraping in the suite's lock.

After a few seconds, the bedroom light comes on. It's blinding at first, and it takes my eyes a moment to adjust and register that the Bishop is standing in the doorway, his arms crossed. He's leaning on the frame casually, an amused smile on his lips.

"You can remove the Holo-Veil," he tells me.

For a split-second, I contemplate being foolish and denying the truth about my identity. Maybe I can convince him he's wrong and hang onto the illusion that is Ana Miller for just a moment longer.

But I can see in his eyes that Naeva was right—he's read me like a book, and he knows everything.

There's no point in delaying the inevitable, so I simply say, "Revert to Original," disabling the Veil.

I'm almost relieved when my dark hair once again ripples down over my chest. Though I know how vulnerable it makes me to reveal myself like this, it feels surprisingly good to be myself once again.

"It was the blood sample, wasn't it?" I ask, slipping out of the bed to stand facing the Bishop.

His smile intensifies when he says, "It was many things, Ashen. You needn't concern yourself with any of it."

Needn't, I think, *is a word young people don't use. Yet it doesn't sound wrong from his lips. Something about him seems so wise, so mature.*

How did he become this way?

He steps into the room and slips over to the dresser, where a small vase of flowers sits in front of a silver-framed mirror. The Bishop feels the petals with his fingertips, watching me in the mirror's reflection.

"I've known from the moment I first laid eyes on you that you were a liar, Miss Spencer. What I didn't know was just how extraordinary you were beneath that Veil. I feel like you've walked into my life at exactly the right moment, like a gift from the angels."

I open my mouth to speak, but I have no idea what to say to that. His words were a series of extraordinary compliments, yet they felt like wounds inflicted one at a time, with malicious intent.

When I remain silent, he strides over to me, taking my face roughly in his hand and studying me.

"You are more beautiful like this," he says, his dark eyes looking me up and down. "I much prefer you in your natural state, Ashen. I've seen you in those videos of yours, covered in makeup. But your natural beauty is intoxicating, Crimson Dreg."

I wince at his invoking of my nickname.

Another wound.

I struggle to control my voice in a weak attempt at bravery when I ask, "What are you going to do to me?"

"I'm not going to kill you, if that's what you're worried about. You'll find, in fact, that I don't make a habit of killing unless someone has wronged me personally. I'm far too invested in most people to want to end their lives. They are so much more useful to me alive than dead."

"Then we agree on something," I tell him, mustering the strength to pull my chin away from his grip. "But you didn't answer my question. What are you going to do to me?"

A sly smile pulls his lips into a frustratingly charming curve. "I'm going to study you and figure out all your quirks. I will likely insist on spending some time with you. When that is done—when I have obtained what I want—I will find another use for you. In the meantime, the one thing I know is that I'll be bringing you to the Behemoth tonight. There will be no battle for you. No Choosing Ceremony. You have already proven your worth, albeit accidentally."

"I see," I tell him, unsure whether to be overjoyed or frightened at how quickly everything seems to be falling so tidily into place. "And where will I stay in the Behemoth?"

"I have a place in mind. Somewhere I can watch over you. I'm sure you understand that I can't let you roam freely among the Aristocrats who live there. Then again, no one in the Behemoth roams freely…which you'll come to learn once you see the inside. All of that aside, I'm well aware of the Duchess's hatred for you. She'd murder you the second she laid her eyes on you." He lets out a laugh then. "I saw her staring at you tonight, trying to work out who you were, and whether you were worthy of speaking to her son. If she'd only known Ashen Spencer was in her presence. The fireworks she would have unleashed then…"

"Tell me something," I say, not nearly as amused as he is. "If she had tried to kill me, would you have let her?"

The Bishop moves close to me again, so close that I can smell his skin, the heady musk of it, distracting me for a moment.

"I would kill her if she laid a hand on you," he whispers. "But it won't come to that. You are mine, Ashen Spencer. Don't forget it."

Mine.

The word sends something skittering through me—a deep, creeping fear, combined with a sense of profound safety. It's as though a large, terrifying lion has wrapped a protective paw around me and is shielding me from threats…

And yet I know he will eventually kill me himself.

"Come," the Bishop says, holding a hand out.

I glance at my bag—the one that contains the clothing Shar provided. The Bishop nods and says, "Bring it if you like. There's no harm in keeping those clothes. My men will scan the bag for weapons and make sure you aren't armed when you enter the Behemoth—though your body is your greatest weapon, of course."

When I tighten, he adds, "It's all right, Ashen. I've heard what you can do, and I suspect that I know how you acquired the skill. It's one reason I wanted the Davenports in the Behemoth. That Finn is something special. I watched his mother tonight, inflicting her own twisted sort of mayhem on poor Maurice, knowing she'd acquired her abilities because of her son's genius. I am actually counting on your friend Finn to provide me with similar gifts."

I narrow my eyes. "Finn never wanted that for his mother. He's not going to weaponize you, either. Not if you hurt me or keep us apart."

At that, the Bishop seems to get angry for the first time. His voice grates in his throat when he snarls, "It doesn't matter what *he* wants. You need to understand that, Ashen. The wants of one young man are inconsequential to me. My concern is not for individuals, but for the future of the entire human race."

His chest is heaving slightly, his voice tight. But he takes a step back and inhales deeply before adding, "You will see when we're inside the Behemoth. I will show you everything. I will make you understand that you and I are not on opposing sides of a war. Neither of us is pro-Directorate or pro-Aristocracy. We are, both of us, pro-humanity, believe it or not."

I take a deep breath, contemplating my next words carefully. The Bishop is powerful—probably more powerful than anyone I've ever met in my life. But he's just revealed a weakness in his volatile temper.

The best way to deal with him is to stroke his ego. To soothe him. To...

"Don't," he half-growls. "I know what's in your mind. Just...don't."

I recall with hideous, sudden clarity what Naeva told me about his people-reading abilities.

"Sorry," I tell him. "I just...I want to find common ground with you. If we really are on the same side, I want to understand how we can help each other."

"Ah. But you see, that's where you're confused," he says. "It's not about you or me helping one another. It's about the world. It's about the future. It's about ensuring that no one deserving of a long, happy life ever suffers again."

Something in his voice, in his words, hits me like a gust of wind, sending me reeling. All of a sudden, I've forgotten how terrifying he can be. His vision for the world and the promise of it sound so beautiful. The thought that we could create a world in which no one is ever in pain...it's almost unfathomable.

Yet something tells me the Bishop could achieve it.

No, I think. That vision is entirely inconsistent with what I witnessed tonight. For the second night in a row, I watched a man die horribly, painfully. Both deaths occurred at the whim of this man. He could have stopped them, but he didn't.

Instead, he watched with pleasure as the life drained from those people.

How does he expect me to believe he wants to create a better world?

"You'll see soon enough," he tells me as if answering the question I never asked out loud.

He holds his hand out again, and this time, I pick up the rucksack and reach for him, ready for whatever may await me inside the Behemoth.

INTO THE VOID

THE NEXT FEW minutes whip by in a flurry of activity. The Bishop escorts me down the hall to an elevator that shoots us to a sub-level of the former hotel, where he guides me into a dark underground parking lot.

I'm surprised when no one escorts us—no armed security, no guards. Despite the fact that the Bishop knows about the Surge, he's not afraid I'll strike him down. *Why not,* I wonder. *What makes him so confident that I won't kill him?*

As I stride next to him, I can feel the answer in the air—a sort of crackling energy between us, an invisible, powerful aura surrounding him like armor.

Is he gifted like me, like Finn? Like the Duchess?

If he is, what frightens me is that I have no idea what his gift is.

In the parking garage, various figures stand by the exits, their eyes scanning the subterranean area. One of them nods at the Bishop as we head toward a car that looks like something the richest of the rich used to drive around when I was a child—the sort of high-priced sports car you only see once in a blue moon. Low to the ground, aerodynamic and no doubt outrageously expensive, it makes me want to gag with its opulence.

"No driver?" I ask as the Bishop opens the doors with some kind of remote device.

"*I'm* the driver," he tells me. "We could, of course, have someone else take us to our destination. But I wanted you all to myself, Ashen, if only for a few minutes."

The way he says the words is jarring, and I can't entirely tell if he's flirting with me or simply taking me prisoner. Maybe it's both.

I slip into the passenger's seat, tempted to ask him about Naeva, if only to remind him that he has a girlfriend. But I resist the foolish urge. *Don't be stupid. You want to see Finn again, don't you?*

As the Bishop drives us out of the garage and weaves the car down the once-bustling Manhattan streets that are now littered with discarded or abandoned vehicles, he tells me a little about his hopes and dreams—always without revealing any actual details.

"My goal in life is to cure the greatest disease in the world," he says. "The one inflicted on almost every human in existence."

"What disease would that be?" I ask him, curious to see if he's about to try and convince me the Blight is still a threat. *I already know about the Cure. I know about the lies.*

But he doesn't answer the question. Instead, he asks, "What do you think people fear most as a species, Ashen? Go on, take a guess."

I think about it for a moment before saying, "I'm not sure. War? Death?"

I look over to see his lips playing their way into a grin.

"You would think so, wouldn't you? But in a massive survey conducted inside every Arcology in the country, the answer was not, in fact, death."

"Oh? What was it, then?"

"Old age."

"Old age," I repeat with a snicker. "I take it the people surveyed were Aristocrats, not Dregs."

"Why do you say that?"

"Because Aristocrats have the luxury of fearing old age, whereas Dregs are terrified they'll never so much as reach adulthood. The Wealthies have been killing us off for close to a decade. Old age is *not* a disease any of us fear, believe me."

"Fair point," the Bishop chuckles. "Yes, very astute of you. It was indeed a survey conducted among the wealthy. I wanted the opinions of those who live relatively normal lives, people who expect to live past fifty."

My brows meet as he speaks.

"Normal lives?" I spit. "There's nothing 'normal' about them, except that they've been brainwashed into thinking it's normal to lock yourself away in a glass tower far from those poorer than you, and to watch murders for entertainment."

I know I shouldn't speak to him in this tone of voice, but I can't contain myself. Something inside me is being stretched thin like a rubber band about to snap.

Fortunately, he doesn't seem offended.

"Ah, but inside the Arcologies," he says, "it *is* normal to live a relatively healthy life. Whether you approve of it or not is not the issue at hand and not the subject of our current conversation."

"Fine," I sigh. "You said people were afraid of aging. So what?"

The Bishop turns my way, offering me a cheeky grin

before pulling his eyes back to the road. In the distance, the Behemoth rises up like a mountain, towering above Manhattan's tallest buildings as though it's laughing at them.

"Age is a curse," he says. "Our minds often stay sharp well into our eighties and nineties, but our bodies fail us in cruel ways. Our bones deteriorate. Muscles atrophy, and joints develop painful arthritis. In our golden years, when we should be enjoying life more than ever, we suffer chronic pain and decrepitude. And, on a more superficial scale, our skin shrivels and we lose the beauty that we once possessed. Oh, we can shield our shriveled faces behind Holo-Veils, but they do nothing to rectify the pain that comes with the passage of time. Even you, Ashen, will one day find your body betraying you, strong as you may be now."

"That's optimistic of you," I tell him with a scoffing laugh. "You're implying I'll live past the end of next week. Frankly, if I make it to the age where wrinkles are even a remote possibility, I'll be delighted."

"If you make it to that age," he says, his voice low, "I suspect you'll begin to miss the beauty that makes you so striking right now."

I find myself shrinking in my seat, pulling my eyes to the window. I don't think myself beautiful, so how could I possibly ever feel nostalgic for my lost looks?

Still, the compliment silences me in a way that isn't entirely comfortable.

"I'm not sure what your point is," I tell him curtly.

"You may soon understand," he tells me. "In the meantime, I will be keeping a close eye on you, Ashen. I have a feeling about you—a very good one. I genuinely hope you'll find our relationship mutually beneficial."

K. A. RILEY

I nod once, though I can't imagine how either of us could possibly benefit the other.

He drives until nothing surrounds us anymore except for the Moth, rising up like a monstrous shadow before us.

Unlike the Arc, which appears to hover several stories above the ground thanks to some clever holographic manipulation, the Behemoth seems built into the very foundations of the city, as if it's taken root to become an immovable force.

As the Bishop approaches, a red beam flashes in our direction then seems to scan the vehicle. A memory comes to me of the Bishop's men using a device to scan Finn's face when the Air-Wing landed just before they snatched him away.

When the scan is complete, the Bishop flips a switch on the dashboard and turns to me, telling me to hold on tight.

"What? Why?" I ask, but the question is answered when our vehicle shoots upwards like a rapid-express elevator.

But there are no cables supporting us. No elevator shaft.

We're simply flying through the air. I want to ask how, but then I remember last night's gallows, the enormous metal structure lifting into the air, seemingly weightless.

"Mag-lift," the Bishop explains, once again fully reading my concern. "But I suspect you've already figured that out. The entire interior of the Behemoth incorporates the same tech, which you'll see very soon. Every residence, every office, every laboratory is moveable, separate, autonomous. There are no 'stories' per se. Only free-floating structures suspended hundreds of feet in the air. It can feel rather frightening at first, but you do get used to it, trust me."

"That sounds horrifying," I tell him. Who the hell wants to live inside a residence that isn't supported by anything other than a magnetic field?

Then again, we're currently nearly a hundred feet in the

air, and for whatever reason, I have no fear of plummeting back to earth.

After a few seconds, the vehicle stops ascending. Out the front windshield, I spot a large window opening up to welcome the vehicle.

As I shoot one final look out the passenger window, I see something in the distance—a bird flying toward us, its wing-span broad as it flaps slowly, silver wings gleaming in the early morning light.

I force myself to look away, afraid that if I so much as think about Atticus, the Bishop will somehow know.

Rys knows where I am. That's all that matters.

The only question is whether Rys will have any way to find me once I'm inside, or to contact me. I'm about to become the prisoner of a man far more powerful than the Duchess ever was. The thought, for some reason, is both frightening and oddly exciting...though part of me wonders if my excitement only comes from my proximity to the man himself. The spell he casts over his victims, the drug he forces on us all.

There's another source of excitement stirring inside me, though. A sort of raging, morbid curiosity driving my mind to distraction as the Behemoth's magnetic field lures our vehicle inside, easing us into the eerie darkness of the strange prison. As we move inside, it occurs to me that the atmosphere here is entirely different from that of the Arc. Whatever exists in this strange place, at least there's no pretense at recruiting Dregs with the promise of a wonderful future.

If what Adi told me was true—if there are thousands upon thousands of Dregs inside the Moth who have lost contact with the outside world—I want to know why.

When our vehicle has come to a stop on a smooth pad

inside, the Bishop takes control again and drives to what looks like a parking spot whose white floor is lit up from below. But once the car has stopped, a series of walls rise from the floor to seal us inside.

A sudden, terrifying burst of claustrophobia prompts me to grab the door handle, but the Bishop chuckles and shakes his head.

"It's all right," he assures me. "It's my private Transport Cube. It takes me exactly where I want to go. The Behemoth is enormous, as you can already see. Transports are essential for getting around."

I go silent, nodding, and wait as we ascend.

A few minutes pass before the walls finally come down and a door slides open before us to reveal what looks like the inside of a small, private garage.

The Bishop pulls the car forward then stops, turning my way.

"That wasn't so bad, was it?" he asks.

"No. Not so bad," I admit. "Where are we?"

"My residence. Come, I'll show you around. Then you'll be taken to your quarters."

Quarters, I think, wondering what they'll look like. Somehow, I don't picture myself ending up in the sort of luxurious residence the Aristocracy probably occupies.

When we exit the vehicle and head through a door into a large, brightly lit kitchen with marble countertops and about four different ovens of various shapes and sizes, we end up in an elegant living area where I spot Naeva sitting on a large, white sectional couch. She's wearing a long, revealing black dress, and rises to her feet as we step into the room, slipping over to the Bishop and pressing a hand to his chest as she kisses him.

"I thought you'd never arrive," she says in a plaintive voice before shooting me a look of confusion. When she asks, "Who is she?" I'm impressed at her acting skills.

Right, I think. *We're not supposed to know each other.*

But as it turns out, she's almost too good at acting. Other than her physical appearance, she doesn't seem remotely like the woman I spoke to at last night's ceremony.

That person was self-assured, cunning, clever.

The Naeva who stands before me reminds me of a puppy playing with a squeaky toy. Her eyes dart around the room, her attention constantly being taken over by some object or other. She can't seem to focus on me for more than a few seconds before she starts staring off into the distance, a finger twisting in her hair.

"You spoke to her last night, after the Choosing," the Bishop tells her. "She had blond hair then, and her name was Ana."

"Ah," Naeva says, scowling slightly as she sizes me up. "This is your true face, is it, Ana?"

She's scrutinizing me in a way that renders me supremely uncomfortable, as if she's trying to assess whether I'm more or less pretty than she is. I'm not sure if it's part of her act—part of the persona she's projecting to the Bishop.

"Actually, my name is Ashen." *But then, you know that. You told me as much last night.*

She smiles, and there's something unreadable behind her eyes. She's far too good at playing the role of the snooty, bubble-headed lover, and I find myself wishing I could escape this place.

"Ashen," she says, mulling it over as if she's never heard the name before. "I like that."

"Do you know who she is?" the Bishop asks her. "Does she look familiar to you?"

Naeva looks me up and down again before shaking her head. "*Should* I know her?"

"Not necessarily, my love. You aren't really one to follow the goings-on of the Directorate—it's one of the things I enjoy so much about you. But it may interest you to learn that Ashen here helped to head the famous rebellion in the Arc."

I half expect Naeva to recoil or shoot me another exaggerated look. Instead, she reaches down to the coffee table to pick up her wine glass. "Interesting," she says dismissively, as if she wants to change the subject.

"I didn't really head it," I say, not entirely sure why I'm responding at all.

"So you're just some rebel," Naeva replies, though her eyes are locked on the Bishop, not me. "Why is she here? She sounds like a traitor, darling."

He takes her by the waist, kisses her on the cheek, and says, "She's more than just a stubborn Dreg. She has...gifts."

Naeva eyes me again before shrugging, taking another sip of wine, then sitting back down on the couch. "Where is she staying?" she asks, her voice dripping with resentment.

"In the apartment block," the Bishop replies.

Apartment block, I think. For two words that are utterly innocuous, they have a threatening aura to them.

"Can I come with you when you take her there?" Naeva asks.

"I wasn't going to escort her myself, love. I thought I'd have my men do it."

"Please! I want to see," Naeva says plaintively. "I haven't seen that part of the Behemoth."

"I can't say no to you," the Bishop replies with a laugh. He throws me a brief look, and if I didn't know better, I'd swear he was attempting to gauge my reaction. "Fine. We'll go together, then."

"Now?"

"Fine." Turning to me, the Bishop gestures. "Ashen, please come with us. We'll show you to your quarters."

"Where are the Davenports staying?" I blurt out before we've taken two steps.

The Bishop turns and glares at me, and in his eyes I see a look I haven't witnessed before. It's fiery, almost painfully intense, and it tells me in no uncertain terms that I have no right to ask such questions.

"You know I won't tell you that," he snaps. "Frankly, you're fortunate to be conscious right now. Most people in your position are not granted the privilege of seeing inside my residence when they're brought into the Behemoth. Most are sedated until further notice."

I swallow and cower a little, terrified of the strange power that still seems to crackle invisibly in the air between us. It's a threat that I can't see or touch, but there's no question that it's very real.

My tone is sheepish when I hang my head and say, "Right. Yes. Sorry. I forgot my place. Forgive me."

Forgive me? I think when I've spoken. *Why am I asking for his forgiveness?*

But when I look into his eyes, I understand.

He's forcing me into submission. Turning me into a servant without so much as issuing a command. I am willingly cowering before a man whose only hold over me seems to lie behind his eyes.

I'm not sure anymore if the reason no one leaves the Behemoth is because escape is impossible.

I'm beginning to think it's because they don't want to sever their bond with this strange, mysterious man.

THE RESIDENCE

THE BISHOP GUIDES us down what looks like the main corridor of his large residence. Ahead of us, at the end, it looks like the hallway ends in pure darkness, and at first I wonder what it is that we're approaching. As we near the end, I realize what I'm seeing is a huge set of sliding glass doors that lead out into what looks like a pitch-black void.

As we approach, the Bishop says, "Transporter," and a large, glowing glass box rises up from the void like an elevator with no shaft or cables and aligns itself with the sliding doors to await our entry.

I can already see that it's larger than most elevators—maybe twenty by twenty feet, and entirely transparent, including the floor and ceiling. The strange glow that covers its every surface comes from a source I can't identify. Given that the alternative is to be planted into blackness, I'm admittedly grateful for it.

As I step inside, I realize the darkness surrounding us is the Behemoth's interior, a massive shaft devoid of light, except for that coming from a series of floating steel structures that seem to hover here and there without any support. Each is separate from those around it, isolated entirely from contact.

"You're wondering why it's so dark in the Depth," the Bishop says.

"Depth?" I repeat.

"It's what we call the main section of the Behemoth—the enormous shaft at its center."

"I am a little curious," I confess. "I thought the Behemoth would be bright. It's such a huge building—and aren't there a ton of windows?"

"Opaque windows," the Bishop replies, slipping a hand onto Naeva's back as she leans into him, her expression blank. "The only means to see the outside world here is either to take a drone out, which is largely forbidden, or to head to the roof, which no one wants to do for reasons you can imagine."

He's right, I can imagine that the Behemoth's roof is so high in the sky as to feel like the air is thin, the wind is powerful, and there's no peace to be found.

I almost want to ask how people inside this massive place keep themselves sane. It's oppressively dark and depressing, as far as I can tell. The Bishop's residence is nice, of course. But the idea of never seeing the outdoors is one that suffocates me.

Inside the Transport, there's no keypad or other visible means to control its trajectory. When we step in, the Bishop simply says, "Blocks, Residence Seventy-Three," and the glass box begins a slow descent.

I look down, which turns out to be a huge mistake. My eyes are greeted by the distant lights of what look like a hundred different box-like structures floating far below us, suspended in the darkness of the massive pit. I can't help but remind myself that the Transport is kept afloat only by a magnetic force, and that if it were to fail, we would plummet hundreds of feet to our horrific deaths.

"What are the structures we're seeing?" I ask as we move through the interior space, effortlessly navigating our way between the various floating buildings. I realize as we move by that many of them are quite large—as big as some apartment buildings.

"Residences, offices, laboratories, you name it," the Bishop explains. "Each is unique, and each serves its own purpose."

"How do the Wealthies move from one place to the other? Do they all have access to these Transports?"

The Bishop smiles at me, but I detect a flash of annoyance behind his eyes. "You don't need to know anything about the inner workings of this place just yet. You're still a prisoner here, Ashen. But if you choose to cooperate, I'll offer you the information you seek. I promise you that much."

The Transport moves along for what feels like ten minutes during which Naeva drapes herself around the Bishop's neck and begins to make purring noises into his chest.

All right, I think with a roll of my eyes. *The act is very convincing. You can stop now.*

I find myself missing the woman I met last night—the one who seemed so conspiratorial, so ready to lunge into a quiet war of our own. The one a few feet away from me now feels like she's been drugged or lobotomized, and I'm not entirely enjoying her presence.

The Bishop, though, looks perfectly delighted with her behavior. I would almost guess he was proud of her, although I'm not entirely sure why.

I pull my eyes away and stare out into the vast chasm, hoping we'll get to our destination sooner rather than later.

The part of the Behemoth the Bishop referred to as the "Blocks" turns out to be a series of concrete-walled residences scattered at random far below the Bishop's residence. The Transport slips this way and that, weaving through the hovering cubes until it stops at one marked with a large number seventy-three on the outer wall.

"Do you want to tell Ashen about these apartments?" the Bishop asks Naeva.

"May I?" she asks excitedly.

"Oh, yes. I think you should."

Naeva leaps over to me and reaches out, her cold fingertips caressing my arm for only a moment as she begins to speak as if reading from a script. "These residential cubes are where the Chosen stay—the ones who are studied for their Gifts. They're not super-pretty, but they grow on you—or so I hear."

The Chosen. I remember that word from when Adi was first telling me about Stella. It was what they called people with so-called "Gifts" like my ability to heal.

Stella ended up in a coma.

I can't help but wonder if I'll suffer the same fate.

"Will I be allowed out?" I ask, staring at the grim cube that is Unit 73.

"Not without supervision—at least, not just yet," the Bishop says. "But your residence contains all the necessary luxuries for a pleasant stay. Exercise equipment, food, drink, a fully equipped kitchen. We want you to stay strong and healthy."

"Right," I tell him. "Why is that, exactly?" *If I'm nothing but a prisoner, why do you care if I'm healthy, let alone strong?*

"Because you and the others who occupy this incredible

building are essential if we want our ongoing project to succeed. *You* are what makes the future bright, Ashen."

He doesn't expand on the thought, and I think better than to ask more questions.

The Transport slips into position, connecting itself to a steel sliding door on the cube's side until it has locked itself in place. When the doors slide open, Naeva turns to me and lets out a squeal. "Welcome home!" she sings before bouncing into the cube toward what is apparently going to be my home for the foreseeable future.

"Inside," the Bishop tells me, "you'll find clothing, as well as everything else I mentioned. There's even a television that broadcasts old local shows. Like I said, no view of New York."

"I didn't expect a view," I tell him. It would have been nice, of course, to be able to connect with Atticus, to let Rys know I'm all right. But prisons aren't exactly designed to offer such luxuries.

The Bishop guides me down a narrow, short corridor and into what looks like a small studio apartment. Inside is a bed, a dining table with two chairs, a tiny kitchen, and a door that likely leads to a bathroom. The decor is sparse, painted in dull shades of white and beige, and it depresses me immediately.

"This place is terrible," Naeva says with a pout. "It could definitely use a woman's touch."

"Or a blowtorch," I say under my breath. *Does it really have to be so grim?*

"I'm sorry it's not more beautiful, Ashen," the Bishop tells me. "But as time passes, I expect you'll find it more and more appealing."

"I'll survive."

"Yes. I think you will." He pauses for a moment before adding, "May I ask you something?"

"Of course."

His eyes lock on mine, and once again, against my will, I find myself softening as though I've just had a sip of delicious hot chocolate on a cold day. A sense of calm overwhelms and relaxes me, despite the fact that I should probably be enraged.

"I'm about to lock you inside what's essentially a large prison cell," he says, "away from Finn and from everyone else you care about. Yet you haven't fought me. Why is that?"

"Fought you?"

"The Surge," he says. "You could have..."

"Oh. I see."

"I'm just saying, you could have tried to kill me. To escape. You seem remarkably nonchalant about all this. I'm impressed by your restraint, truth be told."

"Let's just say it's not the first time I've been imprisoned," I reply.

"Ah, yes. But you managed to escape the Arc. More than once, from what I understand. You won't find the same ease of movement here, I'm afraid."

"Well then, what's the point in trying to fight my way out? If, as you say, I can't do anything about my situation, I may as well accept it."

With that, the Bishop smiles, reaching a hand out to stroke my cheek. I should slap his hand away. But instead, I find myself smiling back, savoring his touch as though he's just applied a soothing balm to a painful wound.

He speaks again, his voice silken in its smoothness. "I will keep my promise, by the way. If you do manage to cooperate, we may soon find a way to move you up the social ladder. You don't know how badly I want that for you. I wish to work with you, to pick your brain. Not to mention how badly I'd like to get that Finn of yours on our side. You two are valuable in ways you can't possibly imagine."

"But he *is* cooperating." The mention of Finn has inspired just enough willfulness in me to prompt me to speak up. "He's with his family, and he's not trying to escape, right? He's accepted his life as an Aristocrat in spite of the fact that it was never one he wanted. Please—whatever you do to me—don't hurt him."

The Bishop's eyes go wide. "I wouldn't dream of hurting either of you. I need his mind as well as yours. I just hope you two can begin to understand the importance of our work here. It will be so much easier to accomplish what we need to if you get on board."

"I'd come around more easily if I knew what the work was. I don't know anything about this place, other than the bits of information you've divulged—which don't add up to much."

The Bishop glances at Naeva, who's busy mindlessly poking at a remote control for the old television set.

"I'll tell you what. Tomorrow, I'll come here personally and escort you through some of the most important locations in the Behemoth. I'll show you the good work being done here, and over time, you can decide if you'd like to be a part of it. I am giving you a choice, Ashen. You can be a prisoner or an active participant. If you're the former, you may stay as long as you like, but you will not be permitted to see Finn."

"And if I'm the latter?"

"Then you'll soon find the world opening up to you in ways you've never imagined in your wildest dreams. I will make sure you have ample time to spend with the young man you love. I know what it would mean to you."

With that, he turns to leave, taking Naeva by the hand.

I watch them go, wondering how much lying I'll have to do to convince him I'm on his side.

When they've left me alone, I walk over to the kitchen area and open the narrow refrigerator. It's impeccably organized, filled with various beverages from juice to iced tea to some sort of protein drink. Fresh vegetables fill the crisper, and several pre-cooked meals await in foil-covered containers.

I'm not sure if it was custom-designed for me, or for that matter, how anyone would *know* what I like to eat in advance of my arrival. All I know is that every bit of food inside the fridge looks delectable.

I pull out a small meal of chicken, broccoli, and rice, as well as a bottle of some kind of red juice, and when I've heated the food and grabbed a few dishes, I seat myself at the small table. I look around, dismayed at the lack of decor in the place but oddly grateful for the lack of windows. The cavernous interior of the Moth isn't something I particularly want to be reminded of—nor do I want to remember that I'm in a residence that's floating a hundred or more feet from the ground, relying on a mysterious magnetic force to keep it from plunging into a wild free-fall.

Suddenly ravenous, I dig into my meal and devour it in about four minutes flat. Even as I finish the last bites, I look around again, struck by how the walls seem to have changed color since my arrival.

No—not changed, exactly. They're still neutral, still a light shade of beige. But I find them strangely pleasant now, as if beige is rapidly becoming my favorite color.

I rise to my feet, making my way around the small apartment, my fingers caressing the couch, the chairs, the counter-tops. Eventually, I lie down on the bed, staring up at the ceiling.

This is actually pretty great, I think, my mind swirling with pleasant thoughts. *I have my own place for the first time in my life.*

I don't have to worry about a thing.

I think of Finn then—of the fact that we're being kept apart. That he must be worried about me.

But as quickly as it came, that thought wanders away.

No, some part of my mind insists. *He's not worried. He's happy, just like me.*

Happy...

With that word dancing around my head, I fall into a deep sleep.

29

SETTLING

WHEN I AWAKEN with a jolt sometime later, I'm convinced I've only been asleep for a few minutes.

But the clock perched on the nightstand says 4:00 p.m.

After a quick calculation, I determine that it's been well over eight hours since I drifted off.

I sit up and stretch my arms over my head, the strange, euphoric feeling overtaking me again. I find myself chuckling as I mutter, "I guess this place does that to a person," before slipping out of bed.

I open the dresser drawers, scanning for clean clothing. Sure enough, there are items of every sort to be found. Shirts, socks, underwear, jeans, all mysteriously laid out in my exact size.

An assortment of shoes and boots are tidily lined up next to the dresser, though I'm certain they weren't there when I went to bed.

Has someone been in here?

I tell myself it doesn't matter. All I care about is that I'm safe...and weirdly, unnaturally happy.

Humming to myself, I grab a few items of clothing—a red shirt, a pair of blue jeans, gray socks, and underwear, and lay them on the bed before heading into the bathroom to get cleaned up.

The shower itself is small, but the water pressure is impressive. When I'm out, my feeling of innate bliss only increases as I grab one of the bath towels only to discover that it's luxuriously thick, fluffy, and feels like a warm hug.

I laugh, uncharacteristically amused by my own pleasure. I'm not normally so at ease in a strange place. Hell, I'm not normally so at ease *anywhere.*

As I throw together a sandwich in my well-equipped kitchen, I contemplate how strange it is that while I may be a prisoner in this place, I'm not scared. I don't fear the Bishop, though I suppose I probably should. For all I know, he may watch me for a few days, figure out I'm useless to him, and hang me in Brooklyn as a warning to Adi and the other Dregs.

But even as I contemplate that potential fate, my heart doesn't hammer with fear.

I suppose that's a good sign.

As if recalling a pleasant dream, my mind turns to Finn. I want to finish what he and I came here to do, of course. To get Merit away from their parents and head back out west, where we can start our new life together.

But something is telling me I need to stay in this place for a time. I want to find out about the so-called "good work" the Bishop mentioned. What exactly does he do in this place? Why the secrecy? Why is it that every residence is isolated from everything else inside this gigantic building?

As my mind bends and twists to think about the Behemoth's denizens and our purpose here, I find myself unable to contemplate anything else. The Arc, Kel, the Consortium—

they're all part of a past that's quickly turning into a fog. In spite of my initial reservations, all I want now is to help the Bishop so he'll let me in on the secrets of the Moth. I want to reconnect with Finn, to feel his lips on mine. To share with him this strange, addictive bliss I'm feeling in this odd new place.

If I could only see him, life would be perfect.

I'm startled out of the fantasy by the sound of a knock on the wall that must be coming from somewhere near the Transport doors.

"Hello?" a voice calls out. "Are you decent, Ashen?"

At this point, I'd know that voice anywhere.

It's the Bishop.

"I'm in the kitchen," I call out. "Just finishing breakfast—or lunch, or whatever this is!"

A second later, he's standing before me, pushing a strand of dark hair behind his ear. I see a now familiar, unreadable glimmer in his eye as he stares down at me, his lips curving into a smile.

I examine his irises, which once again look blue with the central ring of gold. But instead of feeling disconcerted, a burst of admiration floods me, as if I'm staring at a beautiful work of art.

"Good afternoon, Ashen," he says, his voice smooth and charming as always.

"I wasn't sure you were coming," I tell him, happier than I want to admit to see his face. "You must be so busy…"

He nods. "I was, in fact, considering sending someone else to you. Naeva has been…" He pauses, tilts his head as if he's contemplating how to explain, and concludes, "Well, let's just say she's been a handful over the last day or so."

"I can imagine," I reply, surprising myself by saying it out loud. But it's the truth. The woman is supposed to be some secret rebel infiltrator, after all, and she behaves like an irritating gnat, constantly poking at this and that, pawing the Bishop like he's a toy for her to play with.

"She may seem a little...flaky," he tells me, slipping around the small apartment, eyeing the bed, the dresser. "Her mind occasionally wanders in ways that aren't entirely wonderful." He turns to look me in the eye. "Do you know, I can usually read people's minds? Not literally, of course—the mind doesn't function like a book, with coherent sentences racing through sets of tidy pages. But I can generally sense when someone is lying to me, when they're being honest, when they're on my side. But Naeva, she's different. I've never fully been able to read her, and I suppose it's what I enjoyed most about her."

Enjoyed? *Why is he speaking about her as though she's now part of the past?*

I stare blankly at him, unsure how to respond.

"Don't worry," the Bishop says with a laugh. "I haven't broken things off with her. Quite the contrary. I'm hoping she'll be a part of my life for some time to come. She's a sort of...experiment of mine."

My inner bliss shifts then to a quiet warning. *What does that mean? Has he done something to her?*

I stare at the Bishop, my body tense. I can't quite bring myself to smile right now, though I am slightly afraid he knows what I'm thinking.

"Listen, I'm not here to discuss Naeva," he says, changing the subject to my relief. "I know you want to see Finn as soon as possible...and I know you wouldn't be stupid enough to jeopardize either of your lives. I would like for us to work together, Ashen. There are many reasons I wanted to bring you to this place. But one is that I believe you and I could be useful to each other…politically."

"Politically?"

He nods. "I am not a member of the Directorate, as you know by now. And though you have served as the face of a rebellion, you are not exactly a warrior. Your power is in your sincerity, your goodness. To many, you are the face and the voice of reason, of justice, of good winning over evil." He steps toward the blank wall above the dresser and waves a hand in the air. A projection flares to life in front of him. It's fuzzy at first, but I quickly begin to make out flashes of movement, as if a film is unfolding before my eyes.

Rising to my feet, I watch as a battle rages on a broad avenue. I see people in street clothes battling armed soldiers in uniform. The unruly crowd hurls home-made firebombs as the soldiers fire powerful weapons back at them. Bodies from both sides lie strewn about the street, victims of a never-ending fight for supremacy.

"That's Broadway," the Bishop tells me.

"Broadway? Like where…" I begin, but I know without asking that it's the street where tourists used to flock to attend musicals and plays for top-dollar prices. "I was under the impression Manhattan wasn't inhabited by Dregs."

"It's not just Dregs who challenge the Directorate forces in this city, Ashen. It's the Wealthy, too. These conflicts are not something I desire, to be clear. I am striving to unite the world, not break it down. Still, when an Aristocrat challenges the order of things, I feel it's my duty to make an example of them."

"You mean like Soren McNamara," I say. "The man they hanged the other night."

"Yes. Soren was put down for the good of all of us." He says it like he's talking about an old, long-suffering pet in need of relief.

"Why does any Wealthy challenge the Directorate?" I ask the question sincerely. After all, they still have their homes, their lives. Plentiful clothing and food.

Then I remember what Adi told me—the exorbitant taxes the Bishop inflicts on the city's Elite.

"You think it's because I've imposed financial restrictions on them," the Bishop chuckles as though he's looking directly into my mind. "I suppose it is, in part. But to be fair, some began protesting the Directorate the very second construction began on the Behemoth."

With another flick of his wrist, he makes the projection disappear.

"Others protest simply because it amuses them," he adds. "They don't like seeing soldiers in their streets—the military presence represents a loss of autonomy, of power, at least in their minds. But what it comes down to on the most fundamental level, Ashen, is that people of all walks of life are addicted to rage."

I stare at him for a long moment, contemplating the words. I can't find any reason to dispute him. Ugly as the truth is, he's right. People love being angry. They love to have a target, whether it's a political party, a celebrity, or some other common enemy, to rail against.

It's a pastime that will never cease to amuse us as a species.

For the first time, I'm beginning to understand why the Behemoth has such a strange, exclusive membership requirement, and why the residences are kept separate from one another.

The Bishop knows that letting too many people fraternize could eventually lead to mutiny or rebellion, as happens eventually in almost every close-knit society. There is no such thing as paradise on earth. No such thing as a "happy place." We are all, in our own way, content to be malcontents.

But none of that explains what it is that goes on inside this building, or what lurks in the multitude of residences and other structures floating around the darkness of the Behemoth like errant organs swimming their way around a massive body. It doesn't explain what happened to Adi's sister, Stella, or Shar's vanished son.

And it *certainly* doesn't explain why, ever since I set foot in this residence, I've been feeling happier than I've felt in ages.

A voice somewhere deep inside me tells me to enjoy the ride. To play the Bishop's game, to learn to trust him, to go along with whatever he asks and help him.

The trouble is, I'm not sure if the voice is coming from me or from him.

"Let me fulfill my promise to show you around the Behemoth a little," he says, seeing my body tense up. "And then you can begin to judge for yourself whether you think I'm worthy of your time."

30

THE MED WING

I SLIP on a jacket and a pair of ankle boots, and accompany the Bishop into one of the Moth's Transports, which is docked at the entrance to my residence.

This one is a pure silver box, mirrored on all sides to create hundreds of replicated images of the two of us. A strange, elusive army of Ashens and Bishops, dark-haired rivals who may yet find common ground.

Once the doors have sealed, the Bishop speaks out a command.

"Medical Level Fourteen-C," he says authoritatively, and instantly, we shoot sideways and then down, my stomach lurching as we go.

"Sorry to take you for such a drop," the Bishop says. "I'm afraid it's some distance to the wing we're off to see—a couple of miles, in fact. But it will be worth it. I am intent on showing you the best of this place."

"You never told me why," I say, my unease increasing with the feeling of hurtling through space.

"Why what?"

"Why me? I'm only a Dreg. I can't offer you money or know-how. I'm not some high-powered executive like the King, or a scientist like the Duke. You say you want a political alliance, but I'm not a politician."

He turns to face me, stepping close. There's a look in his eyes that inspires a cold, shuddering fear at my very core. He looks angry, though not with me, exactly.

Once again, I sense that odd, protective paw wrapped around me, the lion shielding me from the rest of the cruel world only to claim me for his own. "Never describe yourself as 'only a Dreg.' Never let anyone think you're an expendable commodity, Ashen. Or trust me, people you thought were your closest allies will be rid of you quickly. You need to make yourself invaluable, or you'll have no leverage in this world."

I find myself wondering as I stare at him who he really is beyond that mask of perfection. Because I'm realizing as each moment passes that what I see on the surface isn't real. It *can't* be. Someone this young, this unscarred by life, can't possibly have taken control of a structure like the Behemoth and all that goes on inside.

It's unfathomable.

Whatever the Bishop is under all the smoothness and polish, he's got to be more than just the young man I see before me.

As if he's studying me, he reaches out and slips a hand onto my cheek, his fingers digging into my hair. I feel the chill of a ring against my skin, in stark contrast to the almost unnatural warmth emanating from his gaze.

I should pull away, or at least flinch under his stare. But instead of intimidating me as he usually does, something in his touch acts as a tranquilizer, forcing me into a sort of immediate, euphoric submission.

For a moment, I wonder how he does this—how he charms and mesmerizes me without so much as a word. He's like a thief who steals away stress and replaces it with comfort.

Even when I want to hate him with a passion.

It's both disconcerting and utterly addictive, and right now, the last thing I want is to fight it off.

"Ah. We're here," he finally says, pulling away as the Transport's door opens.

He guides me down a long white corridor toward a set of glimmering steel doors. Etched in each is the same flowering tree I saw on the uniforms of the guards who questioned me on Brooklyn Bridge.

It represents "Life Itself," Adi told me. Appropriate for a medical wing. A bit strange for the uniforms of armed guards, though.

As we approach, the doors split apart with a wave of the Bishop's hand. I watch him move, his gesture fluid, and let out a quiet chuckle.

"What is it that amuses you?" he asks, but he doesn't seem annoyed. Just curious.

"You're like a wizard," I tell him, laughing louder this time. "I know it's ridiculous to say. But..." I wave my hand in the air, imitating the way he opened the doors, and he laughs, too.

But he doesn't explain how he does it—why everything in this building seems programmed to read his body language, his voice, his mind. Something tells me those same devices would go into lockdown if I tried to offer up commands.

Beyond the doors, we come to a massive, brightly lit room that isn't just long, but wide. It stretches as far as the eye can see, and I estimate that it takes up several acres of real estate. The room's walls glow white, though at first, I can't figure out the source of their light. The ceiling is high above us, but it's smooth and devoid of a single fixture.

All around us in organized rows are several long series of desks, tables, and storage units. On some of the tables are what look like biological samples in petri dishes and other clear containers. People in white hospital-style clothing move about the space, some wearing strange, obtrusive eyewear to study the genetic material.

"The goggles have a built-in microscope function," the Bishop explains as we advance. "They can see everything. Cells, disease, Gifts."

"Gifts?" I ask. "You mean…"

"Yes. I mean Gifts such as yours. It's in these labs that we studied the blood that was taken from you and discovered how you heal. Your blood is a roadmap for our scientists."

"Is that what you do here? Study these 'Gifts?'"

"We study humanity," he says. "Specifically, the wonders that make us unique—the traits that make some, let's say, *superior* to others."

Normally, I would cringe at the use of the s-word, but for some reason, the way he says it warms my heart. I fight the feeling, telling myself I should be disgusted. But as much as I try, I seem unable to conjure a single negative emotion.

"What about the ones who are *inferior?*"

"The Undesirables have their uses, of course. But here in the Medical Wing, we focus on the positive. There are wonders out there, Ashen—wonders you can't even begin to imagine. There is a future in our world brighter than anyone has ever imagined. And I want you to be a part of it. You and Finn, both. Each in your own unique way."

He brings me to a table some distance away, where a

woman in a medical coat is staring at a screen. On the left chest pocket of the coat is the same tree I've seen elsewhere.

"May I?" the Bishop asks, and the woman nods and smiles, backing away. The Bishop points to the screen, which shows an image of something I can't quite identify.

"Would you tell our guest what she's seeing?" he asks.

"A genetic marker of a subject who is impervious to all strains of the common cold," she replies with a grin. "Complete and utter immunity. One of the first ever detected."

"I didn't know there was such a thing as natural immunity to a cold," I say, leaning in to take a closer look.

"There are people in this world immune to every illness imaginable," the Bishop says. "And we are setting out to uncover each and every one of them."

"That's...amazing, actually," I reply.

"Wait until you see what our cancer researchers have done. You'll be stunned." The Bishop gestures around us. "This vast room is filled with scientists and with miracles. Every sample in this wing is from someone with a Gift. These are the healthiest, strongest humans imaginable, and we have a piece of every single one of them—including you and Finn. This all happened thanks to the cooperation of brilliant individuals such as yourselves, Ashen. You are walking, talking miracles, and we appreciate what you're doing for the world."

"You're saying my blood is here somewhere, then?" I ask him.

"Somewhere, yes—though we've already isolated the marker that makes you heal quickly. We're already putting it to good use."

I hesitate for only a second before saying, "It's Finn."

"Finn?"

"He's the reason I heal," I blurt out. "At least, I think he is.

You were right when you said he's a genius. And if he knows I'm okay, he'll cooperate, I know he will. Let me talk to him, and I'll persuade him to help you. This work you're doing here is something he would want to be part of."

"Of course he would," the Bishop says. "And of course I will let you see him."

"What?" I stammer. "Really?"

"Yes. But not just yet. Give me a few days—one week, at the most. One week to show you the wonders of this place."

My heart sinks. A week. A week in this Arcology, with its strange, isolated residences. A week, disconnected from everyone I care about.

Finn will worry. So will Rys, when Atticus sees no trace of me for days on end.

"Ashen," the Bishop says, laying a hand on my cheek once again, "I promise, the time will pass quickly. Do this one thing for me, and I will see to it that you and Finn have plenty of time to spend together."

Under the touch of his fingers, my worries melt away. Suddenly, seven days seem like no great sacrifice. "Sure," I say. "Yes. Of course."

"There's something more I want to show you. A special wing, with special patients. I feel, however, that I should warn you—they are not doing so well."

I nod and accompany him down a long hallway to another set of silver doors, which open at his command once again.

In the next corridor is a series of white doors to either side, what look like patients' charts hanging on each of them.

"I'm going to take you to see two patients," the Bishop tells me quietly, stopping in front of the first door to the left. "Remember—I'm bringing you here for a reason. Try not to despair."

I nod, a sense of unease building inside me once again.

He takes me through the first door, where we come upon a frail woman lying in a hospital bed. Her face is deeply lined with wrinkles, her skin pale, her eyes sealed shut. Her breath comes in shallow, hoarse waves.

I would estimate her age to be ninety or older. Her body looks so fragile, so irreparable, and all I can think when I look at her is *She doesn't have long to live.*

"Age," the Bishop says softly, "can be cruel. If she were anywhere else in the world, she would die in a matter of days. But it doesn't have to be so."

I stare at him, horrified that he would say such a thing in front of her. But she doesn't seem to hear him as her apparently unconscious form continues to struggle for breath.

"What's going to happen to her?" I ask quietly.

"You'll see soon enough. But come, I have one more patient to show you."

I hesitate as I turn to leave the room, unsure if I like the idea of wandering around to stare at distressed patients as if they're paintings at an art exhibition.

As I'm headed toward the door, I spot a framed photograph on the bedside table. It's a portrait of a young woman, her eyes large and blue, her brown, wavy hair flowing around her shoulders.

I pull my eyes back to the struggling patient.

That's you in the photo, I think. *I can tell.*

The juxtaposition between the two versions of the same person makes me sad, and I follow the Bishop, eager to leave.

MARCO

IN THE NEXT room is a young boy of eight. He's lying in bed, purple circles under his eyes, his skin translucently pale.

He lifts his head weakly when we enter, issuing us only the briefest of smiles before his body convulses in a coughing fit.

I realize as I'm looking at him that he reminds me of my brother Kel. Except Kel is vivacious and healthy, able to run around with other children his age, whereas this poor boy...

"What's your name?" the Bishop asks him as he steps up next to the bed, his tone soft and kind.

"Marco," the boy says weakly.

"Marco. What's your favorite kind of toy?"

"Dinosaurs." The boy gestures to the table next to us. On it are several plastic dinosaurs of various sizes, arranged tidily, probably by a parent.

Once again, I find my heart breaking. It's one thing for a woman in her nineties to be suffering the pain that comes with aging, but to see this small child, so young, in constant pain as he is...it's enough to crush my spirit and rob me of any residual pleasure I derived earlier from the Bishop's strange, soothing effect.

The boy looks up at me as if he knows what I'm thinking and says, "It's all right. I know I'm very sick."

I chew on my lip and nod. "I hope you get better soon," I tell him, struggling to keep my voice in check.

"They say this place works miracles," Marco replies with a smile. "My parents brought me here yesterday because the hospital in Manhattan couldn't help me."

I look over at the Bishop, freezing in place for a moment when I see his eyes fill with tears.

Tears.

How is this man—this strange, enigmatic creature who, by all accounts, is a monster—on the verge of weeping? Have I misread him? Is there some goodness to be found inside him, after all?

I reach out to take Marco's small hand. It's cold and skeletal, and I try to will all my strength to pass to him through the miracle he was promised. I know it's an impossible wish. But I want him to live so badly that it hurts.

We leave Marco a minute later with promises that we'll be back to see him tomorrow. As the Bishop and I head back up the corridor toward the Transport, I'm silent in my grief.

Once we're on the Transport and the doors have sealed, the Bishop reaches a hand out and touches my shoulder. "People get sick every day, Ashen. People die all the time. But I am here to end all of it. Do you understand?"

I shake my head, fighting back my tears. "No!" I tell him. "I don't. You can't fix terminal illness and old age. It can't be done, no matter how much you might think otherwise. That boy…"

I can't say anything more. My voice breaks and I bury my face in my hands.

The Bishop steps closer and takes me in his arms, and to my utter shock, I press my face into his chest and let the tears come.

Two nights ago, I watched this man from afar while he ordered the horrific death of an Aristocrat. Last night, I watched him revel in a drawn-out, vicious battle to the death.

How am I here now? How am I in his arms, letting him console me? What kind of upside-down world have I wandered into?

"Come back with me tomorrow," he says softly, in the same calming voice he used to speak to Marco. "We'll see him again. You'll see the miracle unfolding. I promise you that."

I pull back, shaking my head and wiping my eyes. "I don't see how…"

The Bishop presses a finger to my lips, his strange eyes staring into mine. He brushes my hair from my cheek, slipping it behind my ear, and for the briefest moment, I think he's going to kiss me.

I pull back instinctively, my loyalty to Finn suddenly foremost in my mind.

No. I'm not going to let you do this to me. I refuse to desire you as everyone else does.

You will not manipulate me in this way.

But in the end, he doesn't kiss me. He simply looks into my eyes and says, "Right here, right now. I promise you, Ashen, you will see very soon that miracles are a daily occurrence in this place."

For the second night in a row I sleep like the dead, exhausted both emotionally and physically after the day's events. As I drift off, all I can think about is Finn. How much I miss him, how if I play my cards right, each sleep will bring me a day closer to him.

But it's the Bishop I see in my dreams. His face. His voice. His touch. It's as if he's snuck into my bedroom and injected himself into my bloodstream, stealing away my ability to focus on anything else.

The sensation of infiltration isn't entirely unpleasant. In fact, I feel blissful, just as everything has felt since the moment I first set foot inside this strange residence. In the dream, the Bishop doesn't touch me, and there's nothing particularly intimate in our interactions.

He's just…there. Part of me, of my mind, my body.

He's in my blood.

When I wake up to see him standing a few feet away, I find myself smiling as I stretch my arms over my head.

"Time to go pay Marco another visit," he tells me, seating himself at the foot of my bed and handing me a cup of tea.

I sit up and take a sip. Part of me wants to beg him to let me stay here, in this comfortable apartment. I'm not sure I have the strength to go see Marco again, suffering as he so clearly was.

But then I remember our promise to the young boy that we'd be back.

"What about the woman?" I ask.

The Bishop sucks in his cheeks, sighs, and tells me, "She's gone."

I'm not sure what he means, exactly, but when he doesn't say more, I assume she's died in the night.

I nod solemnly and brace myself for the day to come.

"I'll let you get dressed," the Bishop tells me. As he's turning to head toward the alcove by the Transport doors, he turns back and says, "By the way, Finn is doing incredible work already. I thought you should know."

"I have no doubt," I tell him.

I dress quickly after picking out a pair of gray pants and an off-white silk blouse. Showing up to see Marco again in jeans and a t-shirt seems disrespectful, somehow. And if the old woman next door to his room is really gone, it seems doubly so.

When I'm ready, I head into the Transport to see that the Bishop is waiting for me with a plate of pastries. I take a lemon danish and eat it greedily before thanking him.

"I want you to enjoy your time here, Ashen. It's not all grim and wretched, I promise. The Behemoth may be a cavernous, dark affair, but there is a good deal of light to be found here."

I'll believe it when I see it, I think as he commands the Transport to take us back to the Medical Wing.

When we've arrived at the dock and the doors have slid open, the Bishop stops for a moment and turns my way. "I think there's a gift shop here somewhere," he says, guiding me down a corridor to our right. "I thought you might like to bring Marco something."

"He mentioned he likes dinosaurs," I reply, though the thought makes me sad. It's not like he has the strength to play with them, after all.

Still, when we get to the shop, I pick out a stuffed triceratops, which the Bishop holds up for the shopkeeper. She waves him on as if to say *You don't need to worry about money,* and we make our way to Marco's room.

The Bishop knocks once, and a nurse opens the door a crack, smiling when she sees us.

"How is our patient?" The Bishop asks.

"Very well," she replies. "Are you ready to see him?"

He turns to me, awaiting an answer.

"Sure," I say. "I guess…"

With that, the nurse opens the door wide. Clutching the dinosaur, I step inside only to see an empty bed.

I'm suddenly sick with worry.

Where is he? What's happened to him?

Is this some kind of vile joke?

"Is that a triceratops?" a high-pitched voice asks from somewhere behind me.

I spin around to see Marco sitting on the floor, playing with his dinosaur toys. His cheeks are rosy, his hair glossy and clean. The dark circles have vanished from under his eyes, which are now bright and sparkling.

It's all I can do not to drop to my knees and throw my arms around him.

"You're looking well, young Marco," the Bishop says. "And it is indeed a triceratops. Ashen here brought it for you."

I step forward, handing it to the boy.

"Thank you so much!" he exclaims, hugging the plush toy to his chest.

"How…how are you feeling?" I ask, still stunned.

"Great!" he replies. "The miracle happened!"

"He's still a little weak," the nurse says. "But much better. He'll be running around soon."

"I…I don't…" I begin, turning to the Bishop, who takes me by the hand and tells the others we'll be in the hallway.

He leads me out, closing the door behind us.

"Do you trust me a little more now?" he asks with a playful raising of one eyebrow.

I nod. "How did you do that?" I stammer.

"Believe it or not, Marco's miraculous recovery was partly your doing."

"Me?"

"Your blood. The sample we took. Healing comes in many forms, Ashen—knife wounds are one thing. Cancer is another. Admittedly, Marco is a bit of a guinea pig for us, but I'd say the results are impressive, wouldn't you?"

I nod again, speechless.

Whatever happens to me in this place, whatever wild ride I'm in for before I leave New York, knowing one young boy's life was saved because of my presence might just be enough to make it all worthwhile.

Each morning for the next five days, the Bishop and I return to see Marco, and each day, he looks healthier and stronger. He is soon able to walk, to run, to bounce around, and by the last day, the nurse tells us he's ready to be returned to his parents in Manhattan.

There are other patients, too.

One is a woman who has suffered a traumatic spinal injury and was told she would never walk again. Within two days, she's jogging on a treadmill in her room as tears of joy stream down her cheeks.

Another, an older man, lost an arm in an accident at a factory…and by the fourth day in the Behemoth's Med Wing, he's been fitted with a prosthetic that looks exactly like actual human flesh. The Bishop tells me it has bound itself with his nerve endings and muscles to form a new organic structure.

After each visit, the Bishop escorts me back to my residence, where time seems to pass in a fog. I'm aware of the hours I'm spending alone—hours without Finn, without any human contact. Yet I find myself perfectly content and devoid of boredom, as if everything is happening so fast that I'm not even aware of my own lack of activity.

On the final morning, when the Bishop and I have said goodbye to the young boy for the last time and made our way back to my residence, I ask him, "Who are Marco's parents, anyhow? I assume they're Aristocrats?"

"Believe it or not," he says, "they're Dregs. His father is a driver, his mother a maid. They aren't wealthy, by any means. But when I heard their story, I was moved. I wanted to help."

I watch his face carefully as he speaks, trying to read him, to figure out if he's lying. But I detect no hint of a falsehood or insincerity.

Either the Bishop is a brilliant actor, or there really is some good in him.

"Thank you," I say. "For what you did for him. It's mind-blowing, really. I only wish..."

"You wish everyone could be saved."

"Yeah. I do."

He strokes a finger over my cheek and says, "We're working on that. In the meantime, I believe I made a promise to you I need to keep. It's been nearly seven days, after all, since we brought you here."

My eyes go wide. "You mean..."

He smiles brightly. "Yes, Ashen. Tonight, you and Finn are invited to my residence for dinner. Wear something nice. And cheer up, would you? Life's too short for sadness."

I let out a quiet laugh as he makes his way back to the Transport.

Any sadness I was feeling has vanished.

The only thing that matters now is that in a few short hours, I'll be back with Finn, where I belong.

3 2

DINNER PARTY

THE BISHOP REMAINS true to his word.

At seven o'clock that evening, I'm escorted by one of his servants, who brings me in a long-distance Transport equipped with comfortable leather chairs, books, and even a television set airing old films, to what he refers to as "The Grounds."

"You're lucky to get to see the Bishop's main residence," my guide tells me as we slowly ascend hundreds of feet.

"The residence I've seen isn't his main one?"

The servant lets out a chuckle. "Hardly. Few people ever see the Grounds, actually. The property takes up one entire level of the original Behemoth—it's not a separate structure like every other residence and office in this place. Imagine an area almost as big as old Central Park...which is long gone, of course."

Gone. Yes. I'd forgotten the Behemoth was actually built on top of that iconic park, decimating it in the process.

It's no wonder Manhattan's Elite protested when the Moth was built.

When we finally arrive after our long vertical journey, we step out of the Transport into a level that reminds me of the King's property inside the Arc. Green, rolling lawns stretch out before us, leading up to what almost looks like a small town made up of various stone buildings, including an enormous gothic mansion. Above us is what looks like clear, cloudless sky, the sun setting in the distance to cast a pretty pink tint on the horizon.

My guide leads me up a gravel path until we reach the front door, which sits open as if inviting us inside. I suppose security isn't a huge concern of the Bishop's; it's not like anyone can simply walk up a flight of stairs and break into this property. In fact, I'm still not entirely sure if anyone other than the Bishop and his closest servants are able to control the Transports.

We step into the house to be greeted by a broad corridor, its walls a rich, dark red. There are no doors to either side, no windows, nothing—until we come to the end, where my escort presses a hand firmly to the wall, which shimmers away to reveal a large, elegant dining room. The space is painted dark green with white moulding around a vaulted ceiling, and beautiful, expensive-looking oil paintings on the walls. It has the appearance of a dining hall in a stately old manor house, which, I suppose, is exactly what this is.

I wander about the room, glad to have chosen a long black dress to wear for the evening. I'll admit that I put it on with Finn in mind. It's elegant, shapely, and perfectly cut, and the second I slipped it on, I thought of the hungry look that sometimes makes Finn's eyes narrow in the most delicious way.

But standing in this space, it occurs to me that wearing

anything less than the most lavish outfit would feel utterly wrong.

Another servant, a tall man with a beak nose and slicked-back hair, gestures me to one of the dining chairs. "The Bishop and his lady will be here soon. For now, would you like a glass of wine?"

Wanting to keep my wits about me, I reply, "I'll just have a glass of water, thank you."

"Very well."

The man disappears through a side door just as another door opens. My heart somersaults in my chest when I see Finn stepping into the room. He's alone, dressed in a black suit with a dark gray shirt.

The second he lays his eyes on me, he leaps over and takes me in his arms, pulling me to him almost violently before pressing his lips to mine.

"Are you all right?" he asks, cupping my face in his hands. "When they told me you were brought to the Behemoth, I was so worried—I thought..."

I shake my head to silence him before he says anything critical of the Bishop. "I'm fine!" I insist. "Actually, better than fine."

I almost want to tell him how oddly happy I've been since my arrival in spite of my isolation from him and everyone else I know and love. How strangely devoid of worry most of my days and nights have been.

But the truth is, seeing and touching him now brings me a joy far deeper and more real than anything I've felt in the last week.

"The Bishop has been showing me around," I tell him. "Finn, this place is amazing. Better than anything I could have dreamed of. The medical breakthroughs..." At first, I can't find an adjective to complete the thought. "They're miraculous."

Finn seems to relax a little, his look of concern softening into a smile. "So you've seen some of the Moth," he says. "You've seen the work they're doing here."

"A little, yeah. Enough to convince me this place isn't even close to what we expected."

With a chuckle, Finn says, "I'm not sure what I expected, exactly. All I know is that I'm about ready to murder both my parents. Living with them again after everything...it's a little tense, to put it mildly."

"I don't doubt it. But you're busy, right? The Bishop said you were working on some project or other?"

He nods. "It's kind of amazing," he says, looking around. "It's not something I can talk about, not even with you. Let's just say the Bishop's promises that he's trying to make the world a better place aren't entirely off-base. Still, I'm not sure..."

With a smile, I interrupt, "I'm as surprised as you are, but I have to hand it to him...after what I saw this past week, I'm going to keep any skepticism to myself."

"I should certainly hope so," a voice barrels out from the far end of the room.

The Bishop is striding in with Naeva on his arm. He's smiling, though the expression in his eyes isn't entirely compatible with the one on his lips.

But it's Naeva who draws my gaze. I haven't seen her since my first few hours in the Behemoth and I've been worried about her ever since. The way she behaved was so...

I shake my head, telling myself she looks fine, unscathed, perfectly healthy. Her hair is swept up in an elaborate style, her eyes brightly glancing around the room as though she's never seen it before. As the couple walks toward us, it occurs to me that she has a good deal in common with him—an almost impossible perfection that makes me both want to stare and avert my eyes.

Together, they're overwhelmingly perfect.

"I'm so glad you're both fully on board with what we're doing here," the Bishop continues. "I thought we might have to resort to a few negotiation sessions, yet here we are, a small, happy family, ready to change the world."

Family, I think as I watch him pull out a chair for Naeva before taking a seat at the head of the table. *I'm not sure I would go quite that far.*

"Yes. Here we are," Finn says, taking me by the hand as if to reassure me.

"I believe you both realize by now how much we can help each other. There is an entire world of wonders waiting for us out there—a world in which the disaster that was the Blight can be wiped from memory. Where famine, poverty, disease can be eliminated, once and for all. A world in which nature can return to its former glory while humanity thrives in its rightful setting."

"Which is?" Finn asks, a note of skepticism in his voice.

The Bishop gestures to the surrounding walls. "This," he says. "This Arcology is a wonderful place, don't you think? It offers privacy for every resident—a place to grow, to thrive. We grow food here. We are making massive medical and technological breakthroughs daily. The Behemoth is Heaven on earth. I suppose my dream is to have every person on the planet take up residence inside such a place."

"What about those who wish to live out there?" Finn asks with a nod of his head toward the wall, and I become all too aware of the fact that I haven't seen the actual sky in a week.

"You were in Brooklyn with me only a few days ago," the Bishop says. "You've seen what happens when people are given the freedom to take charge of their own territory. It's mayhem out there, a literal war zone. And much as you may disagree with me, it is not the Directorate or the Blight that caused the chaos in our city. It's disease, poverty, anger at the systems that have been in place for far too long."

"So, what's your plan?" I ask cheerfully, my hand holding onto Finn's, squeezing as if to say *Let's play nice, okay?*

"My plan," the Bishop replies, "is to create a world in which each and every person has a place, a purpose. Each individual will thrive, all while being used to the best of their own ability. No one will be left behind to fester in squalor, regardless of their financial status. There will be no such thing as a Dreg or a Wealthy."

I glance over at Finn, who doesn't look entirely displeased with the Bishop's words.

With that, our host claps his hands together. "Come, let's have something to eat."

On cue, a servant steps out of a side room, wheeling a cart displaying four plates covered in what looks like steak, potatoes, and an array of colorful vegetables. As Finn and I take our seats, he lays one in front of each of us.

But before we can dig into our meals, the Bishop flicks a hand in the air and a holo-screen appears above the table, showing what looks like the blueprint of a large building.

"What's this?" I ask, trying my best to conceal the fact that I'm famished.

"My plan for further construction inside the Behemoth," the Bishop explains. "I fully intend to add many more residences to this structure—each isolated from the other, of course. That way, we can ensure that unnecessary conflicts don't arise."

As he speaks, he twists his hand this way and that, and more images appear above the table. Three-dimensional renderings of multi-level, lavish homes, with children running around inside and adults congregating happily in various rooms.

"The residences will be occupied exclusively by carefully chosen specimens such as yourselves. People with something to offer—Gifts, whether biological, genetic, or merely theoretical. I have no doubt you're aware that many Aristocrats are incapable of having children, thanks to a blunder with the Cure."

Finn and I look at each other before I say, "We know that, yes."

"So you will believe me, I hope, when I tell you I am not looking to fill this place with Wealthies. We need to think of a future population, which means we need Dregs as badly as we need anyone. I plan to assemble the greatest minds in the world inside the Behemoth, to take advantage of their varied and plentiful Gifts. What I want most of all is to continue to improve the lot of humanity."

The Bishop locks his eyes on mine, sending a quiet shudder of fear through me when he says, "And the plan begins with the two of you."

POLITICS

"IT...BEGINS WITH US?" I say, squeezing Finn's hand harder. I look from the Bishop to Naeva, who looks as though her mind has strayed a thousand miles away. "What plan are you talking about, exactly?"

The Bishop reaches for a bottle of red wine, pours himself a glass, and takes a swig before replying. "My plans extend far beyond the city of New York. It's time to establish a truce between the Directorate and your friends in the Consortium. I wish to work toward a common goal, one for which I need your help and the help of all your allies inside the Arc."

"And what goal would that be?" Finn asks. I can hear the protectiveness in his tone, as well as a strong hint of cynicism.

The Bishop glances at Naeva. "Would you like to tell them, my love?" he asks.

"Absolutely," she replies with a smile, her eyes suddenly bright. "He's talking about immortality."

Finn and I exchange another look, and this time, I find it almost impossible to conceal the fact that I'm on the verge of guffawing. As much as I want to have faith in the Bishop and the good he's accomplished in the Moth, it's all I can do not to reply, "You're telling us you're planning to create a race of vampires?"

But Finn doesn't look quite so amused.

"Please explain," he says simply, issuing a polite smile.

The Bishop tightens a little, laying his palms flat on the table. He takes in a breath before saying, "Over the last several days, Mr. Davenport, you have seen some of our research on cellular regeneration and replication. You know by now that we have managed to get human cells to recreate themselves faster than ever before. Yes?"

Finn nods. "I have been looking at that, yes," he says.

"And Ashen has witnessed some of the effects of this miraculous work. Haven't you, Ashen?"

"I…" I hesitate, then turn to Finn, nodding. "There was a sick boy. Terminal. I met him one day. I was so sure…" I can't think how to put it. As I look into Finn's eyes, what I'm about to say seems like folly.

"She thought he was on the verge of death," the Bishop concludes. "Which he was. He would have faded to nothing within days, had he remained in the hospital on the outside. But thanks to the research we've done in this place, he not only survived, but he is likely to live a life longer than any human being who has ever existed. You see, I am working toward not only combatting, but reversing the effects of age and of disease. I fully expect all life-threatening illness to be abolished within my lifetime—which, mind you, will be many, many years."

I want to ask how he can be so sure, but instead, I simply nod and smile. The air is tense, uncomfortable. I can tell that Finn isn't convinced by the Bishop's motives. And, much as I want to trust the man, I'm beginning to feel skeptical, myself.

"Why do you need us?" Finn asks, his tone curt. "You've been doing research here for years already. You're well on your way toward the developments you want. So why are we even necessary? You could let Ash go back home to the Arc, to be with her brother…"

"Finn," I say softly. "You know I wouldn't leave you here."

Instead of responding, the Bishop gestures to our plates. "Everyone, eat. Your food will get cold. When we're done, I'll clear everything up. I promise you that much."

Finn narrows his eyes at the Bishop, but after I've released his hand, he finally picks up his fork and knife and slices into his steak.

I follow suit, and for a time, the four of us eat in silence.

I'm still scarfing down my meal when Finn says, "Let's say Ash and I give you everything you want from us, Bishop. What are you going to do for us in return?"

Horrified, I peer over at the Bishop, who looks mildly irritated. Still, he smiles when he says, "I will keep Ashen and your family safe."

"I want more than that," Finn retorts. "Much more."

"What?" The word shoots out of the Bishop's mouth like a bullet, almost so fast that it feels violent. But after a moment, he seems to settle.

"You heard me," Finn says, his voice still astoundingly calm.

"What exactly do you want?" the Bishop asks, his tone softening.

"I want you to stop killing people in the streets. And no more Hangings. No Choosing Ceremonies."

I almost cry out a warning.

Finn, what the hell are you doing, making demands of the man who's got us locked up in this place?

But to my surprise, the Bishop chuckles then full-on laughs. "Done," he says. "No more killings."

I'm speechless. *That was so...easy.*

Finn takes another bite before swallowing it down and adding, "I also want you to promise you'll release Ash when we're done helping you. She's been through enough at the hands of Aristocrats and the Directorate. It's time to end the cycle. She's no one's prisoner. She's not a servant or a pawn. Do you understand?"

At that, the Bishop stares into my eyes, and I feel myself mesmerized as I look back at him. "I have every intention of releasing her," he says, "provided she offers the cooperation I'm hoping for."

"What about Finn and Merit?" I ask without thinking. "We came here to New York to bring his brother home—not to end up locked inside another Arcology."

"Finn will be free to leave with you, of course," the Bishop says. "I only ask a few weeks of your time, perhaps a little more. During that time, I will allow you two to see one another daily. I will even persuade the Duchess to let you spend a night together here and there, if you'd like."

I shoot Finn a sideways glance, and I can see that he knows what I'm thinking. *The Duchess will never say yes.*

"It's never going to fly," Finn says, his voice sharp. "You don't know my mother..."

To my surprise, the Bishop rises to his feet, walks over to Finn, and lays a hand on his shoulder, squeezing. "Your mother will do as I ask," he says, leaning down so his face is next to Finn's. "She is my guest in this place. She is only here because I allow her to be. Do you understand what I'm telling you?"

Finn's entire body seems to go limp, relaxing under the

Bishop's touch. All the tension that has built up inside him seems to disappear into the ether as he nods.

"I will provide Ashen with a beautiful, well-appointed residence," the Bishop continues, heading back to his seat. "And I promise you, she will find it more and more appealing as time passes. Provided, Mr. Davenport, that you prove your worth over the next days, which I have no doubt you'll do with flying colors. In the meantime, I will be asking for a little of Ashen's time. I have a project in mind for her."

I glance at Naeva, who's staring into space again. She's completely disengaged from this conversation, but when the Bishop reaches for her hand, she takes it and smiles at him, her face glowing.

Almost immediately, the Bishop pulls away and claps his hands once as if to conclude the conversation.

"Come," he says, rising to his feet. "All of you. I want to show you a little more of the good we've done here in the Behemoth." Pulling his eyes to mine, he adds, "I believe *you* will particularly enjoy this, Ashen."

MIRACLES

WE ACCOMPANY the Bishop and Naeva back down the hallway until we reach a set of doors to a clear glass Transport tucked into what looks like it was once an elevator shaft.

Once inside, the clear cube shoots us downward so fast that at first, it feels like we're in a free-fall. The feeling of weightlessness is disconcerting and slightly terrifying, and I reach for Finn to stabilize my body and mind, reassured when he wraps his arms around me.

Before long, the Transport slows to a crawl, easing sideways to dock at a structure I haven't seen before. In contrast to the ubiquitous silver surfaces in the Behemoth, its exterior is a bright, sparkling gold. When the Transport doors open, we step out into a corridor of similar metallic gold walls. It's opulent—a little obscene, even, and I determine without asking that it must be the domain of someone incredibly wealthy.

The Bishop guides us down the corridor in silence even as a series of small, translucent creatures that look like moths appear out of nowhere to flit around his head.

"Scanner Drones," the Bishop says. "Ignore them."

The moths flick and flutter around our heads, too, and after a few seconds, I notice a white light scanning Finn's face as if assessing whether he's a friend or a foe. Eventually, they move on to do the same to me before disappearing entirely.

"Who exactly are we here to see?" I finally ask, my eyes locked on the Bishop's back. But it's Naeva who answers.

"A very important woman. Her name is Beatrix Hemner."

"Hemner?" I've heard the name, though I can't immediately recall where. But after a few seconds, it comes to me. "As in the Hemner Museum?"

"That's the one," the Bishop says.

The Hemner family has been famous for decades for owning art collections and museums all over the world, as well as for their extraordinary wealth and philanthropy. I suppose it shouldn't surprise me to learn that one of them has found her way into the Moth, though I have to wonder why a woman Beatrix's age would choose to live here.

"Isn't she a hundred years old by now?" I ask.

"Ninety-eight, to be precise," the Bishop asks as we come to a set of gold double-doors at the end of the hall.

On our approach, the doors slide open.

A woman stands on the other side, waiting to greet us. Her face is immediately familiar, with large eyes and delicate features. She's about my height, with brown hair and high cheekbones.

At first, I'm sure I recognize her from old news articles in my father's art studio. But I quickly realize that's not how I know her at all.

No.

It can't possibly be.

I'm staring at the patient the Bishop took me to see on my

first day in the hospital wing—the old woman who looked so frail, so close to the end of her life.

I remember her face so well from the old photo on her side table.

But...I was so sure you'd died.

Yet here she is, standing in front of us, the picture of health.

She looks thirty. Maybe thirty-five.

"Beatrix," the Bishop says, kissing her on both cheeks. "You look incredible."

"Thanks to you," the woman replies with a glowing grin. Her voice is a little raspy, betraying an age that doesn't entirely coincide with her smooth skin or bright eyes. She turns our way as Finn and I exchange a look of shock, and laughs. "You're wondering who I am and what I did with the real Beatrix."

"Honestly, I'm just confused," I stammer. Is it a Holo-Veil? No. There's no sign of it, no translucence or odd shimmer to her skin.

She looks *very* real.

But how...

Beatrix grabs the Bishop's arm and squeezes, patting him on the cheek with her other hand. "When I came to him, I was ill...and ancient, of course. I had been told I would be dead within a matter of months. That was five years ago now. I'm rather a lot younger than I was, which makes no more sense to me than it does to you. But here I am."

"You're not younger," the Bishop says, patting her hand. "You have all the experience of one who has lived for nearly a century. I would classify you only as *a little improved*."

"I don't understand," I say. "I'm sorry if this sounds rude, but I saw you in your hospital bed. I can't believe you're the same person."

"I suppose I'm not," she replies. "Ah, but time is a cruel disease. From birth, it begins to assault us. We fall victim to age, and with the years comes the inevitability of death." Shooting a look at the Bishop, she adds, "Until recently, at least."

Immortality.

The Bishop spoke of it, and I all but laughed in his face. I thought he was joking, or at least exaggerating. But this...this is proof of...well, *something.*

"Come in, come in," Beatrix says. "I'll have the servants bring you all some tea," We follow her into a massive, bright living space with enormous windows to one side. Through the glass we can see a projection of mountains—the Alps, maybe—that give the comforting impression of sitting inside a warm chalet on a winter's day.

We seat ourselves on a series of couches and armchairs. Finn looks tense, and it occurs to me he hasn't yet offered his opinion about any of this. I can't say I blame him; I'm torn between disbelief and wonder, myself.

Naeva looks vaguely bored, her eyes locked on the mountains.

But Beatrix and the Bishop look downright euphoric.

"I brought our guests here to see you," the Bishop says, "because you are one of our greatest accomplishments." He turns to Finn and me and adds, "She came to us with two types of cancer and heart problems that were no surprise for someone of her late age. But we've mended her."

"How?"

It's the first word Finn has said since we stepped into the

residence, and it comes out curtly and cynically. There is no admiration in his face, no hopefulness.

There is only doubt.

"How?" he asks again, gesturing to Beatrix as if she's a piece of furniture. "This is impossible. You can't reverse a person's age, not like this. The best you can possibly hope for is to slow it down a little. This makes no sense."

"It does if you consider that cellular regeneration greatly decelerates as we age, Finn," the Bishop replies. "And my scientists have found a way to accelerate it to a rate that was heretofore unimaginable—to the point where the cells not only regenerate, but actually reverse time."

"I want to understand," Finn says. "I really do. But what you're saying isn't..."

"Work with me," the Bishop interrupts. "Tell me you're fully on board, Finn, and I will let you in on every one of our secrets. Until then, I can't tell you everything."

Finn leans forward, his expression shifting from full-on skepticism to reserved excitement. He turns to me and says, "Ash—are you confident this is the person you saw in a hospital bed?"

Glancing at Beatrix, I say, "I mean, I can't be sure, but...yes. Even if I didn't recognize her from the photo I saw that day, I remember her face from old articles. This *is* Beatrix Hemner."

The Bishop speaks once again. "We have managed to reverse age and disease in Beatrix, as well as others. We're hoping to offer the same to the masses one day soon."

"The masses," Finn says. "Dregs? The poor? Those who suffer in silence because they can't afford expensive treatments? Those who can't enter these hallowed halls—" As he says this, he flings his arms out to gesture to the obviously incredibly expensive walls of Beatrix's residence. "Is that what you mean by masses?"

The Bishop's neck tenses, and his flawless face turns scarlet. Naeva, suddenly attentive, puts a hand out and lays it on his own, which seems to calm him a little. Still, when he speaks, there's venom in his tone.

"If you don't approve of what we're doing, you and your family are more than welcome to forfeit your right to a residence here," he says. "I would have thought that you of all people might be impressed. What we have achieved here is no small feat. This is, in fact, a thing humanity has been striving for for centuries."

Finn sits back, a strange smile on his lips. "This is a thing that is impossible," he says. "And if you knew anything about biology, you'd know I'm right."

"You're not!" the Bishop snaps, rising to his feet and taking an aggressive step toward Finn.

"Bishop!" Naeva shouts sharply, shockingly, bringing him back from the brink of explosion.

The Bishop runs a hand through his hair, pulls at his jacket, and seats himself again.

"There, there," Beatrix says. "I should be living proof of the possibility of it, shouldn't I? I'm here right now. I exist. Isn't that enough?"

Finn looks at her. Her face is kind, her voice sweet, and he allows himself a friendly smile. "You are here, and I can't dispute that. But what the Bishop claims is possible is not. I mean no disrespect when I say it. There must be more to his methods than what he's told us."

The Bishop clears his throat and replies, "Ah. Well, I'm not a scientist. I am merely a dreamer. I should not have pretended to understand the intricacies of the research as though I was the one responsible for it. My apologies, Mr. Davenport. You're quite right—I'm entirely sure there is far more behind the scenes than what I have mentioned."

"It's fine," Finn says, his voice settling into something more civilized than before. "I simply want to understand what's happening here before Ash and I sell our souls."

"What's happening here," Beatrix says, "is nothing short of a miracle. It has given me new life, and if I have anything to say about it, it will give life to many, many people in the future." She strides over and clasps Finn's hands in hers. "There is so much hope in this place, Mr. Davenport. So much love. I hope you understand that one day very soon."

The way she speaks is so sincere and engrossing that I desperately want to believe she's right—that there really is hope in this place, that the goings-on inside the Moth are all for the good of humanity as a whole.

It's only when we've concluded our visit and Finn and I are following the Bishop and Naeva back to the Transport that I dare to put a hand on his arm, stopping him in the corridor while the Bishop and his companion walk on.

"Do you think she's real?" I ask in a whisper.

"Beatrix?" he says. "Yes. As real as anyone. She's as real as the Bishop—although..."

I can see something in his eyes, something churning in his mind like spinning gears are working their way through a problem.

"What is it?"

"Don't you think there's something *off* about him?" he finally asks, glancing toward the Transport doors at the end of the hall. "I mean, aside from the usual psychopathy of Wealthies."

"I mean, he seems older than he looks, if that's what you

mean," I reply. "But I've looked at him closely. I'm almost certain he doesn't have a Holo-Veil activated. He seems very real. It's almost like he's...I don't know, *more* than human."

"Exactly," Finn agrees. "I suspect he'd be happy to hear us say it, too. It's like...he's *too* perfect. Superhuman, like you said. The question is, who is he really? And how did he get this way?"

I shake my head. "I don't know. But if he can help people—if he can eradicate disease like he says he can, I'm willing to work with him. Even if he *is* a little psychotic. Particularly if he holds to his promise and keeps our people safe."

Finn looks at me dubiously before relenting.

"I'm not convinced a deal with that man will ever be in our best interests. But I'll admit, this place isn't what I thought it would be. I've seen no evidence of the Directorate's cruelty in the Behemoth, and frankly, their labs are magnificent. The resources they've shown me are like nothing I've ever seen. And if the Bishop really does let me in on this cellular regeneration technology..." With a sigh, he adds, "I'll give him the benefit of the doubt, for now. *Only* for now."

"Good," I tell him. "Because I've seen two miracles this week, and you'll probably manage a few of your own."

"Maybe," Finn says, taking my hand as we begin the walk over to the waiting Transport. "But if that bastard tries anything—if he hurts you in *any* way—I'll kill him with my bare hands. That's a promise."

35

MANHATTAN

When the Transport reaches my residence in the Blocks, I say goodbye to Finn with only the briefest kiss.

"When will we get to see each other again?" I ask the Bishop, holding him to the promise he made earlier.

"Tomorrow," he tells me, his tone velvety-smooth. "But not until the evening. I have plans for you both during the day. For now, let's simply say goodnight so tomorrow comes sooner, shall we?"

I glance over at Naeva, who smiles at me for a split-second before her face neutralizes to something entirely devoid of expression. I give Finn a final hug before slipping through the doors into my residence.

As I walk through the short hallway, something feels different about the space. At first I can't figure out what's changed, and it's not until I enter the main area that I see it:

The entire residence has...grown.

At first, I think I'm in the wrong place entirely, that the Transport accidentally stopped at the wrong Block and brought me to someone else's residence.

But then, I see Shar's rucksack hanging from a hook on the far wall, next to a coat rack that wasn't there before. The shoes that were previously next to the dresser line the floor, my jackets hanging above them.

The neutral beige of the residence has altered, too. The walls are now light gray, and a collection of attractive artwork hangs here and there. Landscapes like the ones my father used to paint, as well as other pleasant scenes. It's almost as though someone has delved deep into my soul and extracted the notion of my ideal living space.

The kitchen, too, has grown into something spacious and luxurious, complete with a marble-topped island, an enormous refrigerator, and every appliance I could ever hope for.

Off the kitchen is a living room with a huge, comfortable sectional and a screen on one wall large enough to take up almost the wall's entirety. Right now, it's projecting an outdoor scene. Mountains, like in Beatrix's residence. But these aren't the Alps. These are *my* mountains, the ones that surround the Mire back home.

Tears well in my eyes as I spin around, trying to figure out if I'm dreaming.

But it's all real. I can feel the couch when I reach down to touch its soft upholstery and pick up a cushion. I smell the air, fresh and clean as it is.

The Bishop has kept yet another promise. And I'm beginning to think Finn and I sorely misjudged him this whole time.

He's not a bad man. He's just a complicated one.

Overwhelmed by a sudden feeling of fatigue, I head to the bedroom to get ready to sleep. All I can think as I look around at the lavish bed and other assorted furniture is *I wonder what that man has planned for me tomorrow.*

Whatever it is, I'm more excited about it than I've been about anything in a long time.

"I want you to accompany me into the city today," the Bishop tells me while we drink tea in my new kitchen the following morning.

His words nearly induce me to spew liquid all over him. Swallowing hard, I say, "What?" before wiping my mouth with the back of my hand. "Are you serious?"

"Absolutely. Yes, I know—you thought you'd be locked in here for eternity. But unlike Finn, Ashen, you're no good to me in here. I need you out there." He nods toward the wall and Manhattan far beyond. "And before you ask, I want the people to see your face. There will be no Holo-Veil, no Ana Miller. I want them—Dregs and Aristocrats alike, to see Ashen Spencer. Do this for me, and I will make it worth your while."

I sit in silence for a moment, stunned.

I'll be able to breathe in the outdoors.

Look at the sky.

I may even see Atticus...

I force the last thought from my head. I know the Bishop can't entirely read my thoughts, but he's far too good at deciphering what's going on in my mind, and I'm not willing to risk losing my one connection to Rys, to the Arc, to Kel.

"Why?" I finally ask. "I mean...why would you want to be seen with the Crimson Dreg?"

He laughs. "You may not have noticed, Ashen, but you are rather famous. Come, you know all this. Let's not waste each other's time."

"So what is it that you want, exactly?"

"It's simple, really: If I'm to convince your allies that I'm not the devil himself, I need you by my side. They need to see that we're working together, toward a common goal."

I guess I don't look entirely convinced, because he continues.

"Look, I'm well aware that there is hatred for me running rampant on the streets of this city and far beyond. Fear of the monster they think I am."

With that, the Bishop reaches out and puts a hand on my arm. My skin tingles under his touch in a way that's not entirely unpleasant...except for my acute awareness that I'd far rather be touched by Finn.

"I'm not naive," he adds. "The people's fear is one I've nurtured and cultivated for a long time—but it's a political tool, and nothing else. The time has come to alter my image into something more palatable. The truth is, if I'm to continue my work, it will be much easier with the help of the multitude of Dregs residing in the boroughs around Manhattan. I want them to see that a truce really is possible. I want them to believe me when I assure them there will be no more killings. And the fact is, they will be far more likely to believe such a thing with you by my side."

"It will take more than just you and me going for a stroll through Brooklyn to convince the masses that you've changed," I warn him. "Some of those people..."

"Some of them what?" he asks. "Tell me. It's all right."

For a moment, I contemplate mentioning Adi's sister, but I quickly steer my mind away from her. It's too soon to confront the one thing I haven't had the courage to bring up— the masses of missing Dregs who are hidden somewhere inside the very building where we now sit.

Or is it?

I swallow and steel myself. Thinking of Finn—of his courage yesterday when he confronted the Bishop—I speak again.

"I met a young woman whose sister is missing. She was brought to the Moth a few years ago, and, well, Adi doesn't know if she'll ever see her again."

"Adi, you say?" the Bishop replies.

I nod. "She's one of the Trodden. A rebel." I'm not sure how much to tell him, but I take a risk. "She knows people, and I suspect she has a lot of influence among the Dreg population in Brooklyn—and probably all around New York. If you released her sister, it would help mend the fences. It would also show that you're not mysteriously killing Dregs in here or anything."

"What is her name?" the Bishop asks. "The sister, I mean?"

I realize as he's asking that I don't actually know Adi's last name.

"Stella," I say. "Adrastos is Adi's full name. I don't know any more than that."

"Adrastos," he repeats. "Yes. I've heard of her."

Instead of saying anything more, he rises to his feet and steps away from me, slipping a finger over something on his forearm. A second later, he speaks a few words so softly that I can't make them out.

When a reply comes, his lips curl down, and he looks toward me.

"What is it?" I ask.

He holds up a hand, nodding as though listening to a voice in his head before finally letting his hand drop.

"A slight hitch, but only slight. But there is some good news…" With that, he reaches out, takes my hand, and says,

"We will release Stella in a matter of a few hours. My people just need a little time."

"Time?" I ask. "For what? If she's here, why can't we just go find her?"

A shadow passes over the Bishop's face, but quickly fades. "When Stella came to us, she was ill. It's quite possible that her sister doesn't know, as we only diagnosed her sickness after her arrival."

I recall what Adi and Cillian told me about Stella's seeming comatose state, but I say nothing.

"Part of her treatment," the Bishop continues, "involved keeping her in an induced coma—for the sake of recovery, you see."

I stare at him, half-stunned that he's confirming what they told me. Could it be that all this time, she's been kept alive out of some kind of act of benevolence? If so, why did no one ever tell Adi?

"Has she recovered?" I ask.

"We look after those we bring here, Ashen. She is healthy and alive. But we can't simply snap her awake and send her on her way. She needs time to come out of it. Give us a few hours. Please."

I nod. "Okay. But I have a request."

"Anything," he says, taking a seat next to me again. He smiles with that same intimate, disconcerting look he's given me so many times. Almost warm, but ringed with something slightly frightening.

"Can we tell Adi? It will make her so happy to know Stella's going to be okay."

The Bishop slips a hand up to my cheek and caresses it almost possessively. "Sweet girl," he says. "We'll tell her when we bring her sister to her. It won't be long now."

"And you'll keep your word? No more killing? No more Hangings? You'll tell the Dregs?"

"Better still, you will."

"Me?" I pull back, horrified.

"Come on. I've seen the videos you made to stir up your rebellion. You're a good speaker. You're sincere. You're confident, at least when it comes to matters of justice. Your people respect you."

Your people.

Are they even my people anymore? Who am I now, other than a quasi-prisoner in this strange place?

I want to refuse his request, to tell him no—that my days of public speaking are over.

But something occurs to me.

"On one condition," I say.

Another dark look passes over the Bishop's face for a second before he relaxes and asks, "What is it?"

"I want you to broadcast whatever I say here in New York to the Arc. I need to let them know I'm all right—and let them know what's happening here. They'll be worried that they haven't heard from us. But more than that, it will give them hope for the future, if I tell them what you're doing for all of us."

"I was going to suggest it myself," the Bishop says, seemingly relieved. "Yes, we will absolutely broadcast to the Arc, if you like. If I'm to make allies of you and Finn, I need to let the Consortium know I mean to offer them support—and that means every single member of that organization."

My heart lightens a little, though small, distant warning bells have begun to sound somewhere deep inside me.

"Do we have a deal, Ashen?"

I suck in my lip only for a moment before saying, "It's a

deal. I'll make the video. As soon as you've handed Stella over to Adi and Cillian."

"In that case, I'm off to the Medical Wing to make sure Stella is well looked after. I'll be back in a few hours. Be ready for me."

"I will."

He holds a hand out and I take it in mine, forcing myself to look deep into his eyes as we shake on our promise to one another. They've changed again, from blue to near-black.

If only I knew with absolute certainty what was going on behind those eyes, I think, *I'd feel less like I was making a deal with the devil.*

36

SURPRISE

THE BISHOP RETURNS to my residence at three.

But to my dismay, he's alone.

"Where's Stella?" I ask.

"She just needs a little more time to prepare for her journey," he assures me. "In the meantime, you and I are going to head into the city. There are a few things I want to show you."

"But..."

"Ashen," he says sharply. "You've trusted me until now, which I appreciate. Please—don't lose faith now."

I nod, my jaw tense. *I'll trust you more when I see Stella...*

Still, I accompany him onto the Transport that takes us to the private residence where he keeps his vehicle, and he brings us down on the mag-lift to Manhattan's streets once again.

I find myself exhaling audibly when we reach ground level, and the Bishop lets out a soft chuckle from the driver's seat.

"You didn't wholly trust that you'd ever see the outside again," he says.

"I…" I begin, but he's right, and I can't quite bring myself to deny it.

"It's all right," he assures me. "I'm not a beast, Ashen, but I can understand why you might still think I am. I have a strange life. I'm in charge of a place that feels like the bowels of Hell on a good day, for one thing. I know it's hard to fathom that I can actually keep my promises."

My heart melts just a little then. "I'm sorry," I reply, smiling awkwardly at him. "Really. You've stayed true to your word on every front, and I do appreciate it. I'd just…I'd heard…"

"That *no one ever leaves the Moth.* Yes, I know. But today, both you and Stella will prove that rumor false."

His mention of Stella heartens me, and I look out the window, smiling.

I'm still grinning when we make our way across Brooklyn Bridge, surprised to see how few military vehicles block the way. The armed presence is almost nonexistent compared to a few days ago.

"I forgot to mention that I have a surprise for you," the Bishop tells me as we enter Brooklyn. "I think you'll like it."

"I'm sure I will."

I glance out the window, trying to get a read on the atmosphere on the streets. It feels less dangerous than it did, less threatening than before. The Bishop's expensive vehicle isn't accompanied by a convoy, nor, apparently, does it need to be. The only Dregs in my periphery are wandering the streets, seemingly carefree as they go about what look like normal daily routines. Coffee shops are open, as are grocery stores and other businesses.

"People are going back to work," the Bishop says. "Back to their old lives with the promise of safety."

As I'm watching the buildings go by, a flurry of movement catches my eye—something far above us, flitting from one building to the next.

A flood of relief surges through my mind when I look up to see Atticus's gleaming silver belly.

I see you. And I'm sure you see me.

Now hide.

"Where are we headed?" I ask, hoping to distract the Bishop long enough for Atticus to disappear into stealth mode.

"Your friend Adrastos's neighborhood. A park near her home, to be precise."

Within minutes, we're pulling onto a narrow gravel laneway that takes us to the center of a large green space. All around us are the same damaged brownstones that surrounded me when I first made my way through the streets with Adi and Cillian.

But to my surprise, there are also construction vehicles.

A *lot* of them.

"What's happening?" I ask as a bulldozer makes its way down the street to our right, clearing mounds of debris from the road.

"I'm repairing the damage done by people like Finn's mother," the Bishop says with a disdain that feels oddly satisfying. "Such needless cruelty, all in the name of power," he adds with a shake of his head. "You may despise what I've done in my life, but in my defense, I only end lives out of a sense of justice. I don't do it for sport."

"What about the Choosing Ceremony?" I ask, aware that I'm pushing it a little. "That seems a little like sport."

"That's a matter of choice. I have never forced an Aristocrat to partake, and I never would. *They* make the call." He reaches over and touches my leg only for a moment before pulling his hand away. "I promised you and Finn no more killing. So let's not speak of it. Agreed?"

"Agreed."

Armed guards patrol the streets, keeping any potential threat at bay. But I don't see a single rebel storming out of their house to shout or threaten. And when we emerge from the vehicle, no weapons appear to be trained in our direction, despite the fact that the Bishop is walking in plain view of every window in the neighborhood.

"I don't understand why it's so quiet," I say. "Do the Trodden already know about the truce?"

"They know some of it," the Bishop tells me. "My people have been here for a few days—since even before we agreed to the truce. I suspect many of them are simply waiting in their homes for the main event."

"Main event? I thought we were here to make a video."

"We are. But be patient, Ashen. In the meantime, just enjoy the view. I'm sure you'll agree that our construction crews are working astonishingly fast to rebuild this lovely neighborhood."

We walk another half block, watching bricklayers work wonders, and carpenters whose entire job is to replicate the houses' original window frames and doors.

It's several minutes before a guard approaches the Bishop to ask if he's ready.

"I am," he says, nodding. "We both are."

As we watch, a large truck pulls around a corner some distance ahead and stops in the middle of the street. When the back doors fly open, a camera crew emerges and begins to set up tripods and other gear.

"What's happening? Is this for the video?" I'm about to remind the Bishop that I only agreed to film it when Stella had been freed, but I hold my tongue.

"In part," the Bishop says mysteriously.

A minute or so later, two familiar figures round the corner to our right and head toward us. They approach slowly, cautiously, eyes locked nervously on the Bishop.

It's not until I call out to them that they pull their gazes to me.

"A—Ana?" Adi says, looking surprised to see my real face in such close proximity to the Bishop. "What are you...How..."

"It's all right," the Bishop replies. "I know her real name."

Looking baffled, Adi nods, her lips sealed tight.

"We have a gift for you, Adrastos," the Bishop says. "One granted by Ashen here."

"A gift?"

The Bishop pulls his eyes to the sky, slipping his finger along his forearm to activate his communication device.

"We're ready," he says. "Are you?"

"Coming down," a voice on the other end says.

Seconds later, a drone—an Air-Wing, like the one that brought Finn and me to New York—begins to descend toward us. When it's come in for a soft landing at the park's center, the Bishop strides toward it, telling us to follow him.

Adi shoots me a look, as if she can't quite tell if this is real or a dream, and all I can think is *I understand perfectly, my friend.*

A woman and a man, both dressed in what look like lab coats, push open the Air-Wing's hatch from the inside to reveal a teenage girl, who rises slowly to her feet. Her hair hangs limp around her face and she looks a little disoriented, but her cheeks are rosy, and when her eyes lock on Adi, she smiles and tries to make a sound.

I watch Adi as she cups her hands over her mouth, tears forming in her eyes. Cillian puts an arm around her, pulling her close. Adi turns to me, speechless, before finally managing to say, "You really did this?"

I nod, smiling at her. "The Bishop did. He said she's been ill. They've been looking after her. Adi—I know it's hard to believe, but their medical team is amazing. Your sister has been in really good hands."

There's sudden movement to my right, and I realize with a slight shock that the camera crew has begun filming now—one camera focused on the Bishop and me, the other on Adi as one of the medics approaches her and says, "It's all right. You can come see your sister."

Adi leaps over to the drone as her sister climbs out slowly.

"Stella," she cries, her voice breaking. "I…I can't believe it."

Tears well in my own eyes to see the two siblings embrace after such a long separation. Adi is weeping, while Stella looks disoriented and unsteady on her feet, like a newborn deer. Her muscles look atrophied, her body weak. But she manages a smile, and as Adi squeezes her, I hear her whisper her sister's name.

Cillian stands back and watches the two of them. He's not wearing a Holo-Veil now, and his eyes, too, are wet with tears.

Adi turns my way, her arm around her sister, and says, "I genuinely don't know how you did this. I never thought…"

"I…" I begin to reply, suddenly acutely aware of the cameras fixed on my face. *He wants me to turn it into a moment, I know. To make him shine.*

And honestly, he deserves it for the happiness he's brought Adi and Stella today.

"I asked the Bishop," I say, my voice clear and strong. "He made a promise that he would find a way to bring her to you, and he came through."

This is why I'm here, after all. To show the world the Bishop is a reformed man, one whose interest lies only in helping humankind.

As if on cue, he steps toward us. "I'm sorry, Adi, that you two were separated for so long. Your sister was ill and we had to keep her comatose in order to keep her alive. But she's home to stay now." He gestures around us, guiding the cameras to focus on the construction vehicles working relentlessly to clear rubble and to begin the rebuilding of Brooklyn, which, thanks to their efforts, may never be called *Broken* again.

The Bishop then gestures the camera crew to focus on him as he moves to stand next to Adi and Stella. Looking directly into the lens, he says, "You have my promise, New York, that every Chosen inside the Behemoth will be returned to their families. We thank you for the sacrifice you made when you allowed us to bring them to that place. You cannot possibly know our gratitude. By now, you know we have been working on a series of top-secret projects. I am here today to tell you our work is near completion, and it is time that families be reunited. Let the chasm between us diminish and fade to nothing. We are all equal. We are all valuable. And your beloved family members have done more for the future of our world than you can know."

Easing over to stand beside me, he puts an arm around me and says, "This is Ashen Spencer. The Crimson Dreg. A symbol of rebellion, of triumph. Of good. She and I are working together to restore New York's former glory, to bridge the divide between Dreg and Wealthy." He turns to me. "What do you say, Ashen?"

"I...that's right," I reply, forcing a smile as I realize what he's asking of me. "I promise that as long as I live, I will keep fighting for the rights of Dregs, and of all people. I have seen some of what the Bishop is doing inside the Behemoth, and I can tell you, it's a...miracle. With his help, we can end suffering. We can end torment and pain. The Bishop has vowed that there will be no more fighting, no more Hangings. No more reason for Dregs to fear him or the Directorate. And I have many reasons to believe him—reasons I will show you over the next days."

I focus my eyes on the camera lens. "To my friends and family in the Arc, we will be home soon. We're bringing new technology, new medicine. We're going to change the world, and I can't wait to tell you about it."

The Bishop smiles and signals the crew to shut off the cameras for now.

"That was perfect," he tells me, taking me aside. "We'll film a little each day. When we're done—and when Finn has finished his current project, I will put you two—and his brother—on a drone myself, and send you back out west."

"Really?" I ask. My voice sounds like that of a child, high-pitched and thrilled.

"Really. Now, feel free to wander around Brooklyn some more. My guards will keep an eye on you, so you don't have to worry about a thing. I have a meeting a few blocks away, but I will find you at Adi's. If it's all right with you, I'll have Finn brought to the city, and we'll spend the night at the Palace. I could use a change of scenery."

Spend the night, I think. *With Finn. Outside the Behemoth?*

This day is turning out to be one of the best ever.

I begin my Brooklyn visit by walking Adi, Stella, and Cillian back to their house. Their street, like the one we were just on, is crawling with vehicles that are already working on repairing the broken façades of the brownstones that line either side.

Adi and Stella barely say a word as we make the journey, and it seems that Adi is struggling just to keep her sister from collapsing on the sidewalk. Occasionally, Cillian offers to help, but Adi seems more than a little reluctant to let go of her sister.

"It's fine," she says, a smile on her face that nothing could alter. "Really. It's all good."

When we get to their place, though, she finally lets Cillian help get Stella to the second floor, where they settle her into a bedroom.

"Thank you," Stella says, looking at them both. "I'm so tired…"

"Of course you are," Adi says, offering her a glass of water.

But Stella shakes her head. "I just need to rest for a little bit," she says with a weak smile. "I'll be all right."

"Let me know if you need anything at all, okay?"

"Of course."

Stella's voice is still thin and strained, but it seems to be coming back to her slowly.

When Adi has shut the door, we head down to the kitchen to sit at the table, where all three of us breathe a deep sigh.

"I really can't believe you managed all this," Adi says. "Not just Stella, but the construction, the truce…the Bishop seems like a new man."

"I think he's just realized you catch more flies with honey than with vinegar," I tell her with a laugh.

"Tell that to every Dictator and authoritarian figure who's ever lived," Adi replies with a roll of her eyes. "The Bishop's never been one for a light touch. I figured he'd kill us all before his time was over."

"Tyrants never last, though," Cillian protests. "They instill fear in people, sure. But that fear turns to hatred. The Bishop has figured out that if he can gain trust and affection, he'll survive longer."

"Something tells me he'll survive plenty long enough," I reply with a snicker. I stop short of telling them about the Bishop's secret project, though. I'll leave that revelation for him. The world will be stunned, not to mention immeasurably grateful when they learn what he's about to give them.

Immortality.

Or, at the very least, long, healthy lives.

I wonder with a twitching smile what Illian and Kurt will think when they see the broadcast—if they haven't already. At the very least, it will make for a good story to tell when we see them.

But it's not Illian and Kurt who matter most. It's Kel. He's the one I most want to talk to, to hug, to tell about our strange, unexpected journey here. I can't wait to see the grin on his face when we return with his friend Merit.

I let out a quiet, contented sigh. Things here haven't exactly been easy—I've been stabbed, terrified, manipulated, confused out of my wits, and more. But somehow, my time in New York has gone far more smoothly than I could ever have hoped for.

I tell myself it can't last, that I can't possibly expect my life to be easy from here on in. But with the Duchess locked away inside the Behemoth, Adi's sister returned to her, and a voyage home so close at hand, it's hard not to be excited.

37

DREAMS

ONE OF THE Bishop's drivers shows up at Adi's place a few hours after my arrival. I say goodbye to my friends, though it's difficult to leave when Adi keeps thanking me and giving me hug after hug for what I did for Stella.

With a laugh, I wave a final farewell and step into the driver's silver vehicle.

When we've driven back over the bridge, made our way through security, and entered the Palace's foyer, Naeva comes over to greet me with a smile on her face.

She looks more engaged than she has the last few times I've laid eyes on her, and I take her aside when the driver heads off to summon the Bishop on some sort of intercom device.

"How is everything going?" I ask. "Are you okay?"

"I'm fine," Naeva replies, smiling. "Why wouldn't I be?"

"It's just…" I glance over to make sure the driver is still occupied. "When we spoke that first night, you sounded like you had some kind of plan. You said something about Finn and me being the pieces you needed."

"Pieces?" she says, cocking her head to the side like a curious puppy. For a moment, she stares at me blankly as if she has no recollection of what I'm talking about. "Oh. I remember now. I warned you the Bishop was coming for you." She lets out a funny little laugh and adds, "He didn't like it much when he found out I was lying to him about who I was."

"So he knows," I whisper.

I don't suppose it matters much. He knows I'm Ashen, after all, and he's found a way to work with me. He's probably found a way to work with Naeva, too.

"Of course he knows," she says with a mysterious smile. "There's no hiding anything from that man. He knows every cell in my body. He knows how my fingers move..." As she's speaking, she holds her hands out in front of her face and wiggles her fingers in a bizarre display, staring at them like they're mesmerizing her.

I pull back and narrow my eyes at her. *That was...a really weird thing to say.*

In fact, *everything* Naeva has said to me since that very first night has been strange. I thought her behavior with the Bishop was an act, put on to convince him that she was an unthreatening bubble-head. But now, whispering with me, she seems equally devoid of her former conspiratorial nature.

It's almost like she's had a personality transplant.

"He wasn't angry when he found out who you are?" I ask tentatively.

"Oh, he was definitely angry," Naeva says with a strange laugh, grabbing my arm. "So, so angry. But he's all right now."

I wait for her to tell me more. After all, the man found out she infiltrated his life, his home, his top-secret work. He has murdered people for far less.

But no explanation comes. Instead, Naeva says, "Well, bye!" and wanders over to the elevator. A second later, the door opens, and as if on cue, the Bishop steps out.

Taking his arm in hers, Naeva moans, "I'm tired. Can we head up to the suite now?"

"Of course, my love," he replies, kissing her on the forehead. He shoots a look my way that I can't entirely read. He smiles and says, "Ashen—Finn will be here in a moment. There's a surprise waiting for you both on the fortieth level. I think you'll enjoy it. Consider it a thank you for all that you're doing for our world."

When he and Naeva have left, I hear a sound behind me. Turning to look, I see Finn striding toward me in a pair of jeans and a t-shirt, a grin on his lips.

He takes me in his arms, kissing the crown of my head. "It's nice to be out of that place, isn't it?" he asks.

"So nice. But even nicer to have you here with me."

"Mm-hmm," he says with a little yawn.

"Tired?" I ask, laughing.

"Yes. But weirdly happy. There's something about this city, Ash. It's like...every time I even start getting stressed out or worried, the feeling just fades away like there was never anything wrong in the first place."

He's right. A minute ago, my brow was furrowed, my mind racing with confusion and fear about Naeva's erratic behavior.

But now, it feels like nothing but a brief overreaction on my part. After all, she didn't say the Bishop had done anything bad to her. In fact, she seemed quite content with their relationship.

Finn's right. This place—whether it's the city or something else—has a calming effect like nothing else I've ever encountered.

"I'd forgotten what it feels like to be happy." I pull back to look into Finn's eyes. "This *isn't* a dream, right? Everything is actually getting better. The world is stabilizing. The Directorate has lost most of its power."

"And my mother is holed up inside the most secure building in the world, while you and I can move around New York freely," Finn says with a snicker. "If that's not justice, I'm not sure what is."

I smile, but don't say what I'm really thinking—that the Duchess deserves a far more severe punishment than time in a luxurious residence inside the Behemoth.

Finn hinted to me once that he would kill her himself one day. But I'm not sure the same desire surges through his bloodstream anymore, and I can't say I blame him. She's Merit's mother too, after all.

Besides, he's right—she's locked up without access to other Directorate members. If the Bishop manages to keep her in the Behemoth, she won't be able to hurt anyone ever again.

"Even if this is a dream," I say with another sigh, "it's a good one, and I can't say I have any desire to wake up. In the meantime, the Bishop said there's a surprise waiting for us on the fortieth floor. I think we should go see what it is."

"Agreed," Finn says, putting an arm around me. "Maybe we can prolong the dream a little."

When we reach the fortieth floor, we're both surprised to be greeted by a woman in a white uniform. On her face is the biggest, brightest smile I've ever seen.

She says, "Welcome to Wonderland!" before turning and guiding us down the hall away from the elevator.

The corridor is empty, its walls white and clean. It's devoid of doors except for one at the far end, a hundred or so feet away.

When we reach the door, the woman pulls it open for us, gesturing for us to enter. And when we do, we find ourselves inside a blindingly white room that sends my stomach into a nervous state. It looks too pristine, too much like the Arc's impeccable interior.

I only feel a little reassured when the woman hands me an envelope with our names on it and says, "From the Bishop."

With Finn watching over my shoulder, I open the envelope only to find a note inside that says:

> *This room will shift into the place of your dreams.*
> *All you need to do is ask.*

I look at Finn, puzzled. "Do you know what this means?"

"It sounds a little like we're in a virtual reality chamber?" he says, throwing the woman a look.

"Actually, it's what the Bishop calls *Enhanced Illusion*," she says in a friendly voice. You will find your every sense stimulated and heightened as you make your way to your destination: Sight, sound, smell, even taste and touch will all seem one-hundred percent realistic. It's an absolute wonder, trust me. You'll feel like you're entirely immersed in whatever locale you might select. All you need to do is tell me where you want to go, and I will send you there."

"I have no idea where I'd like to go." I say, glancing at Finn. For so long, we've found ourselves trapped in one place after the other. The idea of this much freedom is overwhelming.

"Do you have any thoughts?" I ask. "Any dream spots on your wish list?"

He shakes his head. "I want this to be your choice," he tells me. "Ash, you deserve the world. I'll happily accompany you anywhere you'd like to go, even if it's the moon."

"In that case..." Smiling, I turn back to the woman and say, "You know what? We'd like to be on a sandy beach—maybe something with a pretty cottage and long, swaying grass. I want to smell the ocean. Taste salt on the air, feel sand between my toes."

She smiles when she says, "Take off your shoes and socks, then."

I let out a laugh and obey her command, and Finn does the same. Suddenly holding a device in her hand, the woman presses a series of buttons and, just as she promised, the room around us transforms completely. The white walls disappear in favor of blue sky and rolling dunes; the floor turns to white, cool sand that eases its way between my toes, neither too warm nor too cold.

I reach down, pick up a handful, and let it filter between my fingers, stunned at how convinced my mind is that we're standing outside right now.

I spin around to see a white wooden cottage behind us, its shutters bright cobalt blue. It has large windows, a white-washed deck, and best of all, a hot tub.

A plate of what looks like cheese and fruit sits on a nearby picnic table, and I wander over and pick up a slice of pear, slipping it in my mouth.

"How..." I begin as I taste its sweetness, but I shake my head. "You know what? I don't care. It's amazing."

I turn to thank the woman, but she's gone, disappeared into thin air.

"Finn!" I yell, spinning around, my arms outstretched. "Isn't this incredible?"

"It is," he agrees. He grabs hold of me, pulls me close, and kisses me deeply. "And you deserve it, like I said."

"You do, too," I tell him, smiling against his lips as I kiss him again.

I pull away to look at the endless ocean, its white waves cresting and crashing against the beach. Unable to resist, I leap over to feel the water on my toes. It's cold but delicious, and I can't help but laugh with delight as a sudden shocking wave slams into my legs, soaking me to my knees.

"I always dreamed of having a little place near the ocean," I confess, turning back to Finn. "A second home of sorts. I suppose it came from living in the mountains. I love them—but I always wanted something special."

"Someday," Finn promises, "I'll see to it that you get your wish. If it's the only thing I ever accomplish in my life, I'll make sure of it."

I kiss him again, this time out of pure bliss and adoration, then I look around. "I just wish there were a picnic blanket for us to lie on…"

A split-second later, a large, cozy-looking plaid blanket appears about ten feet from where we're standing. I bounce over giddily and lie down, my eyes fixed on what I know is only the illusion of a cloudless sky. I can feel the sun's heat on my skin, the absolute perfection of the temperature as a refreshing breeze sweeps over me.

Finn comes and lies down next to me on his side, his face in his hand.

"What are you thinking about?" I ask him, giggling like I haven't done in years.

"You," he says. "And me. And how soon, we'll finish our

work here, and leave this place behind, and walk into a world that's better because we helped make it that way."

As I lie back, I say, "That sounds amazing."

He climbs over me. His lips are on mine then, tasting me hungrily before slipping over to my cheek, my jaw, my neck. As intensely heightened as my senses are right now, nothing is more pleasurable, more wonderful than the feeling of need, of desire, of pure bliss that comes with his touch.

"Let's go for a swim," he says, his lips skimming my shoulder. "Like the old days in the Grotto."

"The Grotto," I repeat. I'd almost forgotten our secret meeting place in the Arc, and the one space where he and I could be completely isolated from the loathsome eyes of the Directorate.

Until his mother ruined it for us, of course.

"How can we swim?" I ask. "It's not really the ocean."

"Great! We won't drown."

Finn leaps to his feet and starts pulling off his clothes, starting with his shirt.

I've seen him shirtless before, of course. But the tautness of his abdomen and the corded muscles in his arms still manage to take my breath away and send a frisson of euphoria shuddering through me.

His pants are next, then his socks. He leaves on his boxer shorts as he stands with his hands on his hips, waiting for me to follow suit.

"Fine," I laugh, pulling my shirt over my head before yanking my jeans off, still worried after all this time that his perfect eyes might find a way to focus on all my flaws.

"Race you!" I leap toward the water, jumping in as a waist-high wave crashes against me. Within seconds, Finn has caught up and taken me in his arms. He pulls me into deeper water which may not be real, but feels exactly as I imagine the ocean *should* feel.

I taste salt on my lips as I wrap my legs around his waist and kiss him with a need deeper than any ocean in the world. Wishing we could remain forever in this place, in this moment.

With a sigh of contentment, I hold on tight to Finn and make myself a promise: *When all this is over, I'm going to make sure every single day feels like this one.*

38

PROMISE

I WAKE UP SOMETIME LATER, unsure how much time has passed.

Finn is asleep. His face is peaceful, his breath coming in gentle, irresistible waves. We're still on our blanket, the sun rising in the distance.

Last night was a gift. A taste of a life I've only ever dreamed of. It's hard not to hope that one day, it will become our reality. Everything is falling into place, after all. Finn has only to finish his project, and we can begin our new lives for real.

Except, that is, for one small, persistent problem:

The Duchess.

As much as I would love to forget she exists, I can't. She is the reason my mother is dead. She killed Peric's parents and then murdered him viciously.

Not to mention the countless others whose lives she's ended.

I will never feel truly free or happy as long as she continues to live a life devoid of consequence.

It's with that thought in mind that I rise to my feet and stretch my arms tensely over my head. As if I've destroyed our beautiful illusion with my dark thoughts, the sandy beach disintegrates below my feet. Finn, sensing something has changed, wakes drowsily from his slumber as the space around us reverts to the bright, white room we were in yesterday.

A door opens some distance away, yanking us both abruptly back to reality.

The Bishop walks in, dressed as always in a perfectly fitted suit. As he approaches us, he runs a hand through his hair, a bright, friendly smile on his lips. I slip self-consciously behind Finn. I haven't even put my clothes back on yet, and this intrusion seems oddly aggressive.

"I hope I'm not interrupting," the Bishop tells us as Finn reaches down to grab his clothes off the ground. "I left you two in here as long as I could. But I know Mr. Davenport must be eager to get to the lab and continue his work. After all, you two must be chomping at the bit to get back home."

"Yes, of course," Finn says. "I *do* want to get to work—we're so close to a breakthrough that it would be crazy to stop now."

"Wonderful," the Bishop replies. "I already have the drone prepared to take us up to the Behemoth."

When I look disappointed, he asks what's wrong.

"I was just hoping to check in on Adi one more time, to see how Stella is settling in."

"I'm sorry, but that will have to wait a few days," he replies with a sympathetic tilt of his head. "Today, Ashen, I need you to accompany me to the Medical Wing with the camera crew. We need more video footage, if that's all right. More evidence of our work here to show our allies across the country."

I nod, remembering our agreement.

"Also," the Bishop says, "I have news for you both—news that I think you'll like."

"What's that?" Finn asks.

"I'll be sending you home sooner than expected. In a matter of days, not weeks."

"But I thought we had a lot more work to do. The research—"

"The research is important, and I appreciate everything you've contributed. But I've been thinking about it, and it's not fair of me to keep you here. You are not prisoners, and those you left at home must be eager to have you both back. So it's only right that you return." He lays a hand on Finn's shoulder and adds, "I want you to continue your work—*our* work—in the Arc. You will be my top researcher there. My most trusted scientist."

As I pull my clothes on, I glance up at Finn's smiling face. He looks prouder of himself than I've ever seen him.

I should be happy too, I tell myself. *We're really going home. I'll be able to see Kel and Illian, Kurt, Kyra.*

Still, something is unsettling me.

At first, I can't put my finger on it. But after a moment, I realize what it is.

If our lives keep improving like this, I think, *there will be nowhere to go but down.*

Finn and I spend the rest of the day inside the Behemoth. He remains in the Science Wing, learning the Bishop's secrets, while I tour the Medical Wing with the camera crew. The Bishop introduces me to new patients, including a young

Dreg girl with the face of a doll who has been told she has a matter of weeks to live. A man with a terminal illness that has caused his body to weaken to the point where it can't support itself. He sits hunched over in a wheelchair, his neck craning with effort to look at us.

I find myself speaking to the camera's lens once again, explaining what I've seen and what the viewers will witness within a matter of a day or two. "Incredible recoveries by people who would never have survived anywhere else," I tell them.

The Bishop, the camera crew, and I visit the same patients the following morning to find that the young girl is bouncing around her room like she's been given a second chance at life. The man who was slumped over in his wheelchair only twenty-four hours earlier is now walking, his shoulders back, his chest broad and powerful.

Once or twice over the next few days, I break down in tears as I speak to the recovering patients, their faces filled with indescribable joy.

As he vowed he would, the Bishop allows me to see Finn every day. Sometimes only briefly, sometimes for several hours at a time, which we spend in my residence. For once, I'm grateful to be isolated from the rest of the Behemoth's population. In my apartment, we have total privacy. Finn and I share the most intimate moments of our relationship so far, our bodies a tangle under the sheets as his lips explore me, and I savor every inch of him.

We whisper shared thoughts of our secret dreams for the future...which now seem like they could actually come true.

As I lie with him, I remind myself how luxurious it is not to feel terrified that he'll be ripped away from me.

We have time now. We have a life to look forward to.

The one thing Finn *doesn't* share with me in our time together are the details of his work in the Bishop's labs.

"It's top-secret," he says sheepishly. "But you already know most of it. I can tell you I'm beginning to understand how the Bishop's scientists are able to create entire new cellular structures for the people who are ill. It's pretty astounding. There are still a few things slightly beyond my grasp, but I'm sure they'll let me in on them sometime soon."

I stroke a hand over his cheek, prouder than I can say as I look into the eyes of the man he's become. Finn is helping to save lives, to grant people a new chance at a full, rewarding existence.

"I love you," I tell him. "So much that it almost hurts."

"I love you back just as much," he says. "And I can't wait to get home with you and finally start living."

On the seventh day since filming began, the Bishop shows up at my residence as usual, and I remind him of his promise to let me venture into Brooklyn for a quick visit.

"A very good idea," he says with a smile. "But first, there's something I need to talk to you about."

"What is it?" I ask nervously as I pour him a cup of coffee.

He takes off his jacket and drapes it over the back of a chair before loosening his collar and fixing me in his gaze. Standing before me like this, he looks like a model from a high-end fashion magazine, and I find my cheeks heating. I pull my eyes away, a little irritated that he always manages to have this effect on me in spite of my unwavering feelings for

Finn. After all this time, it still feels like this man has a hold on me that's inexplicable and a little frightening.

I told him once that he reminded me of a wizard. And if I actually believed in such things, I'd be convinced he really *was* a magic-user who had cast a spell on me and every other person he ever came across. *But,* I remind myself, *spells aren't real.* They're mere fantasy, inventions crafted by creative minds.

What the Bishop does to me is far more insidious than magic, anyhow. It's almost palpable, and most *definitely* real.

"You and Finn have been very kind to me since your arrival," he says. "Helpful, obliging, trusting, even—which I realize must be very difficult, given all that's happened to you both over the course of your lives."

It's a perceptive thing to say, and I'm surprised at how much I appreciate his words. "It isn't the easiest thing to trust people in positions of power," I confess. "But you've given us a lot of reasons to trust you. What you're doing in the Behemoth is nothing short of incredible, and I know Finn is proud to be part of it, as am I."

"I'm glad," he says. "You can both be happy to know you'll go down in history for your various contributions."

I take a sip of the café mocha I made before his arrival. "We're not doing it for personal glory, you know. We're doing it because we both want to make the world a better place."

"Of course you do," he says, seating himself next to me, close enough that our knees are nearly touching. "Which brings me to your pending departure. I know how eager you are to get home and see your brother, and it would not do for me to keep you here. But I also know there's a loose thread hanging about—one that must be irksome."

"Oh?" I say, tension building inside me as I take another sip. "What thread is that?"

The Bishop smirks, his dark eyes seeming to pierce the more delicate layers of my skin. "Come on, Ashen. You know full well I'm talking about the Duchess."

So there it is. The bitchy elephant in the room.

When I say nothing, he continues. "You want to see justice done—and in your mind, justice is not being served if she remains in this place."

I put my cup down, tightening. I've thought almost those exact same words, and it's eerie to hear them come out of his mouth.

"I will admit," he continues, "if she were useful, I would insist on keeping her here. But she's nothing more than an overly ambitious Directorate member who would happily kill me if it meant gaining one extra ounce of power for herself. She is of no interest to me, and I am the first to acknowledge that the world would be better without her in it."

I take another swig of my drink, curious to see where this is going.

"I vow to you now," the Bishop continues, "that I will hand Merit over to Finn before you leave. But I will also give you the Duchess."

At that, I nearly spit my coffee all over the counter. "Really? You're serious?"

He nods. "You, of all people, should have the honor of doling out her punishment, don't you think? She has wronged you so many times, Ashen, and I dislike her intensely for it. So she will be my gift to you."

It's all I can do not to throw my arms around him and squeeze. "Thank you," I gush. "I can't tell you how grateful I am for this."

I don't say it out loud, but I'm also relieved. If we can get the Duchess back to the Arc, then Illian and Kurt can decide what to do with her. As much as I fantasize regularly about choking the life out of her, right now I'm not entirely sure I could do that to Merit.

I tell myself I will be satisfied so long as I know she'll finally face the punishment she deserves. And if that punishment is being locked in the Arc's Hold for the rest of her days, I won't complain.

"Don't thank me yet," the Bishop says, a hint of mischief in his tone. "You may find her a handful."

"I can deal with her."

"Yes. I'm sure you can."

When I've finished my coffee, I ask, "Is it really okay with you if I go to see Adi today?"

"Absolutely. I'll summon a driver right away to bring you down to the city." As he's speaking, he flicks a finger over his wrist. "There. Done. He'll be here in a minute. I only ask that you come back by this evening."

"Of course," I tell him. "I won't be long. I just want to see how Stella is settling in."

"I'm sure Adi will have a good deal to talk to you about," the Bishop says, stirring his coffee slowly. "I must admit, I'm quite curious to hear what she has to say."

Something in his tone slightly disconcerts me. It's almost as if he already *knows* what Adi will tell me. But I remind myself that he can't see into the future any more than I can.

When the alert sounds to tell us the driver has arrived, I push myself to my feet and say, "I'll head out, then. I'll see you later."

"Yes, you will," the Bishop says, nodding toward the Transport doors. "Say hello to Stella for me, would you?"

"Of course," I reply with a tense smile.

As I step onto the Transport to greet the driver, a chill runs its way along my skin. With a shudder, I realize that despite his recent kindness, and despite all our conversations since my arrival in New York...

I don't know the Bishop at all.

ADI

WITHIN FIFTEEN MINUTES, the driver, a middle-aged man with salt and pepper hair, is steering us at ground level through Manhattan's streets.

"I'll have you to your friends soon, I promise," he tells me. "But the Bishop has asked that we take the scenic route. He said he wants you to see the recent progress on the reconstruction efforts in Brooklyn."

"Oh," I reply. "Sure. Sounds good."

We cross over Brooklyn Bridge, which is now only monitored by a few patrolling guards on each end. None of them carries the high-powered rifles I've grown used to seeing, and when we drive by, they greet us with waves rather than threatening glares.

"Now this is what I call progress," I say quietly as I glance over to see a mass of Dregs wandering Brooklyn's streets without fear.

"Shops are fully operational again," the driver says. "And restaurants. People are able to work again. The Bishop has opened up a whole new world on this side of the river."

My cynical thought is *The Bishop simply allowed the reemergence of a world that should have never been destroyed in the first place,* but I refrain from pointing it out. The important thing is that the Bishop is making amends. The city is flourishing. People who were trapped inside the Moth are slowly being returned to their families.

To ask for much more would be not only selfish, but foolish.

As we approach Adi's street, I'm pleased to see how much progress has been made on the façades of most of the devastated brownstones in the area. The houses have been returned to their former glory, beautiful and inviting once again.

Finally, after a half hour of exploration, the driver pulls up in front of Adi's place. "She should be inside waiting," he tells me, opening my door remotely. "I believe she's been notified of your arrival. I'll stay here and await your return."

"Thank you," I reply as I step out of the vehicle.

When I knock on the front door, it's Cillian who answers. He looks pleased to see me, but his expression quickly sinks into something less than joyful.

"Nice to see you, Ashen," he says with a half-smile.

"Is everything okay?" I ask as I step inside.

"It's fine. But..."

"But?"

"Look, I'll let Adi talk to you about it. It's not really my place to say anything."

"Okay," I reply slowly as we head toward the back of the house, where we find Adi sitting in the kitchen alone, a cup of tea clutched in her hands. She stands to greet me, a sad smile on her lips.

I look around, confused.

"Where's Stella?" I ask.

"Upstairs in her room," she says. "She…"

She glances at Cillian, who immediately says, "I'll leave you two alone. I'll be in my room if you need me." With that, he takes off back down the hallway, and Adi and I seat ourselves at the table.

"What's going on?" I say quietly. "Is everything all right?"

"It's fine," Adi replies, but when her gaze moves to the window, I see her struggling as she tries to gather her thoughts. "Brooklyn is bustling. Everything is going great—a lot of the Dregs who were crashing in this house have left to look for their own places. It's just…"

"Just what?"

She grinds her jaw for a moment before inhaling. "There's something…*off* about Stella."

"Off?"

Adi nods. "It's hard to describe. She seems like herself, but totally different. Does that make any sense at all?"

"Sure. But of course she's different. Adi, she was in a coma for years. Her muscles have atrophied, and her mind is probably a little addled, too. Who knows what was happening with her brain that whole time?"

"Yeah," she replies, nodding. "But…it's not just that. She just feels…I don't know, *wrong*." She hesitates for a moment then adds, "You have a brother, right?"

"Yes. Kel. Why?"

"Do you think you would know if something was wrong with him? Like, if he changed into someone you didn't quite recognize?"

I ponder the question for only a moment before replying, "Sure I would. But I'd also *expect* him to be distracted or confused if he was in a coma for years. I'm no medical expert, but I can imagine that changes a person, at least for a while."

"I know, I know. I guess I need to be patient. It's just..." She looks at me, tears in her eyes. "Stella used to be so much fun. She had this amazing sense of humor, always joking and goofing around. She was my fantastic sister. Now, it's almost like she's awake but still in a coma. Like her personality is still asleep."

I want so badly to reassure her. To tell her it's normal, that it's to be expected. But as I stare into Adi's eyes, I can sense a deep fear lurking somewhere behind them.

She's right about one thing: no one knows us as our siblings do. We grow up with them, witness their best and their worst moments. We see them unfiltered, warts and all as they laugh, cry, scream.

Adi is probably right to trust her instincts.

"It's possible that Stella changed while she was in the Moth because of her illness," I say. "She's been through a terrible trauma, after all. Give her time. That's all you can do. Give her a chance to come back fully to you." I gesture toward the window when I add, "All the work that's going on out there takes time, too. The buildings were damaged in all the fighting—but they *will* return to their former glory. So will Stella, Adi. She's in there somewhere. I know it's hard, but you probably just need to hang in there."

She nods again, but doesn't look convinced.

Glancing around, she brings her eyes to focus on mine, reaches for my hand, and says, "Ashen...there's something you need to know. Something I should have told you the first time we met. It's been eating away at me ever since that day. Ever since I watched you head over the bridge."

"What is it?" I ask, my heart in my throat, my hand tight under her touch.

What could possibly be bothering her this much? She and

Cillian were kind to me. They helped me, even when I insisted I couldn't help them in return.

"Cillian and I lied to you," she says. "Look—I feel like I need to come clean after everything you've done for me. Stella may not be herself, but you brought her home to me. That's worth more than you can ever know. So please trust me when I tell you we never wanted any part of this. We never—"

She stops speaking, and we both freeze.

Somewhere close by—far too close—I hear the awful, familiar buzz of a Scorp.

It reveals itself in the kitchen window a few seconds later, and Adi and I sit stock-still, our stares locked on the metal creature with the glowing eyes.

The Scorp disappears a few seconds later, flying off into the distance.

"I didn't think they were still in service," I say, slightly irritated at the Bishop for failing to mention they were still monitoring Dreg residences.

"Neither did I," Adi says under her breath. She pulls her hand away from mine and stands up. "I think you should go," she says. "For your own sake."

"But you were about to tell me something," I protest. "You said you lied to me?"

She shakes her head. "It was nothing. I...I'm sorry I misled you on that first day. I'm sorry I used a man's voice to play with your mind. That's all."

I stare at her, puzzled as to why such a small thing should amount to some great weight that's been perched on her shoulders all this time. But I simply nod and say, "It's okay, but thanks, I guess."

She escorts me to the front door, where I give her a quick

hug. "Don't worry," I say. "Stella will be fine. Just look after yourself and Cillian, okay?"

She nods once, then without another word, steps back inside and closes the door.

I glance up at the sky to see Atticus soaring some distance above me before he disappears from view.

Thank you for watching over me. I miss you, Rys.

When I see Finn that evening, I want to tell him about the odd conversation Adi and I had, about the Scorp's sudden appearance. But he seems so excited about the project he's been working on, so upbeat, that I don't have the heart to bring anything negative into our conversation.

"Can you tell me anything about it?" I ask him.

He shakes his head. "No more than I have already. But Ash…"

He has a mischievous glint in his eye as he takes me in his arms and spins me around, then kisses me.

"What?" I laugh. "What's going on?"

"I officially finished my part of the project today. I'm done. That means we can go home tomorrow."

"What?" I almost squeal. "Are you serious?"

"Dead serious. You and I—and Merit, of course—are getting into an Air-Wing early in the morning and flying back to the Arc."

"That's amazing news!" I tell him. I wince slightly when I realize I haven't yet discussed one small detail with him—we're supposed to be bringing his mother back with us as our prisoner. I'm still not sure how to broach the subject, and make a note to discuss it with the Bishop first. I may even ask him to send her with a couple of armed guards to keep her from trying to murder Finn and me during the flight.

But right now, my focus is on Finn and the fact that by this time tomorrow, I'll be able to hug my little brother for the first time in weeks.

"I need to pack up a few things," Finn tells me. "And I promised Merit we'd play some games tonight in my parents' residence. I also need to break the news to them. They know I'm planning to take him with me, and they also know there's no way in hell they can stop me, but it's probably going to get intense. Is it okay if I see you in the morning? I'd invite you, but…"

"But your mother thinks I'm the spawn of Satan and hates me with the fiery passion of ten-thousand scorching suns?" I laugh. "Yeah, I'm fine here alone. I'm just looking forward…"

I stop talking, shake my head, and laugh.

"What is it?" Finn asks.

"I was going to say I'm looking forward to leaving this place. But the truth is, I've been happy here, at least for the most part." I feel it again, the infiltration of quiet joy settling into my mind, my body. A sensation of complete, blissful peace.

When we say goodnight a few minutes later, I watch him slip inside the Transport that will take him to his family's home inside the Behemoth.

As alone as I am, isolated from the world, my heart is full…and I am happy.

40

STORAGE

AROUND EIGHT O'CLOCK THAT NIGHT, an alert sounds in my residence, telling me someone has arrived.

I rise from the spot on the couch where I've been perusing an old fashion magazine and stride over to see if Finn has returned to regale me with tales of his parents' reactions.

But as I approach the doors and they slide open, I see that it's the Bishop who's arrived. He steps into my residence, his eyes glinting in the soft light of the overhead bulbs.

"Oh," I say. "I wasn't expecting to see you."

"I can see that," he replies with a laugh as he takes in my expression. "I assume Finn has told you the good news?"

"That he's finished his work here," I reply with a smile.

"Yes," he says, brushing his hair away from his cheekbone. "I was wondering if you might care to take one last look around the Behemoth to see what he's been helping me with."

A jolt of excitement surges through me. "Really? I thought you were keeping it secret."

He steps forward and takes my chin in hand more aggressively than usual. It's almost a possessive clench, and I wince slightly under his touch.

"Oh, I'd love to make an exception for you, Ashen. You've been so patient with us, after all. Besides, if I wait until you're back in the Arc, how can I show you the parts of this extraordinary place you haven't yet seen?"

I feel myself tensing under his touch, but as he stares into my eyes, my entire body relaxes. The balm that is his presence has once again worked its magic.

"I'd love to see," I tell him as he pulls away, smiling. But the moment I'm free of him, a feeling of foreboding hits, and I find myself hesitating. "M—maybe we should wait until Finn is here. We could go tomorrow morning, before we leave."

The Bishop looks momentarily angry, but he forces a smile onto his lips. "The Air-Wing will depart first thing in the morning," he says. "There won't be time. Besides, Finn has already seen everything he needs to."

Something is telling me to tell him I can't go. To remain inside the residence and wait until morning. But he's right— Finn has already experienced the Behemoth's secrets, and he's only ever been excited about what he's seen. I may as well go for one last tour before I head home.

"Okay," I say, screwing my lips into a smile.

"Good. Come with me, then."

Grabbing a nearby jacket, I follow him into the clear glass Transport, where he tells me to hold on.

"To what?" I ask, but even as I say the words, long, vertical silver handles emerge mysteriously from the glass walls.

"We're about to move fast," the Bishop warns.

I nod, taking hold of one of the handles and bracing myself.

As promised, the Transport shoots down what must be

close to a hundred stories, then makes a sudden stop before altering course to move sideways through the depths of the Behemoth into a darkness even more profound than that of the void where the Blocks are located.

As we hurl at high speed between what look like a random series of onyx cubes, the Bishop tells me we're headed to the Storage Sector.

I immediately picture neatly-stacked piles of Aristocrat furniture, cars, all manner of things, but I can't think why he'd want to show them to me. "What kind of storage?"

"Human," the Bishop says.

I turn to him and laugh, convinced he's joking. "What, like a prison?"

"Not exactly. In prison, the inmates are generally conscious, for one thing."

My hand grasps the handle harder as I stare into his eyes, trying to figure out if he's serious or not.

He clicks his tongue and lets out a low chuckle. "Oh, come on, Ashen. You knew there were thousands of Dregs unaccounted for in this place. Don't look so shocked."

All of a sudden, I wish I hadn't come. I curse myself for not listening to my instincts back in the residence.

Something tells me whatever he's about to show me will crush my soul.

When the Transport finally stops and connects itself to a set of silver doors, the Bishop gives me a final look and says, "Brace yourself. You probably won't like this very much."

I want to ask him to turn us around, to go back to the residence. I want to be anywhere but here.

I don't want to see it. I don't want to know.

Something occurs to me then—something horrifying.

"Does Finn know about this?"

"If you mean *Has he seen it,* the answer is no. But Finn isn't stupid. He has been part of the development of a cellular regeneration program the likes of which the world has never seen. One that samples organic material from thousands upon thousands of individuals. So if he were to put two and two together, he would probably realize one cannot accomplish such a thing without…"

He stops and waits for me to finish the sentence for him.

"Without those thousands of individuals."

"Bingo."

When the doors slide open, I'm greeted by a nightmare.

41

MIRROR, MIRROR

I TAKE one step forward then double over, heaving with nausea. The Bishop reaches for me, but I slap his hand away.

"Don't!" I practically scream as I straighten up and force myself to look out at the space around us.

We're standing on a narrow platform that extends for ten or so feet. We seem to be inside some kind of silo. It's a round, dark, enormous space that instantly coats the marrow of my bones in frost.

Suspended along the perimeter are thousands of objects that look like clear, egg-shaped pods. And inside each pod is a human being floating in some kind of clear liquid.

Their limbs twitch; their eyes are open...but they seem to stare at nothing.

"Impressive, isn't it?" the Bishop asks.

"It's repulsive," I snarl.

To think I once raged against the Directorate for bringing Dregs into the Arc and forcing us to train, to serve them, to battle for our lives.

The Dregs who were brought to the Moth never so much as had that chance.

"Is this where you kept Adi's sister for all that time?" I ask, my voice trembling. "Is this where you kept Stella?"

"Oh, Stella is still here somewhere," the Bishop says casually. When I look at him with confusion, he adds, "The *real* Stella. Not the one currently sitting in your friend Adi's home."

Feeling like I've stumbled into some twisted horror show, I back away, moving toward the Transport. But my hands meet cold steel, the doors sealed tight behind me.

"What do you mean?" I ask.

"My research," he says, "and Finn's, has involved cellular regeneration. The fighting of age, of disease, of any number of ills. But it's so much more than that."

He flicks a hand in the air, drawing a pattern with his index finger. Almost immediately, the platform we're standing on begins to move, descending several stories. There's nothing for me to grab hold of, nothing to steady me, so I push myself down until I'm on the floor, my face buried in my hands.

"I don't understand," I say, my voice shattered. "I don't know where you're taking me. Why…"

"Ashen, you have done more for me than you could ever know. I must say, you're one of the more sincere people I've had the pleasure of meeting in my life. Oh, there was that Ana deception in the beginning, but you're a terrible actor—I'm sure you know that. Even if I hadn't orchestrated the whole thing, I would have seen right through it immediately."

"Orchestrated," I say quietly as the platform continues its downward trajectory.

The Bishop steps over and kneels down next to me.

"When a stolen Air-Wing showed up near New York City many days ago now, the Duchess came to me. She told me she suspected her son was inside. Naturally, I was curious. But all the more so when he turned out to be quite a genius. Then, of course, I discovered there was a second passenger—a young woman. My men managed to sedate her with a dart to the neck, but the Trodden got to her first." He holds his right hand up, palm facing the sky. "I paid Adi a visit while you were still under the effects of the sedative. I made a deal with her that day—one that would eventually lead us to this moment."

"You're lying," I tell him. "She would have told me. She and Cillian…"

I stop myself.

Adi was trying to tell me something when I visited her. Something about a lie. She was on the verge of confessing…

When the Scorp showed up.

"You know I'm telling the truth," the Bishop says. "Deep down in that very sincere Ashen Spencer heart, you know. And if, for even a second, you doubt Adi's ability to lie, consider for a moment what you might do to save your brother."

With his left index finger, he draws a pattern on his right palm, and a holo-screen springs to life in the air above it. The platform we're on slows down, but I hardly notice it as two holographic figures fizzle to life above the Bishop's hand.

I see Adi and Cillian, standing on the front porch of their house in Brooklyn. As Adi speaks, I realize I'm watching a conversation unfold from the Bishop's perspective.

"What are you doing here?" Adi asks. I see fear in her eyes, but something else—something I know all too well: the same awe that everyone feels in this man's presence.

Including Finn.

Including me.

A spell he casts with his face, his eyes, his voice.

"You have something I want," the Bishop says. "Locked in a room in this very house."

"Fine." Adi turns away as though she's about to oblige him by retrieving what the Bishop wants. "I'll get her for you."

Her, I think. *She means me. He came to see her that day...*

"Stop," the Bishop commands, and Adi freezes. He reaches for her, taking her wrist gently, and as if incapable of doing anything else, she turns back to face him. I see her relenting, melting under his touch as I've done myself more than once. "I don't want you to retrieve her," he says. "I want you to earn her trust."

"Why?" Cillian asks, his stance protective. He positions himself in front of Adi as if hoping there's a chance he'll be able to prevent the Bishop's charms from getting to her. "Who is she, anyhow?"

"That is of no consequence to you," the Bishop says coldly. "The less you know about her, the better. As far as you're concerned, she's nothing more than a refugee in this war-torn city."

"If you want her, why not just take her? You know perfectly well we don't have the strength to fight you off. You could make this easier for all of us by just going inside and snatching her away right now."

The Bishop shakes his head. "I need to observe her in her natural habitat," he says, describing me like I'm some species of rodent. "I want to watch her as she learns the power dynamic in this city. I need her to *experience* it as someone briefly occupying your world. I need her to see you as allies, at least for a little while. I want her to see me as a tyrant. I want her to believe she's doing something honorable when she comes to me willingly. Perhaps, if you're very fortunate, she'll even offer to help you with your own plight."

"Plight?" Adi says.

"Your sister," he replies. "The young woman in that house of yours is the only chance you have of ever seeing Stella again. Do you understand me?"

"We understand," Cillian says, taking Adi by the hand.

"Good. When you've earned her trust and shown her a little of your world here, I need you to get her to Manhattan."

"You actually think we can get her across the river?" Adi laughs as she eases closer to Cillian. "Your men would shoot us dead if we came within a hundred feet of the bridge."

"Very true," the Bishop's voice says smoothly. "But you're a clever young woman with a vivid imagination." He hands Adi a small package in plain brown wrapping. "I have every faith that you'll get her to me. But she must believe it was her choice—that it was ultimately her doing."

Adi looks like she's about to protest again, but the Bishop holds up a hand, stopping her.

"Everything you need is in that package," he says. "You can speak freely as you formulate your strategy. Slander me if you like. Tell her I'm the devil himself. It will only make it easier in the end for me to convince her I'm not so very bad."

Adi and Cillian exchange a look, but say nothing. I can see their fear, their confusion, as they try to make sense of the Bishop's plan.

"I have already contacted your friends Trace and Shar," the Bishop tells them. "They know what's at stake, and that any act of disobedience, any betrayal of my plan, will result in death. Shar will equip your guest with any clothing and disguise she needs. Trace knows his task already—you simply need to convince the young woman that she's in need of a tattoo, and he will administer it. An Aristocratic implant, as it were."

Implant.

My insides wither, my fingers reaching for the back of my head, touching the uneven surface of my tattoo. I feel it then —the rigid, distinct rectangular outline of something under my skin.

"It's a neuro-implant, in case you're wondering," the Bishop tells me, closing his fist and putting an end to the holo-projection. "Connected to your brain by the finest filaments. Trace is adept at injecting them by now; he's done it for me a few times. I pay him for the service, of course." His smile is so smug, so self-satisfied, that I wish I could punch it off his face. "The implant has allowed me to listen to you, monitor you, study you. It's how I have seen the world through your eyes for days now, Ashen. How I've managed to compile a massive database of your emotions, your thought patterns, your moods."

He reaches out to touch my face, but I pull back, my lip curled into a snarl.

"Don't you dare put your hands on me," I tell him. "Don't ever touch me again."

I look into his eyes, which have turned a light, unnatural green. For once, he doesn't seem daunting, warm, charming.

All I feel when I look at him is coldness.

"I recorded all of it," he tells me, ignoring my hostile expression. "Every moment you spent at the Hanging, watching me. Watching your beloved Finn. Watching a man die. Every touch of your fingers to Finn's face when you were finally reunited, every kiss. Every second you two shared—the tone of your voice when you told him you loved him. The change in your heart's rhythm when he spoke to you."

"Why?" I ask, my voice a sharp blade. He has violated both Finn and me. Stolen our privacy. Taken our most intimate moments from us. *But why?* "What reason could you possibly have to monitor me that closely, to record me like that? You knew I was Ashen Spencer all along, for God's sake. What were you trying to prove with any of this?"

The Bishop's lips curl up into a smile that's so inhuman as to make me shudder. "I wasn't trying to prove anything, Ashen. I was trying to *create*. And create I did, with the help of your beloved Finn."

"I don't understand," I moan, weakened by confusion and sorrow.

"You will," he tells me. "Very soon, in fact."

The Bishop waves a hand in the air, and the space around us lights up. By now, the platform has come to a complete stop, and I see that it's connected itself to a large glass room that looks like the Transport the Bishop was in when he arrived at my residence tonight. Its doors are open, welcoming us eerily inside.

Standing at the other end of the room is someone so intensely familiar that when I see her, I feel like I'm staring into a mirror.

"Ashen Spencer," the Bishop says, "meet Ashen Spencer."

4 2

ENDGAME

THE BISHOP TAKES me by the hand and pulls me forward, and I'm too stunned to resist.

My mind goes cold as the chamber's glass doors slide shut behind me. I should be angry, scared. I should feel *something*.

But there is nothing inside me as I stare at the figure who looks so much like me and yet isn't me at all.

She stares back, an odd, kind smile on her lips that I know I've issued many times to many people. A smile I've never seen reflected back at me, and one that sends my blood into a deep freeze now.

"Impressive, isn't she?" the Bishop asks, stepping forward and laying a hand on the other Ashen's shoulder. "She is what's called a Replik. A near-perfect copy of an existing person—with a few genetic enhancements."

"She looks just like me," my doppelgänger says in my voice, as if the Bishop's words were directed at her.

My voice. A sound stolen from inside me.

An entire life stolen from me.

"I don't under—" I begin.

But I stop myself.

The truth is, I understand completely.

I know what's happening here. It may be devastating, unfathomable. But I understand it. This is why the Bishop told Finn we could leave earlier than planned. He doesn't need me anymore, because *he has me already*. He is in possession of a version of Ashen Spencer that will do whatever he wants, whenever he wants her to.

"Cellular regeneration," I say. "It wasn't about anti-aging or curing disease. It was about...this?"

The Bishop lets out a stifled chuckle. "Oh, it's *all* about fighting age and disease," he insists. "Do you have any idea how much money is tied up in those two business ventures? I'll make a fortune from Wealthies looking to live longer." Gesturing to the other Ashen, he adds, *"She's* simply a bonus feature."

"She's a clone, isn't she?"

He shakes his head. "A clone would have taken a great deal longer to produce. Ashen here is simpler in many ways. A synthetic skeleton covered in organic material grown incredibly rapidly, thanks to the blood sample we took from you—and other organic samples, taken in your sleep. Each cell in her body is derived from your own, each memory in her head is one of yours—so she is, in essence, an improved version of you. Every little detail matches you, even her emotions. Her love for Finn, for your brother. They're very real."

"What..." My voice is shaking as I repeat the word. "What are you planning to do with her?"

"Use her, of course," he says. "Don't get me wrong, Ashen. You have served me extremely well. You've been wonderful, in fact. Making those videos for me and letting the Consortium know what a good man I am. I'm so *very* grateful. But Ashen Two-Point-Oh—that's what I call her, you know, for fun—will take over now. She will be venturing back west with Finn and Merit and dismantling the Consortium for me from the inside."

"Why are you doing this?" I ask, still staring at my own face on another body. "The Consortium would have supported you. I would have made sure of it. Why would you want to dismantle them?"

A creeping smile slithers its way over the Bishop's lips. "I have been watching the goings-on inside the Arc for some days now, thanks to our friend the King. He still has access to much of the security system that was in place there for years, you know. He's proven quite useful here in New York."

"So what? Are you telling me you've seen something that convinced you to create a second version of me? Do you know how insane that sounds?"

"Your friend Illian isn't convinced you're acting in his best interests, Ashen," the Bishop says. "I've been watching him. In fact, he has no desire to allow me anywhere near that place. But trust me when I say that by the time I get to the Arc, they'll welcome me with open arms."

"Why? What's changed?"

"Today, we disabled much of the electrical system in the Arc," the other Ashen tells me, her voice animated as if it's good news she's conveying. "The Arc is at the Bishop's mercy now. When Finn and I arrive with him and Merit, we'll save the day and restore the power. We'll tell them it was the Bishop's doing."

"So you caused a blackout," I reply. "And you're going to

turn the lights back on. That's not going to persuade Illian—"
I begin, but the Bishop raises his hand to silence me.

"That's not the best of it," he says. "Illian's partner—Kurt, I
believe his name is?"

"What about him?" I snarl.

"He's fallen ill over the last few days. Gravely so." He pouts
as if in mock sympathy, which only riles me more. "He's in the
hospital inside the Arc, and no one quite knows what's wrong
with him."

I grind my jaw, a murderous rage welling up inside me.
"You..." I growl.

The Bishop laughs. "I'll heal him, of course. Make him
good as new. And after a few days spent watching the man he
loves hanging around at death's door, Illian will most
certainly change his tune. If all goes well, the Arc's denizens
will be eating out of my hand in a matter of days, if not
hours."

"They'll know you're not a friend," I growl.

"Like *you* knew?" he asks. "Haven't you realized by now,
Ashen, that I can be a friend to anyone I choose in this
world?"

"It's okay," my doppelgänger says. "They'll trust me. I'm the
Crimson Dreg." She smiles and her cheeks flush in the way
mine have thousands of times over my life, as if she's embar-
rassed by her boasting.

For some reason, that one small thing infuriates me more
than anything else.

"You're not the Crimson Dreg. You're nothing of the sort!"
I shout. "They'll see right through you, you cheap-ass knock-
off!"

But even as I say it, I know I'm wrong. The Arc's residents
don't yet know the secrets behind the Bishop's research, his

experiments, his vile collection of stolen bodies. Even *Finn* doesn't know what the monster has done.

Finn thought he was helping with research that would save lives, not steal them away. Had he known the Bishop was creating a carbon copy of me, he would have murdered him on the spot.

"You know what?" the other Ashen says, her tone slightly irritable. "I don't think they *will* see through me, actually."

"There's a reason you're sending her to my home and not me," I say, turning to the Bishop and ignoring my irritating twin. "You must have thought I would try to stop you...but what is it that you're planning?"

When he stares at me, his chin raised, and falls silent, I continue. "There are millions of people inside the Arc. What are you going to do to them?"

"Assess them for their biological value, of course," he replies with a shrug. "Those who are worthy will be kept very much alive and thriving. Those who are not? Well, you can imagine I don't intend to waste resources feeding and housing them."

"The Consortium won't let you do this," I tell him through gritted teeth. "They won't let you stick needles into their people or brand anyone you deem unworthy. They're free people and intend to stay that way."

"Freedom is an illusion, Ashen. Do you really think anyone inside the Arc is truly free? No, of course you don't. The only true freedom is that which *I* will provide. The freedom to live without illness, without the perils that come with aging. For the right price, I will offer that life to anyone, whether they be a Dreg or a Wealthy. You think I'm a tyrant, but I'm the opposite. I'm the purveyor of a new, *literal* Renaissance. A rebirth of humanity. And you can take pride and solace in the fact that you were instrumental in bringing it about."

"I had no willing part in any of this," I snap. "I thought you were helping people. Curing disease. Saving lives. Punishing the cruel. I stupidly let you charm me over and over again..."

The Bishop lets out a quiet laugh then, and I want to kill him. I raise my hands, palms out, steeling myself to summon the Surge.

My doppelgänger does the same, mirroring my movements exactly.

"Careful now, Ashen," the Bishop warns. "I should probably tell you that you are no longer in possession of the powerful weapon Finn gave you. But your twin here is another story."

"I don't believe you," I snarl.

With a smirk, he says, "You don't have to believe me. Go on—try it."

He reaches a hand out to tell the other Ashen to back away, and waits as I thrust my palms out once again.

But the familiar crackle of energy is gone. There is no blue orb blasting from my body. No weapon hurtling through the space between us.

He's stolen the only power that could possibly have saved me.

I take a step toward the Bishop, but before I can get close to him, he flings a hand in front of his chest. At first, I think he's trying to stop me. But then I see it: a strange, almost transparent wall forming between us.

An Aegis wall.

Finn's ability. *You've stolen it too, you lying, deceitful bastard.*

He's imprisoned me fully now, cutting the glass chamber in half and killing any hope I had of escape. With a jolt of fury and anguish, I realize this glass room will probably be my coffin. I leap forward, pounding my fists against the Aegis wall.

"Leave us," the Bishop says, turning calmly to the other Ashen. "Send the others in. It's time."

She obeys, exiting the chamber via a door at the far end and disappearing down a hallway to the side.

"I told you your friend Finn was a wonder," the Bishop says with a snicker. "His design of Aegis tech is extraordinary. He'll do good work in the Arc for me, too. You should be proud."

"Finn is far from stupid," I tell him, ignoring his barbs. "He'll catch on quickly. He'll know that...*thing*...isn't me, for one thing."

"Maybe," the Bishop shrugs. "Probably not, though. Even you, Ashen, aren't so skilled at telling the difference. You thought Naeva was real, too."

"Naeva?"

He smiles. "The woman you met the night of the Choosing Ceremony—the one who betrayed me by warning you I was coming for you—she was admittedly very real. And she was right about one thing: I was intrigued by her—she was so very unreadable. But in the end, I was able to hear every word she said to you on the last night of her life, thanks to that lovely implant Trace gave you."

"You had her killed."

"Yes, yes. Of course I did. She betrayed me, Ashen." He says the words with such spite, such rage, that even with the Aegis wall protecting me from him, I'm filled with terror. "She warned you what I was about to do—which means she would eventually have warned you about the Repliks, too. I couldn't risk having her ruin everything."

It's all I can do not to vomit.

I think about Naeva's "acting" after that night, after the Bishop brought me to the Behemoth. How different she seemed, how bizarre and flaky.

Of course she was odd. That person wasn't her at all.

She wasn't even a person.

"Is that what you are?" I ask, stepping forward and pressing my palms to the Aegis wall. "Are you one of them?"

His eyes light up at the question and he lets out a boisterous laugh. "Let's just say I'm the product of many years of thorough genetic research and a few clever experiments. I am a greedy man in possession of many, many Gifts. Some physical, others mental. I have you to thank for a few of them, Ashen. Your healing power...*my God.* It came along at exactly the right time. You were like a present sent from heaven." He pulls a small folding knife from his pocket and slices into his hand, holding it up for me to watch the blood trickle down his palm.

But the stream of crimson ceases quickly to flow, the wound sealing itself almost immediately, far faster than my stab wound healed.

"I tweaked your ability a little, I'll admit," he says. "But you gave me everything I needed. So thank you."

"Are you going to kill me?" I ask, fed up with his games.

"No," he replies. "Where would the fun be in that? Besides, I've told you I don't kill people myself. I'm going to let someone else do it."

"Of course you are," I retort, resisting the desire to roll my eyes. "Your executioner, perhaps?"

"Hell, no. Someone far more interesting than him. I think you'll enjoy this, actually. It's somewhat...poetic."

Just then, three figures appear on the other side of the

glass door behind him. All three are silhouetted against the bright light of the surrounding walls.

"I have a gift for you, Ashen. A final, lovely gift," the Bishop says. "I do hope you enjoy it."

It's then that I understand exactly what he has planned.

43

TRAPPED

THE DUCHESS IS STANDING on the other side of the Aegis wall.

I tell myself this is a good thing—that Finn will notice when she's not with him and Merit on the Air-Wing.

But then I remember. *I never told him we were going to bring her back to the Arc.*

Her face is bleeding, her left eye swollen almost completely shut. But she still musters the energy to say, "Hello, Ashen," as if she's somehow looking forward to what's to come.

This isn't how any of it was supposed to happen, I think as I stare at her. *This isn't how it was meant to end for us.*

"You two have a very special bond," the Bishop says. "And frankly, I no longer have any use for either of you. But it amuses me to think how much you despise one another, if I'm to be honest. So I'm giving each of you the gift of the other. But now, it's time for me to collect Finn and Merit—and Ashen Two-Point-Oh, of course—and leave for the Arc. It's a little early, granted, but I'm ever so eager to get to my new friends." With a wave of his hand, he adds, "Goodbye, you two. Don't kill each other too fast."

He turns and leaves, followed by the two guards who escorted the Duchess. The door seals behind them, and almost instantly, the glass chamber we're in begins an ascent through the darkness of the Behemoth, rising painfully slowly as my enemy and I stare at one another.

"We need to help them," I tell her. "Finn and Merit. They're walking into a trap."

"Finn chose this," she says, disdain dripping from her voice. "He chose to leave the Duke and me, and steal our youngest from us. Whatever consequences await him are his own doing."

"What about Merit?"

"Merit will be fine," she says. "Your friend the Bishop will probably protect him, if only to stay in Finn's good graces. I just wish he hadn't sent that ghastly version of you with my sons, though. Even a mere *replica* of you is repugnant."

"Charming, as always," I say, wishing I could slam my way through the Aegis and into her. "Damn it. How long is this wall going to be here?"

"Until morning," the Duchess replies haughtily.

"How the hell do you know that?"

"Because that bastard told me," she snaps, gesturing to her swollen eye. "When he did this to my face. All I know is that you and I are going to die high up on the roof of this horrible place. He said he wanted us to be as close to Heaven as possible, *so the fall would be all the harder.*" She lets out a quiet, bitter chuckle. "The man is a psychopath."

"You would know."

She leers at me then, her eyes narrowed, and I realize with

genuine amusement that this is the longest, most human conversation we've ever had.

"Maybe we don't have to die," I say, more to myself than to her, turning to look around. "Maybe there's another way."

"What way is that? Climbing down a building that's hundreds of stories high?"

Our glass prison is still ascending at a snail's pace, and something tells me it will continue to do so until morning. It's a slow-burning torture, a means to assault us both with the anticipation of our battle to come.

"I don't know," I tell her. "But there has to be another way."

"There's *no* other way," she says, slumping down to sit on the floor. I notice for the first time that she's uncharacteristically dressed in jeans and a sweater, as well as a pair of knee-high black leather boots. She looks almost—*almost*—human. "Sometimes, Ashen, you just have to accept your fate. You and I have each escaped death on multiple occasions. One of us will kill the other in the morning. The survivor will likely die of dehydration. It's not a pretty truth, but it's still the truth."

I seat myself too, leaning back against the thick glass wall, and wonder what Finn would think if he could see us now.

"Did the Bishop steal your power from you?" I ask wearily. "Your...fire?"

The Duchess turns to me and shakes her head, lifting a hand, palm up. A small but deadly-looking ball of flame appears in the air, twisting slowly around as if she has perfect control of it.

"I get it," I say. "I see what he's hoping for. Well, may the best woman win."

"Or the worst," she replies with a snicker.

So strange, to be speaking to the Duchess almost as if we're friends.

Of course, all that will change the second the wall between us comes down.

4 4

SHOWDOWN

I FALL asleep with my head against the glass wall and wake only when I hear the sound of two familiar voices.

I leap to my feet to see that the Duchess is standing a few feet away, still on the other side of the Aegis wall. Her face is pointed in my direction, but she's not looking at me.

It takes me a moment to realize that hovering between us, faint on the air, is a projection of a scene unfolding slowly.

I see myself with Finn, standing inside what looks like a large white chamber. We're holding onto one another tightly, and Merit is with us.

Only it's not us. Not really.

Finn is with the other Ashen. The Replik. This is happening now.

I watch my doppelgänger press her lips to his as they prepare to board the Air-Wing for their flight home.

I want to be sick as it sinks in that this video is the Bishop's final, cruelest insult. He's gleefully showing me that Finn has been taken in by the new, improved version of me. That he's about to leave New York with her, wholly oblivious to the fact that she's not even human.

The video stops suddenly when somewhere above us, I hear a loud, low grinding sound. A flood of light pours over us, and the Duchess and I both pull our chins up to see that part of the Behemoth's massive roof is cracking open.

"We'll soon stop moving," she tells me. "And the wall between us will come down."

I pull my eyes to the Duchess. She's beaten down, weary. I see exhaustion in her face, as if she can hardly be bothered to despise me right now. But she's still dangerous.

For a moment, I almost feel sorry for her. But I remind myself what she did to my mother. To Peric, to his parents. To so many others.

She may lack energy, but I don't. I despise her as much as I ever did, and I will fight until my last breath to bring her down.

Even if I know I don't stand a chance.

As I'm watching her, contemplating how many more minutes of life I may have, a hatch opens next to me—some sort of stealthy compartment in what looks like a clear glass wall.

Inside the small opening is a silver dagger that I recognize immediately as the one Finn gave me so long ago, the one I left with Adi and Cillian.

At first, I wonder if they somehow managed to get it to me. But no—that's not possible. This was the Bishop. It's one of his sick games. For all I know, he killed them both to acquire it.

I reach for the blade and immediately see something else in the wall's opening—something made of silver fabric, folded neatly into a square.

It's my silver stealth uniform. The one Finn created

for me.

I pull it out, and as the Duchess watches disdainfully from beyond the clear wall, I slip out of my clothing and slip into it. The uniform won't protect me from fire. But it may just buy me a few extra minutes of life.

By now, the glass chamber has emerged from the roof, which begins to seal up under our feet. The wind howls fiercely around us, shuddering the glass chamber just enough to make me nervous.

To my right, I hear a high-pitched sort of whistling, and I slip over to examine the wall. Almost instantly, I understand where the sound is coming from. The wind is gusting through a small, round hole in the glass, designed to allow air into the chamber.

I stick a finger through the hole, wondering if there's any way I could shatter the glass.

Bad idea. Even if I could, where the hell would I go?

I continue to slip around the walls, feeling every inch I can reach to assess for weaknesses. There has to be a way out. A way to free myself from this hideous prison.

But I can find nothing. Even the door embedded in the glass wall seems to have disappeared.

I take the blade in hand and smash its hilt against the glass, but it fails to give.

Sensing that I'm living on borrowed time, I pull the uniform's hooded veil over my head and face, and press my fingers to my palms to activate its stealth mechanism. The Duchess looks over with a disinterested glare, seemingly irritated that her life just got slightly more complicated when her opponent disintegrated.

Seconds after my transformation, the Aegis wall shimmers away, leaving us each vulnerable to the other, and I move against the chamber's side wall, trying my best to hide from my enemy.

As if on cue, the Duchess stands up and steps back, her arms extended, her skin crackling red and white in preparation to summon deadly flame. As if to test herself, she hurls a small fireball that passes inches from my head.

I force myself to hold my breath. *She doesn't know where you are. That was a lucky shot.*

Inhaling a deep breath, I tread softly toward her until I'm close enough to strike. She spins around as if sensing that I'm near, but looks disoriented and pained, her one eye still swollen shut.

With one quick burst of energy I lunge at her, moving swiftly, and manage to slice into her side with my blade before slipping away into the far corner of the room.

She howls in pain, clutching at the wound. But I know without so much as looking that it isn't life-threatening or even debilitating.

Damn it, I say under my breath.

She flings another fireball, this one far larger than the first, and I can feel its searing heat as it explodes against the wall next to me.

Again, I lunge, and again, I swipe the knife, this time across her upper arm.

She collapses then, falling against the wall and wincing in agony.

I'm about to run at her again when a flurry of sudden movement to my right distracts me, and I hear a familiar voice calling my name.

I spin around to see that something is hovering in midair just outside the chamber's walls…

An owl.

LEAP OF FAITH

"I WILL KILL YOU, ASHEN," the Duchess moans. She's still sitting on the floor, her head pressed against the wall. I can see the blood trickling down one arm as her other hand clutches at the wound. "I will take your life. Do you hear me?"

I want to shout something back at her. But instead, I turn my attention to Atticus, who's hovering just outside.

"Ash!" Rys's voice calls out again.

I have no choice now. I have to say something. I need to let him know where I am.

"I'm here, Rys," I call out, drawing the Duchess's eyes. But she doesn't get up or move to attack. For the moment, at least, she's down for the count.

But I can't imagine she'll stay like that for long.

I press myself to the wall. "Rys—they've disabled the electricity in the Arc!"

"I know," he calls back. "When the power started glitching, I knew something was up. I know those systems inside and out, and I knew the only person who would be able to shut them down was the freaking King. So I figured something was wrong. I climbed down a Conveyor shaft to the tunnels and got the hell out of there. Only problem is, *everything* is shut down now—blast doors, you name it. I can't get back in. I'm hiding out in Sector Three."

"How did you know I was here?"

"The Tracker in your uniform. I couldn't make sense of it. I saw you leaving this morning—I mean, *Atticus* saw you flying out on an Air-Wing with Finn. Only I knew it wasn't you."

"Because of the Tracker?"

"No. Because you never once looked for Atticus. The Ash I know would have looked for him."

"But she's like me in every way," I tell him. "He's building these creatures—these Repliks...He's going to use her to—"

"She's *not* you," he protests. "And Finn will figure it out. It's only a matter of time."

"I'm not sure it matters," I moan. "I'm locked in here with *her*." I gesture toward the Duchess, who's slumped against the far wall, muttering to herself. "We'll both die in this box, and no one will ever find us."

"Not true. *I* found you, Ash. And I'm going to get you out of there."

"But..." I begin. "Look, there's no way out. I've already tried breaking this damned glass. It's too thick."

"There's always a way out. And the Bishop may be the most diabolical genius in the universe, but I have something he doesn't."

"What's that?" I ask with a half-hearted snicker, my eyes locked on my enemy.

"A freaking robot owl."

As I watch, Atticus's belly cracks open and out comes what

looks like a small metal arm with a whirring blade attached to its end.

Only the blade isn't made of steel.

"Stand back," Rys tells me. "Laser coming through."

He's not joking. A thin, razor-sharp red beam has already begun slicing through the thick glass. I stand aside and watch as he cuts a window into the cube's wall.

I watch as the glass tumbles inwards and lands with a hard thud on the floor. It doesn't shatter or even crack, which only reinforces the extraordinary stunt Atticus has just managed to pull off.

The window is large enough for me to climb through, but the wind feels as if it's going to blow me off the roof if I'm foolish enough to step outside.

"If I come out there," I say, looking at Atticus as if he understands me, "what then? It's not like there's a door out here to some magical stairwell. Even if I get back inside the Behemoth, I'll just fall to my death."

"You're not going back inside," Rys's voice says, cutting through the wind as Atticus flaps up and perches on the cut-out window. "Ash, do you trust me?"

He's asked me this question before, and I've hesitated. But this time, I don't need to think about my answer.

"Of course I do."

"Good. See the far corner, to the right of this window?"

I look over. The corner he's talking about must be a hundred feet away, at least. But it's far closer than the roof's other corners, which have long since disappeared in a distant bank of thick cloud.

"I see it," I tell him.

"Good. Climb out the window and make your way over there."

I look back toward the Duchess, who is on her feet now, her hands pressed against the wall.

I didn't kill you, I think. *But I'm leaving you for dead. That's the best deal you can possibly hope for from me, you evil bitch.*

Atticus is a few feet away, fighting at the wind with his enormous wings as I manage to toss the dagger through the window and pull myself out. I land with a hard thud on the gravel that coats the Behemoth's enormous roof, but I don't seem to have injured anything.

The wind whips at me like I'm standing on the peak of Mount Everest, and I cover my face with my arm as I begin to slog my way toward my destination.

As I finally reach the edge of the building, I press my hands to the parapet lining the roof, grateful that it's there for support.

I glance down, only to see that Manhattan and the surrounding boroughs are invisible. All I see is a thick wall of clouds.

"What am I looking for?" I shout as Atticus hovers next to me, still fighting the wind.

"You're not looking for anything," Rys says. "But I will find you. For that, you're going to need to deactivate your stealth mode."

"Wait—what?"

"You said you trust me, right?"

"Yes, but—"

Sighing, I press my hands into my palms and show myself as Atticus flaps next to me, Rys's voice slicing through the wind.

"I need you to jump, Ash. Right from this corner."

I look down again, wondering if I've missed something. Is

there a window cleaner's scaffold hanging along the wall or something?

"Rys…" I say. "Are you trying to kill me?"

"No, Ash. I'm about to save your life."

"I don't see how. I—"

A shriek cuts through the air from somewhere behind me. I spin around to see the Duchess running at me, her skin cracking open with heat, her eyes glowing a horrific, cruel orange menace.

There is nothing human in her right now. No sign of a woman who cares for her husband, her children. All I see is pure hatred.

She intends to use the last of her strength to end me.

I reach for my blade only to remember that in my eagerness to get away from the Duchess, I left it on the gravel next to the glass chamber.

I'm weaponless, and the Bishop robbed me of the one power that could have saved me.

Still advancing, the Duchess holds her hands out in front of her chest, a massive ball of fire swirling between them.

"Ash," Rys says, "I promise you on my parents' graves…I will not let you die if you leap. But you need to do it. Right now."

As he's speaking, Atticus swoops at the Duchess, distracting her for only a few seconds before she swats him away and refocuses on me.

She's too strong, I think. *He can't hurt her.*

I know now that I have only two options.

I can die by my enemy's hand, or take control of my own fate.

"One day soon," I say under my breath, "I *will* kill you, Duchess. That's a promise."

Without another word, I leap up onto the parapet, close my eyes...

And jump.

End of Book Four of the Cure Chronicles

ALSO BY K. A. RILEY

If you're enjoying K. A. Riley's books, please consider leaving a review on Amazon or Goodreads to let your fellow book-lovers know about it.

Dystopian Books:

The Cure Chronicles:

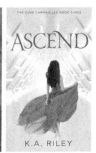

The Cure
Awaken
Ascend
Fallen
Reign (Coming in June 2022)

Resistance Trilogy:

  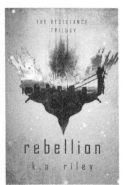

Recruitment
Render
Rebellion

Emergents Trilogy:

  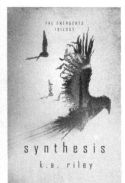

Survival
Sacrifice
Synthesis

Transcendent Trilogy:

Travelers
Transfigured
Terminus

Academy of the Apocalypse Series:

Emergents Academy
Cult of the Devoted
Army of the Unsettled

The Ravenmaster Chronicles:

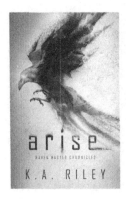  

Arise
Banished (Coming in January 2022)
Crusade (Coming in April 2022)

Athena's Law Trilogy:

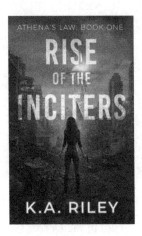

Book One: *Rise of the Inciters*
Book Two: *Into an Unholy Land*
Book Three: *No Man's Land*

Fantasy Books

Seeker's Series:

Seeker's World
Seeker's Quest
Seeker's Fate
Seeker's Promise
Seeker's Hunt
Seeker's Prophecy (Coming in 2022)

To be informed of future releases, and for occasional chances to win free swag, books, and other goodies, please sign up here:

https://karileywrites.org/#subscribe

Made in the USA
Las Vegas, NV
08 December 2024

13407733R00193